Also by Alys Einion and available from Honno

Inshallah

ASH

by
Alys Einion

HONNO MODERN FICTION

First published in 2018 by Honno Press,
'Ailsa Craig', Heol y Cawl, Dinas Powys, Vale of Glamorgan, Wales,
CF64 4AH
1 2 3 4 5 6 7 8 9 10

A catalogue record for this book is available from the British Library.

Published with the financial support of the Welsh Books Council.

ISBN 978-1-909983- 82-3(paperback)
ISBN 978-1-909983-83-0 (ebook)

Cover design: Rhys Huws
Cover image: Rhys Huws
Text design: Elaine Sharples
Printed in Great Britain by Gomer Press

For my Jo

Today I will find out if my daughter is alive or dead. Prescience and portents... the clouds are sun-kissed pink, a carpet of vapour below me, as insubstantial as dreams. Today and every day I am drawn, inevitably, to the conclusion of a story begun so long ago I can hardly remember who did what to whom, what my role was. But I am unable to say if this is an ending, or a beginning. All I know is that if she's alive out there, I have to find her.

The last child of my body. Please, let me find her.

Flesh Tint

A hymen is like trust. Fragile, invisible, it takes less than a second to break it, and then it is gone forever.

My name is Ash, and ash I am; the burned traces of age-old dust and sand and sudden death without resurrection. I am the grey ash-cloud and the thick film on the surface of things. I am the frozen hollows within, shaped in the form of the long-forgotten.

Ash. Aisha. Ashley, Asha, Ashana; I could be any of these, but here, in this place, the sun and moon and bright stars see only that single syllable, sound only that sibilance. Ah, sshh. I am the very essence of burned bridges and dreams in flames, and if there is a phoenix to rise from this cloud-pillow-soft pile of once was, then I have never seen her.

I stand, feeling every part of my skin, dragging my body up from the stinking stained mattress under the rotting carcass of a shed at the edge of the disused railway.

It was easy, in the end, to shed the burden of virginity. Here, now, with the wind tearing at the walls and their lacework pattern of holes, with damp and stale smells, unmentionable odours, and this stickiness inside me and on me and the brief pain and then...

Nothing.

I had expected there to be something, something that I was supposed to be saving myself for. He is already outside, the boy I finally let do the one thing that they all want. It wasn't so hard, after all, just a few moments and his sweaty face and his cold hands on my skin grabbing my hips. The first person ever to touch my body like that, this body I hardly know still. All these curves and swells

3

and the dark thatch between my legs, and his recoil of distaste.

"Don't you shave? I mean, don't girls shave...?"

As if I let him down somehow, by not being what he wanted me to be, not being the girls on the porn sites panting and pouting. Flash of anger. But I wanted it done.

"Just do it, for fuck's sake."

And by then he was ready, if I wasn't. But I've been ready for this so long, this great mystery, this bodily transformation. Ready for the moment I no longer have to live in fear of something I don't understand, something unknown and unknowable that somehow defines me utterly. Ash is the taste in my mouth as he grunts and thrusts and within moments it was done.

A sheepish look as I emerge through the doorway. The uneven ground makes me stumble.

"Give me some of that." The cigarette is bitter and harsh but I swallow the cough that hides in my throat and relish the spin and buzz of nicotine and wait for the rest of me to catch up now that I have done what needed to be done so I can get on with the rest of it, the rest of this business of being a woman.

"If you tell anyone..."

He looks at me, down to the floor, then away. Right. He's already texted his mates then. Well, better now than later. Now they know, they won't be teasing me about that any more.

"Oi, Ash, what's it like to be the only virgin left in school?"

"Lesbo! Rug muncher! Why don't you get yourself a girlfriend?"

"Hey, Paki, what you savin' yourself for anyway, an arranged marriage?"

4

Rain, bitter and cold, burns, acid on my cheeks. I shrug the hood of my jacket up, tuck my hair under. "I'm going home."

"Do you want me to walk you?"

I can see he doesn't want to. His name is Jadon and he's fifteen. Technically, that means I just raped him, because I am 17 and legal and he is still a minor. I know this because we did consent at school last week. Again. While the girls in the class giggled and played with their phones and the boys looked red and sheepish and made loud jokes, Mr John helplessly warning the boys they should shut up or else.

"No, I'm good."

Every step hurts, aches, like the cold has eaten into my flesh and tears at my bones as I put one foot in front of the other. These awful, cheap boots *she* bought me, that stupid smile on her face, triumph and hope and something else, the something that I always want to crush, somehow, because it comes from her and from whatever it is that makes her need me so much, need me to love her.

All these years she treated us like baggage, something to be carried around and then set down whenever and wherever she wanted. Shahid says she just had to make a life for us; him and my other brothers talk about the past, about bad things that happened, and sometimes, Shahid reminds me that she saved us. But from what? For what?

Empty. I keep waiting to *feel* something. Pain in my heels, the broken-down boots rubbing and aching my feet. There's never any money. Cheap boots and cheap clothes and I can't even get a Saturday job because she is so afraid of something happening to me. She's has been painting that fear onto me for years, blood-red rivulets

5

dripping down and gluing my eyes shut and my mouth shut, painting me into the landscape of her nightmares.

I never asked for this, did I? I never asked her to do what she did, to bring us here where we don't belong. It's easier for me, I barely speak Arabic, but Shahid and Abdullah and Mahmood, and even Yusuf, still speak it when she isn't around. One day Shahid told me he feels like he doesn't really belong anywhere. He can't relate to the Muslim men he meets, and he can't relate to the white boys he went to school with and works with. It's like everyone around him has assumptions about who and what he is. Abdullah doesn't talk much, it was always Shahid who had the words, and Abdullah following him around. Mahmood, well, he doesn't talk to any of us, except me, though not so much these days. I don't think any of us feel like we belong anywhere.

Strange streets that lead to home, diamonds of light reflected in dirty puddles, the sky far above growing closer as I climb upwards through the town. Navigate the paths through puddles of neon and the smells of takeaways, thick and oniony, cold air and damp weight through my clothes, the thin fabric of this coat I keep for school, for 'best' though it was a freebie, a foundling, abandoned in the park late one evening and now it's mine and in it I blend in, I think, this black plastic coat and these leggings and the boots that should look right but they don't. Plastic. She won't buy leather. The collapsing heels squish, a little pain against my ankle.

Cold, night like spirit shadows wrapping around me, a cloak to hide within, no one will touch me now. The secret within me, powerful and tainted, the taboo of black magic, rebellion made flesh. This is my body, not given for you. I gave nothing. This is my body and I control it.

6

Up on the hill, the house with its red brick porch and crumbling mortar, mish-mash of styles, a long-ago house that huddled and squatted jealously over its patch of land, the fields and orchards eaten by the ravening town. The garden gate's screech, wet rust on the pads of my fingers, faint light from an upper window. She is in her 'studio' then.

Good.

If she's in one of her frenzies now, caught up in the 'creative flow', I can slip inside, unseen and unknown. The dead place inside growing, spreading, black-ink stain, barren landscape, ravished land. Slash and burn. I have burned through the final barrier of freedom. I am no longer a virgin.

Why prize virginity so? Why spend so many resources on controlling a woman's sex? I never understood it. I don't know. It is nothing, really, just one moment and then the next, and all that is gone is that weight of expectation.

I should feel something, shouldn't I?

There's a gap in the streetlights, creating a strange illusion of light and dark – from further down the street the house is lit up, but now, at the door, there's that patch of shadow. Cold brass of the old knocker and the shove and kick to open the warped wooden door. I could go around the back, through the kitchen – she never locks that door now, though once upon a time every door was triple-locked and every curtain shut. That was before, before this house and all its crumbling memories and the ghosts of every argument we have ever had still echoing from the stained plaster and the fading paper, glancing off the cracked tiles in the hallway. Mud and patches of plaster and paint on the mosaic floor. It was once beautiful, you can see that, but years of careless residents have cast it into ignominy.

A scaffolding bridge covers the gaping and ragged hole that looks down to the cellar, with its ladder leading down, smell of dust and old earth and the leavings of rats and spiders, no doubt, though she swears it's clean enough. Mum just looks at it with that closed smile, rueful, defensive. She's like this house with great gaps and absences and things half-started or never finished. Slash and burn and run away, that's her; inviting the storm and casting us adrift. This is where we washed up, in the end, the shipwreck of her life casting us all like so much flotsam on an alien shore.

She's upstairs, the kitchen deserted but for the lamp in the corner, smelling of burned toast and coffee and stale cigarette smoke and damp and that other smell, old and thick and ashy on my tongue. Greasy tidemarks on the stained wooden countertop. Hungry, I am hungry, and I should cook, because if I don't she'll ask.

"Ash?"

Who do you fucking think it is, Mother? Why does she always have to come downstairs when I get in, and say something stupid?

My mother. Tall and windblown even though I doubt she has set foot outside the door in days, because she doesn't much. Doesn't go anywhere unless she has to, just wraps herself in these walls like some strangely fitting coat, squats between their misshapen limbs like a child in the lap of a monster it has grown to love. Who can love this... the heavy cast iron pan, blackened with age and a thousand meals, these battered wooden cupboards sagging and damp, the floor greyish black with dirt and years of footsteps?

"Good. You're cooking dinner."

"Yes, Mum." Say as little as possible, don't provoke the

8

beast. Tall and stooped, her hair fly-away and messy, her glasses dirty, still wearing the faded tie-dye t-shirt she's had on all week, and those shapeless jeans that flap around her ankles. Witch-like, vague. The hand that holds her cigarette shakes.

"How was your day?"

"It was OK." Why does she try to talk to me? She doesn't know me, or anything about me. I hate this, her trying to act like my friend. If she knew, right now, what I have done, she wouldn't be so cheerful.

There are some leaves in a bowl on the side – spring greens and some slightly slug-eaten cavallo nero, and some very small leeks. Someone has dropped them off for her, no doubt, one of her weird and wonderful friends with "something from the garden". The fridge yawns a fetid smell of old cheese and something gone off. I find a mouldering avocado half and toss it into the compost bucket, pull out some soft carrots and even softer onions.

Crusted to the wood with years-old grease and crumbs is a gas ring, industrial size, orange rubber pipe leading down to the bottle underneath, half-hidden behind the dirty yellow gingham curtain under the counter. I remember a friend coming here once – coming to call for me – and her horror as she traced the outlines and then filled in the details of this our life, and how she laughed. The next day in school it was all anyone could talk about, how Ash lived like a pig, like a gypsy. That was when they started calling me Gyppo and dirty Paki and I shook my head because they were right, weren't they? Normal people have hobs and ovens and microwaves and gas cookers, and central heating that works, not gaps and scars on the walls where radiators used to be, patches of old paint and paper telling their own history.

Light the gas, I don't jump at the roar, not any more, and put on the skillet, throw in some dark oil from the cracked bowl, the kind that would have held Chinese soup or fragrant oriental tea, and is now covered in a layer of grease and burned bits of food. Hot oil smell and hot metal and chopped onions and the carrots and leaves. She watches me, greedy and critical. This is all there is to eat, this and the packets of rice and pasta in the cupboard, and the jars of lentils and beans that take longer to cook. She doesn't cook, not when she's painting, and she forgets to shop. She told me a year ago she wasn't cooking for me anymore, that I should be doing my share in the house. Carl's mother doesn't ask him to cook for her. Carl's mother shops, every Friday night, in Waitrose. Not that I want her cooking, not now, because she would watch me eat. But I want this done, this ritual requirement that will make her think she has won. Another small victory, me cooking for her and her thinking I will eat too. Camouflage for the real victory

"Thank you, love," she smiles. "I'm in the flow right now, things are going well. Talk later, yeah?"

She takes her bowl of vegetables up to her studio, and I look at mine. Feel its weight in my hand. Pressure and expectation, but no desire. This will make me feel fat and heavy and ugly and bad, and wrong, because I couldn't say no. Because if I eat this I am weak, not in control any more. If I eat this I am like her.

The broken window rattles, blasts cold air at me at the bend in the stairs; the light on the landing is bleak, a single eco-bulb, bare and dusty. Cold here too. She has lit the fire in her studio. I can see the flames casting shadows on the wall, smell the wood burning. She will be sitting by the fire, with her books and her papers and the bowl of stir-fry. Tapping away on her ancient laptop talking to one of her freakish friends in far off places, or staring madly at a canvas dripping clots of paint onto the floor.

The door to my room squeaks and sighs on mismatched hinges, and when I see it I see painted layers of memories and for a moment I feel different to the version of me that last stepped through this doorway. That girl, the one before, with her dreams and her books, always reading too much, all those things too advanced for her age. That's what the teachers said, in the primary schools, in the first few years of high school. As if my hunger to know and to understand was wrong, and my mother wrong for indulging it. Books on every subject, classics, textbooks, anything and everything that caught the attention of my magpie mind. Maybe they were right. Was it that that set me apart from everyone else, so strongly that it's as if they sense it, my difference?

Close the door, wood grain and old pain under my fingers. Kick off the boots, feeling the ridged floorboards. I painted them myself, and the rag rug was a present – birthday or Christmas, soft ridged cotton on my raw skin.

The sigh-slap sound of a message on my crappy phone. Shahid. Checking in. If he knew.... Well, he probably wouldn't say much. But he might, and it's different for boys. And they will find out soon anyway, my brothers, Snapchat and Whatsapp and FB and it will be everywhere, that Ash, the dirty gyppo, is a slut. Ash puts out.

I'd rather be known for that. Not for the other things they call me.

All because of *her*.

I leave the bowl on the table by the bed, jumble of makeup and schoolbooks, half-empty glasses of water. Smell of the vegetables. My stomach clenches. Hunger, constant hunger, this daily fight, and I am weak with the walking and the end of a long day and with what has happened. This anti-climax.

Maybe just one mouthful...

Standing beyond that bowl are all the people who call me fat, the girls with their pale willowy arms and tiny hips and their knowing smiles. Words rise like steam. Fat. Elephant girl. Jugs. Dolly. Thunder thighs.

No.

Saliva in my mouth.

No.

Just one bite, it won't matter, just a mouthful.

No.

They all hate me, they despise me, but they can't beat me, because I am better than them, I can do this now, and no one can stop me. No one is stronger than I am.

Fat girls have no willpower.

Wrong.

I have more than you will ever know.

I have to stay strong. I have to change, I can't be this person, the fat girl, I can't be who they say I am. If I eat this, they win, and that means they're right about it all, that I'm just a fat nothing.

Ping, the screen of my phone lights up. Carl.

<Did you do it?>

He is the only person I told.

<Yeah>

<What was it like?>

<Dunno. Nothing to say really.>

<You ok?>

<Yeah. Glad it's done now.>

<Congratulations>

<Thanks>

I don't look any different. The mirror tiles I stuck to the back of the door cast a mismatched reflection, but I look the same. Same long hair, poker straight, same brown eyes and coffee-coloured skin, same mouth, same pointy chin and cheekbones. Carl calls my face heart-shaped, says that all the classic film stars would have killed for cheekbones like mine. Yeah, right. That's why I had to practically beg a kid two years below me for sex.

Flick the switch, turn on the speakers, playlist on. Drum and bass, drown it out, that noise, that never-ending noise of her and now she can't call me and ask me to come downstairs for nothing in particular, because I can't hear her. Peel off the school skirt, the polo shirt, hide from the mirror now, clothes over the back of the spindle-legged chair, pants with their rust-stain already old, already drying. Something flying away from me, gone between one breath and the next, this thing they made out was so important. Loosen the bands around my chest, one after the other, sudden ache, itching in the ridges the crepe bandages leave in my too-soft flesh, sore spots along my ribs where the sports bra has been digging in.

I never wanted these breasts that hang and ripple every time I move, monstrous growths. Her chest is flat, so flat, so why, why me, why this shape, why rounded hips and thick thighs and these huge breasts, the look on the woman's face in the bra shop when I took my birthday money, telling me I needed at least a D cup, I was big for a girl my age?

Big.

Big girl.

That's what the boy said tonight. "I've never been with a big girl."

Small, make me small, make me smaller and flatter and

let me turn sideways and disappear into the shadows and not exist. Make it so they don't see me, don't know me, don't find me amongst all those ranks of blonde and blue eyes and creamy skin. Make me invisible.

Lie on the bed, do sit ups till the muscles burn. Crawl onto the floor. Plank for five minutes and the sweat bursts from my skin. Every bit of me hurts, the pressure of my elbows on the wood, pain bringing tears to my eyes, searing across my belly. Dragging pain between my legs. Panting, collapsing on the cold rug with its ever-present dampness. Hands running over the soft and yielding fat under my skin, a vision of lifting that skin and just cutting it away, cutting and cutting and sticking myself back together, remade.

Thin.

Five salutes to the sun then, penance for stopping and dreaming, feel the pull of sinews and tendons and the stretch of skin.

The bowl of cold food mocks me. No one else can do this. Only me. I turn my back on it, plug my phone in, climb between the sheets, cold, clammy as always, pick up a book from the pile, but my mind skips away from the words, and all I can remember now is the feel of it, the smell of it, the sudden fierce pain of it and the loss.

Tears soak down my cheeks, pooling in my ears. A strangled sob. No. She mustn't hear, she mustn't know, save it for when it has the most power, when telling her will work in my favour. This is my secret.

This and the still-full bowl of food untouched, this is my triumph.

This is the beginning.

This is *my* body.

Burnt Sienna

The beauty of a blank canvas lies in its possibilities, the formless surface, unmarked. Pregnant with all that could be, shape, texture, colour. Life recreated in miniature. It started with nothing, comes from nothing, grows from nothing. And there I was back at nothing, watching my daughter disappear on me just as her brothers have done. There should have been omens, when she was born, some great storm, unseasonal rain, or an earthquake ripping the streets apart. Something that foreshadowed what would happen. But it was an average day, nothing remarkable, just another baby at my breast and another day to get up and keep going. But that was another landscape, painted into the past, a backdrop of bad decisions, fading portraits of people once known, once loved, life driving me ever forward, seeking safety, or something else.

And then there was this, this life I brought us to, the new beginning, the fresh start we all needed. But where are they now? All gone but Ash, and she may as well be, she even rejected the name I gave her. Not Aisha any more. Just Ash.

I could feel it coming, prescience, a warning on the wind, a dream-self screaming soundlessly, vainly. Something was coming, and there was nothing I could do about it.

Soon it will just be me and this house and my painting and my books and the wasted years casting forth empty hopes into this vast sea, where nothing really matters. Nothing has meaning but what has been. Gone, all gone, every one of them now, sliding into the painted shadows and evaporating into memory. I never thought of the future, not in all the years of my captivity, veiled and secret self, living somehow, the life I thought I was meant to have. Now the past is bigger than the future will be, my children grown and nothing to show for it but these marks on canvas, this one thing that is mine alone.

Take me back, I told myself, to where the answers might lie. Let me feel it all again, and maybe then I would understand, maybe then the knowing would come, the reason, cause and effect, that brought me where, finally, I had nothing left.

That is how I saw the past, parcelled up in neat packages of time and connection, wrapped in layers of old news and feelings, bound about with ribbons of desire and love and betrayal and recrimination. Even as I struggled with the pain of unwrapping those layers, untying knots so tight there seems to be no beginning and no end, Celtic knots of past-times and present uncertainty, even in the face of how hard it was, I had to try. Because then maybe I could make sense of it all, of how I got from that place to this. And isn't that what life is about, in the end? Making sense of it? Maybe I wanted to sleep easy in my bed and not toss and turn on a rack of guilt and self-doubt. Maybe if I could just unravel one thread, one single shining thread that answered my questions, then I could look forward instead of back.

Nothing can call them back to you, the ones you have lost. Nothing can conjure up love, not of the kind I somehow always seemed to dream of, the kind that takes such deep root that it cannot be cut down, a tree swayed by storms but still steadfast. I always wanted it, always longed for it, but that is the kind of love only a mother can give, and like all of us, myself, my children, we cast aside that one love far too easily and spend our lives wandering the world searching fruitlessly for what was ours all along, if only we knew where to find it.

It started with grey carpet tiles, the rough kind you can feel on your skin just from looking at them, memory overlaid on thought and feeling, and me alone pushing the chair and watching the boys run forward towards the 'children's area' which was nothing more than old stained books, long-ago scribbled on, and some broken plastic toys around a few small chairs. The rain outside fogged the windows; the wobbly wheel of the pushchair catching on the worn carpet as Aisha looked up at me in that quizzical, challenging way. Too much like her father, always angry because everything is not going as she wants it to.

"Umma," Shahid called, my biggest boy, broader and taller than his brothers, even than his twin. "Can we play?"

"Yes, love, but please speak English," I reminded him, knowing we were being watched. I took it all in. A few adults scattered about in damp raincoats and wet shoes; smell of people and something like wet dog. Abdullah squatting beside Yusuf, who was tired, always tired, his face greyish pale, and engaging him playing with toys that are too young for him. Mahmood, slender and sharp-faced; distant, coal-black eyes. He perched on a chair and simply stared around. I had no idea what he is thinking. Like his sister, he seemed angry all the time; too often I found myself placating both of them, anticipating what will set one or the other of them off, and avoiding it, whatever it is. Too often I couldn't. There was never enough money, and I knew they were miserable and Mahmood, of all of them, was the least capable of putting on a brave face. And then, the torrent of fire, the fury at being thwarted, for whatever reason. He didn't like the food. She wanted her grandmother. He wanted to go home. None of this was fair.

It started in the cold way she barely looked at me, the lumpy woman behind the screen, scarred plastic criss-crossed with embedded wire mesh, a small area to speak through, and told me to take a number. I waited obediently, sitting on a fixed chair in a row near the boys. Aisha wriggled, demanding to be let out of the pushchair, and I unclipped the harness, watching her waddle off in her charity-shop tights and dress, the jersey fabric bobbly with someone else's life. The ache in my legs, my arms, the strange, fuzzy, dizzy feeling in my head, I thought it would clear, but it had been weeks since we landed, long enough to get over jet lag.

Fear in my mouth, bitter; knowing that this is the beginning of something that will never stop and that once I begin, I have to go on, I have to give a name, and I have to tell the story of what was and what is and what will never be again because of me.

Fleeing domestic violence. That's how they described it, the agencies I talked to. Escaping another country where women have even fewer rights than they do here, but not higher expectations. I had to find the words, find the right way to make them believe. After the weeks of wandering, I needed to stop moving, find some stillness.

I watched them, my boys, their quick brown eyes and their bewilderment, the clothes that didn't fit right, didn't look right as they huddled in their jumpers and jackets, still cold, and the smell of wet carpet and dust and years of bodies sat in these chairs, indenting the cheap vinyl covers and tearing at tiny holes to make larger rips. What had I done, bringing them from all that they had: a home, security, family, and even, somehow, despite their father's shortcomings, something like security? I knew, how could I not, that they were wondering why, when it would stop, this wandering and this waiting. When would life begin again?

As if reading my mind, Mahmood turned to me. "What is this Umma? Why are we here?"

"This is the benefits office," I said, in English, though he had spoken in Arabic. "This is where we ask the government for money to live on, until I can get a job."

His expression was too much like his father's, cold and

18

hard, intense somehow, as if he was trying to find ways to refute what I say, trying to locate and seize on something, anything, that would allow him to argue. Through all of it, from the very first moment they realised that we weren't going back, he had been fighting me in every possible way. If he had had the money and the means, he would have called his father and told him where we are, ask him to take him home.

Tears that never came before, pushing up from some inner well of grief and worry. The enormity of it all, suddenly, the reality of what I'd done. I threw myself at this escape, propelling all of us forward into uncertainty, moving towns three, four times, terrified of being found. Does every mother feel this, sooner or later, the sense of futility and the hopeless burden of responsibility? My children. And I *had* to love them, was compelled to take care of them; conception makes this indenture inevitable as sunrise and sunset and I couldn't complain, for there is no love like it.

That was all there was, just me and five needy animals who wanted food and comfort and love and entertainment every hour of every day. I had nothing to give them except this time, this waiting time as the wheels of bureaucracy ground so slowly and the steel-faced woman behind the desk, her grey-blonde hair straighter than stair rods and just as unyielding, gave me that look. Just like the look in the police station when I tried to report domestic abuse, thinking that they would help us, and the look in the first refuge we went to when I said I had five kids and they said they couldn't house us, and there I was with nothing but the bags under the pushchair and on my kids' backs and the last of my money in my pocket.

Nothing.

There were days when I wanted to wish it all away, to become nothing. To be invisible. I used to wear *hijab*; at times like this I wish I still did, to sink into its anonymity. To cry unseen. But I couldn't; I couldn't run away from this. That was never a luxury I could entertain, leaving it all behind, because of them. The children who started this in the first place, but that's not fair, they didn't cause this. *He* did.

There was a television screen high up on a wall, behind a wire mesh barrier, a daytime show where improbably thin women and suited men pasted on false smiles and laughed at meaningless jokes. We watched a lot of those shows, closeted in a room in a cheap bed and breakfast with two double beds pushed together, and the boys struggling to get used to the fact that we were sharing a bathroom, all of us, and that that tiny room was our home. I knew I had over-compensated, spending too much money buying them toys and books and a cheap video game that they fought over endlessly. I didn't want to do this, but I had no choice. I couldn't just keep running. But asking for help makes you a target. Going on record means you can be found.

I glanced at the door, stomach churning. As if he could suddenly appear, demanding his children back. I looked at Aisha, and the pressure of it, worry and fear and that desperate need to keep her safe. The strain made me want to cry, or scream. I did this for her, more than myself. I couldn't have left her there, where she would always be some man's property.

That morning, I had woken from a dream of flight, my body somehow lighter than air, hollow bird bones and fleshless form, and I was aware that despite all of my knowledge to the contrary, I was skimming over the landscape freely and at will. Now leaden and aching, I tried to endure the long wait, the increasingly nasty looks from the staff as the children played, making more and more noise as the minutes turned into hours. Ticking clock with no sound, a woman, almost skeletally thin, complaining loudly as she was ejected from some side office.

I approached the desk again. "Hi, excuse me." Even after all those weeks of running, after the escape home, English felt strange on my tongue, the voice not my own.

"Yes?"

Were they trained not to look at you, these workers, to simply not see you, and were they all women with helmet-hard hair and thin lips?

"I was just wondering when we would be seen. It's been an hour and a half already."

"You have to wait for your number to come up." She nodded at the display up on the wall in the corner, two red numbers that I hadn't seen change yet.

Two hours gone. The numbers changed slowly. People arrived, took numbers, sat. Some people were called to the desk. I started to worry. I had only a few snacks with me and Aisha would need to feed soon. Here they looked disdainfully at 2-year-olds who still breastfed. Just another reminder that I was alone and my own world, my old world, was a foreign landscape.

The door kept opening, wind and exhaust smells and sudden swells of noise, the wide glass uncovered, leaving me exposed, and more and more people filled the dark blue plastic seats, and the smell of them, old, unwashed bodies and young unwashed bodies and sweat and aftershave and children made me so sick I wanted to cry. I felt exposed after a decade behind frosted glass and the constant covering of the veil. I couldn't talk to Allah any more, to the god I had prayed to all these years. I used to think my life was fated, that I was following a path set out for me. Now there was no path, just a wasteland of bad decisions, a nightmare landscape where the demons I invited into my life lurked foully, squatting at

21

every crossroads and leering at me every time I thought I was doing the right thing. I should have had a plan, some longer-term goal, but all I could see ahead was a cliff edge, and me stepping off it, clutching the children's hands.

A small woman walked in, slim, almost straight up and down, with short, curly black hair and a masculine, plain face that showcased her kind blue eyes. Men's jeans, proper blue jeans, worn with time and moulded to her body, and a grey jumper over a shirt, and the first thing she did was almost fall over Yusuf, crawling on the floor near the door pushing a broken, three-wheeled plastic truck along and making Aisha laugh with the noise of the wheels.

"Whoops, careful there, fella," the woman smiled, a warm smile that drew lines around her face that spread out like ripples in a pond. The whole effect was one of warmth as she looked around to find out who he belonged to.

"I'm sorry," I said, as he gabbled at her in Arabic and she just grinned down at him. "I have five of them. It's hard to keep an eye on them."

"I can see that!" She laughed the words out, little bubbles of positivity, and it went to my head like wine. Before I knew it she had scooped Yusuf up and was tickling him as she brought him back to the area near the pushchair. For a moment I forgot about the sickness and the horror and the memories that were fighting to sink me, stealing my air and my will. "Are these all yours?"

I nodded. I wasn't used to talking to people. And I was not sure I should be letting this strange woman play with my children.

"Wow, you make beautiful children," she said then, and what else can you do but smile and feel good when someone says that to you?

"Thanks."

"Terrible weather," she gestured at the door, where rain was lashing against the glass.

"Yes."

There it was, that beautifully, wonderfully familiar British obsession with the weather, rooting me back there, in the cold and the wet.

"Right, I'd better get myself signed in." She walked confidently, for a small woman, a jaunty sort of skip in her step, at odds with the huddled, quiet misery of most of the other people sitting down. Another woman walked in, hugely fat, with twin toddlers who immediately ran to play with my kids, and heaved herself into the seat opposite, her wide flesh spilling over the edges of the metal frame. I nodded, and smiled, practising the art of meeting someone's eyes. It had been so long. She nodded back, no smile, settled her arms across her wide belly, and picked up one of the creased magazines from the table.

The small woman was back. "I wonder how long this will take. I'm Dee, by the way."

"Hi. Amanda"

She shook my hand. A small touch, brief, but her hand was warm and dry, her smile unaffected by our surroundings. For the first time in a long time a bit of me thawed out: it was the first real human contact I had had, other than my children, in the long weeks since we fled the sun and the dust and the desert and found our way there.

Not all who wander are lost. The quote came back to me, a book, maybe, something I read years ago, but I couldn't remember which one, or when. All that was lost in the time before, buried with my mother or closed off into a past that could never be revisited, a family I was compelled to avoid because that was the first place he would look. I could never go back.

23

"Oh, now isn't that nice?"

Dee sat beside me, clutching her ticket like an augury of the future. I followed her gaze. Shahid was helping Mahmood and Abdullah to read a book about dinosaurs, and his voice was confident as he pointed out the unfamiliar words. Mahmood looked irritated, but that was usual for him. I blamed myself. Third born, he was difficult from the beginning, after a rocky start and being so sickly for so long.

"I can tell you're a good mother just by watching your kids." Aisha ran over, noticing my attention turning to someone else, and determined to be part of the action. She was long-limbed, and her hair was frizzy in the unaccustomed humidity.

"What about you, little one? Do you like to read like your brothers?"

Aisha looked alarmed. I can tell she doesn't think Dee is a woman – dressed like a man, short hair and no veil. Although of all of them, Aisha was the most accepting of the changes to her world, she was also more alarmed by the differences when she first encountered them.

"My Aisha isn't much for reading books, yet. She's only just past two."

"She looks so much older."

"She's tall." I settled her on my lap where she tried to whisper in my ear. She smelled of the sweet breakfast cereal I had fed them all, hours ago, and of wet nappy.

"Mahmood is the real reader," I told Dee, pointing him out. "The others love to tease him about it. Shahid now, he's the stockier one, he's into engines and technology, and Abdullah is a little more creative. Yusuf just does anything the others are doing."

"Is their father an Arab?"

I frowned. It was a big deal in the Kingdom, getting the

younger ones British passports. "They were born... most of them...in the Middle East," I said, caution winning out over the sense of warmth, the flush of excitement at having someone to talk to. Someone who wanted to listen. "It's been a big change, coming back, but they're managing. Coping, I suppose. They don't really talk to me except to complain about the cold, and the strange food."

"There's a story there," Dee said when I stopped. Her voice dropped. "I hope that one day you'll trust me enough to tell it."

Without warning, my stomach twisted and turned over in that burning, excited way, as she looked at me so intensely, as I felt the warmth of her wanting to know me as palpably as if the sun had come out, the desert sun in winter warming me after a bitter-cold night with no stars.

My number was called. "I've got to..." I looked around at the children, and she said, "Go ahead, I've got this. I'll watch them. You'll only be over there." A nod towards a desk in the far corner. "Go on. I can shout if there's a problem."

I didn't know why I trusted her, but I did. Maybe I didn't have a choice. Thinking about it, as I dragged my tired bones across the room, heavy from fear and the weight of all this responsibility, fatigued from not eating enough and not sleeping and always, always worrying, it just felt like it did when one of the sisters or the other women took charge for a while so I could nurse, or clean, or cook. I had left behind far more than I ever imagined. Oh, I missed it, the connection, the community, knowing there was always some woman there to help out, if I only asked. And sometimes, many times, when I didn't.

Why are officials so unsympathetic? It took a long, long time, showing my passport and birth certificate and the children's passports and birth certificates, and explaining, again and again and again, before I even got to fill in the forms, and then there were more forms, requests for emergency funding, and then forms for housing benefit and to apply for social housing and that look as if I was trying to steal something, as if I was lying. In the end, I rolled up my sleeves, and showed her the scars, and the deformity in the arm that he broke, and I told her that I had to get away before he killed me.

"I am sorry that you have had such a bad experience," she said, her voice wooden, worn down perhaps by years of sob stories like mine and worse, and nothing to do but get people to fill out forms and tell them what they can't have, not what they can. But with five children I was, suddenly, a "priority" and that had to be a good thing.

Then she mentioned social services.

"I don't need that."

"If there is a chance the children will have contact with the perpetrator."

"No chance, no chance at all."

"I know you are saying that now, but we hear it all the time. And the number of women that go back…"

My temper rose, my voice becoming quieter, not louder, and I leaned slightly forward, for once loving my greater height.

"Listen." I forced the words out between gritted teeth; who knew gritted teeth were real? "I just spent two years hiding money and plotting and planning to get out of a country where my husband literally owns me and my children. I've flown halfway across the world, and we've been moving around for weeks to make sure he can't find us. I have been beaten, raped, and nearly killed. I am never going back. My kids are fine. They are fine because as far as I'm concerned, I will do whatever it takes to make sure none of us ever have any contact with that...bastard...again. My sons will not marry someone approved for them and my daughter will not be forced to wear a veil and spend her life hidden. Am I making myself clear? I am not one of your usual cases. If I could work, I would, but I can't. So just help me sort out some benefits and find somewhere better for my children to live."

When I got back from being asked impossibly personal questions and filling in more of their endless forms, Dee was sitting on the floor building a tower out of big plastic bricks, and telling the children a story about the princes who live in the tower waiting to be set free by a warrior maiden who exercises her horse in the woods below their prison. It made me smile that she made Aisha the rescuer, and the boys the ones who needed rescuing. It was the kind of thing I did when I told them stories.

"Hey, you." She smiled up at me as I began gathering up their things. "I was wondering if you would all like to join me for lunch."

"Oh, no, we couldn't."

"You could. Look, I'm going to be about another hour, I think," she flourished the numbered ticket between two fingers, as if she had produced it out of thin air like a magician. "But there's a café near the library on Cross Street, called Flowers. If you want to meet me there... I know the library has plenty of kids' books so if you have some time to kill..."

I could have hugged her. Not only was she offering me company – real, adult, human company, something I had yearned for since we got here – but she had given me an idea of something to do with the kids on a miserable day of cold rain.

"OK, thanks." I wrestled Aisha into the pushchair, pulled the rain-cover over, and then turned around. Dee had managed to encourage the boys into their coats, shrugging off my thanks, giving me quick directions to the library. I herded them out the door, blast of wind and rain, the loud noise of the cars on wet streets, smell of exhaust and rain and the sting of cold air. They walked ahead, chanting something.

"Wait!" I called as Shahid barrelled towards the pedestrian crossing. He halted, holding out his arms to stop his brothers, and confidently pressed the button. Maybe they were adapting, maybe I didn't need to worry so much. But how could I help it? There was that constant stress and fear, constant pressure, and the ever-present regret. I ached with it, twisting snakes of anxiety souring my gut and spoiling every moment of peace. They were old enough, though; the twins ten, soon to be eleven, Mahmood nine going on forty. Old enough not to need constant watching.

That town was the fourth we had landed in, chosen because I had never been there. It was far away from the first place we stayed, and the second, and the third. I kept us moving to cover our tracks. Just a nondescript English town in the Midlands, grey and stony and worn down, tired-looking, with a small high street full of charity shops and betting shops and plenty of fast-food places, and a medieval Church with an ancient graveyard full of huge old trees that formed a canopy of blossom in the spring. The petals would fall so thickly they looked like snow on the ground. Just another place for me and my babies to hide while I tried to figure out what to do next.

They weren't babies any more, that was the thing. They were young men and children all at once, and though Aisha was still blissfully babyish, the boys had all seen too much, known too much, to expect them to just forget. They had seen their father beat me unconscious, watched my blood pool on the tiles of one home or another. They had felt his

28

hand on them, tasted the constant fear. But I worried it was too late already, that they were already set in the ways of *his* world. I worried that it was too much for us all, the cold and the hunger and the constant running. We were all so tired of running. Aisha had turned two the previous week with no celebration. Even the boys didn't know about birthdays; not properly, not yet. So many new things. I spent my time constantly explaining, mother turned teacher and cultural tour guide.

The library was a sixties cube, all weather-stained grey panels and blue, with dirty windows and faded signs for community groups and events long past. But inside it was different, despite the same kind of industrial carpet tiles that seemed to feature in every council building. They were offset by dark wood bannisters framing the dark wood stairs, and wood-framed windows and partitions separating the adult section and the children's section from the central lobby area, tiled in something that looked like marble. Instantly I breathed out, feeling a calm and release. In the children's room the steel and white plastic shelves held large, colourful books with big writing and jolly pictures, boxes the children could rummage in, and toys, and low tables with an assortment of well-used crayons and pencils, and stacks of scrap paper.

The boys ran to the tables with their little grey plastic chairs with metal legs, and sat down, looking expectant. Oh, they needed so much that I had yet to give them! Aching, wrestling with sudden tears and the burnt taste of fear, I explained what a library was. "It's a place to look at books, and borrow the ones you want to read." I told them to play, and took Aisha out of her pushchair and rocked her little body on my lap as she pawed her way through a picture book. Shahid lined up the cars in size order and entertained Yusuf with stories about them. Mahmood and Abdullah began searching through the books for older children, talking together in Arabic. "English, remember?" I called, to be met with one of Mahmood's black looks. Abdullah nudged him, and his expression cleared, became polite and distant. I sighed. So many conversations still needed, so much work to do to win back his heart.

The clock on the wall had a thick, throaty tick, tick with a plastic second hand moving round and round. I watched it, feeling almost excited. Even though the bruises and scars were fading, even though I had covered our trail as best I could, there was still the fear; jumping at noises in the night, watching shadows, waiting for him to appear. But this woman, Dee, was so friendly. It couldn't hurt, to spend time with someone. There was something gentle about her, though that instant intimacy seems strange to me. It might be simply because I had been away, immersed in a different culture, and forgotten what it was like at home. Ten years is a long time.

Noticing a certain odour, I found the baby-changing toilet, leaving Shahid in charge and telling him not to leave that room or let his brothers leave.

"I won't, Umma," he replied, puffing up his chest.

After changing Aisha I sat on a low chair and let her nurse for a while, angled away from everyone. Other families appeared. Children ran around and some selected books to take to the issue desk. I drifted slightly. So tired, all the time, so very tired, and yet it was as if I couldn't feel anything. This numbness, years of it. Surviving. When would it end?

"Hey there!"

Dee, shaking the rain off her coat in the doorway. The light had changed to a sickly greyish yellow outside. Stormlight. The rain seemed heavier, the wind wilder, but she was bright, grinning.

"I thought I'd come and show you how to get to the café."

"Thanks."

Aisha pulled away and I set her down to run around a little. She ran straight to Dee. "Pincess."

"Yes, sweetie," Dee ruffled her hair and squatted down. "You are the princess. Now, let's find you something to play with, and then Mummy can go and join the library so you can take some books home. And then we'll go and get some orange juice and cookies. I bet you'd like that!"

The café was only a few yards away, a wide room with brick walls and chalkboard menus and a brightly coloured collection of old chairs, painted and mismatched, squishy and cushioned, welcoming us in. It was the kind of place I would have visited *before*. I felt heady and free and defiant. The smell of coffee and hot, sweet cakes, and burnt cheese, and the hiss and bang of the barista, and a clatter but not an unfriendly one, of people and cups and cutlery. I worried about the cost, then decided that I could buy a couple of cans of something fizzy, and get some tap water, and share it amongst the children.

"Don't worry about it," Dee was watching me. "This was my idea. So, it's my treat."

"I'm sorry? No, no, you can't. There are six of us!"

"I can see that!" She laughed. "Amanda, please, you should learn to accept kindness when you see it. Look, I'm having a good week, and the weather's terrible... To be honest, I spend too much time alone. So let me do this for you, and sometime in the future you can do something in return – maybe cook me dinner or buy me coffee, and then we'll be even. OK?"

I gave in. Not for myself, though the thought of one of those toasted teacakes, dripping with butter, made me feel almost faint with wanting. I gave in for the kids, who were

31

miserable and wet, becoming truculent. I knew the boys were starting to question if had made the right choices.

Soon we were spread over two tables pushed together, cups of hot chocolate with marshmallows and cream, hot buttered teacakes, toast, orange juice, chocolate brownies, and cheese toasties, the heady smell of it, the riches. The boys talked loudly, laughing as the sugar and fat hit their brains, Yusuf laughing at the twins' jokes. Only Mahmood sat quietly, reading the library book he chose; not a story book, something about nature. Aisha perched in a high chair, Dee helping her to drink orange juice and eat buttery toast with jam.

The heat, steamed up windows, the hot sweet coffee, the burnt, fatty teacakes... All of it was like a balm, like someone was soothing some part of me that has been twisted and knotted and is now, slowly, untangling. Tears pricked at my eyelids.

"Better?"

Dee's gentle smile, watching me.

"Yes, much." I sipped coffee to hide the confusion and the new heat that flooded my face. The way she looked at me... "It's been... difficult."

"Yet here you are. I don't know what you've been through, but it must be worth it, having these little ones to make you smile."

"It is."

"But you worry about them? A lot more than you should?"

Was it that obvious? Did I bear stigmata or a large red letter to announce my status as battered wife and international fugitive?

"I do."

"So, tell me. I promise you, Amanda, I'm just trying to be a friend. You seem so alone. Do you have any friends here?"

32

I shook my head. "We've been running."

"Their father?"

"Yes."

"I see. When did you get back?"

"Oh, it's been almost two months. I kept moving, at first. I was so afraid he'd find us."

A warm hand on my arm; the one he broke. A flash of memories of his fist flying, him seizing me by the wrist and twisting. Brutal, technicolour images.

"It's OK now. He's not going to find you. And even if he does, there are solicitors, and courts. These are your children. He can't just take them away from you."

I knew this. I knew that I had rights and status, but they were still his children and we were still married.

"So, are you planning to stay here?"

"I think so. We have to settle somewhere. And better somewhere nobody knows us. The money... I had some money, but it's almost gone. I was trying to last out. I thought of changing our names, but there doesn't seem much point. So I thought, somewhere like this, where there are plenty of other people, you know, somewhere multicultural..."

"I get it."

The boys were fully occupied, and Aisha was getting tired after eating. I settled her back in the pushchair and tucked her in, her beautiful chocolate brown eyes gazing at me before she started to slip into sleep. A wave of love, fierce, impossibly powerful. Anything, I would do anything for her, for them, to keep them safe.

My tongue loosened by more coffee and half a sticky-sweet brownie, I opened up to Dee, telling her of living in an Arabic country, of the beauty and the peace and the friendship I found there, of my children's father and his drinking and drug taking, and violence. Not all of it, not nearly. I knew I would never share it all, never put into words all of the pictures and feelings that frame the nightmare within.

"It just seemed to get worse." I looked at the dregs of the coffee, the twisting shapes of the foam on the edges of the cup, as if divining my future, or my past. "And the worse it got, the harder it was to believe I could get away."

"It's a common story." Sadness in her tone. Stories laid upon stories, we must all carry them. I wanted to ask hers, but I didn't dare. This unfamiliar landscape left me cautious and careful and eager and hungry for something I couldn't quite define; but it might have felt like home, or friendship, or even love. Maybe all I need was just to be wanted, just for me, to speak to another adult who saw me, not what I'd done and how many children I had.

"It's been a shock," I ventured as she piled the dirty plates up and made some space on the table, efficiently, as if she had been clearing up after children her whole life. "The way people react to me and my children. Back... back there, a big family is a good thing. Here, people treat me as the lowest of the low, irresponsible to have so many children."

"I know. But it's like everywhere else. A crime to be female."

"I wouldn't wish any of them away, I mean, I love them, but..."

"I suspect you didn't choose to have all those children though."

"Does anyone?"

That soft hand again, electric touch, sweet blue-green eyes and the creases around them, and the paradoxically soft and thick curves of her lips. I was unaccustomed to looking at the faces of anyone other than my children.

"Come on," she said suddenly. "Let's think about getting you all home and dry."

"Oh, it's OK, I can manage."

34

"And I have a car," she replied. Would she ever stop smiling?

"I couldn't."

"Yes, you could. I came into the social to sign off. I became self-employed a few weeks ago, driving a taxi. Let me give you a lift."

Within minutes she had them all corralled into coats and jackets, and we were out in the rain and cutting through the churchyard to the car park; smells of earth and loam and age and whispers of centuries of prayer collecting in the eddies and sighs of the wind. Then piled into a large black cab, and Dee whipping through the traffic as the afternoon melted into a windswept evening. She helped me up the horrible stairs that smelled of cats and of human urine and cigarette smoke, carrying Aisha and the buggy and teasing Abdullah about being the strong silent type.

I wasn't surprised that she showed no distaste for the tiny space we lived in, or that she settled the boys playing games and still managed to find and make coffee while I bathed Aisha and put her to bed, or that she had somehow put together a meal of fish fingers and beans on toast that all the children ate without resistance. I wasn't surprised when she produced a four-pack of bottled beer and suggested that we watch a video with the children until they fell asleep.

But what did surprise me was how I felt, how my hands shook so when she settled near me on the bed and we clinked bottles together and drank to a better future, looking over the sleeping forms of my children, piled together like puppies. Or how alive my skin felt, how the heat of her leg burned through the denim of her jeans and the cotton of my skirt, and how I cried hot tears when she held my face between her cool, strong hands and promised not to hurt me. The touch carried me back to Grace, dearest friend, and to the secret tenderness and the calm I had known only in her presence, back when my whole life was carved by pain and fear. Back when the days and nights melted into one great wheel of endless turning, torturous time and Grace the only relief.

It seemed then that Dee read my whole past in the shadows around my eyes and the lines and creases of my face, and that I had been waiting for her, waiting for that gentle pressure of her cool lips, and the way she brushed my neck with her fingertips as she kissed me, because every part of me rose up to meet her like a wave crashing down on the beach, over and over again.

She came back, again, and again, to visit, to take the children out. She took me shopping, oriented me to the town, small streets and small people and shifting days and nights. Dee, just a woman with a past, just like me. And it seemed like nothing special or unusual, to meet her at the library or in the park, to walk with the pushchair or watch her play football with the boys. Anodyne affection, the attention diverting from the past horror, a comfort blanket to draw up against the nightmares.

Did she whisper "I love you" in the darkest reaches of the night, a soft sigh lost amid the regular breathing of the five bodies littered across the other bed and half of this one? Did I say it too? I know I wanted to, wanted to believe that it was love and that she meant it when she said she wouldn't hurt me. I wanted to believe in the dreams of the future that we shared as a grey dawn broke over the serried roofs of the town, and the morning streets filled with traffic. She held me against the length of her body and stroked my hips and the scars on my arms, and for a moment, just a moment, there was no pain and I was washed clean of it all, the worry and the memories and the fear and I just wanted to stay there, in that moment, forever.

Take that as the reason then, for what came after. The threat of being found was always there; people are too easy to find. I had come back to a world alive with new technology and new ways of tracing people. My ten years in the Kingdom had felt like another world. Take it as a kind of love that made me say yes, again and again, until the day when she came to take us out to the play barn and paid our entry and bought us all lunch again. While the kids ran and climbed and tumbled, and Aisha toddled about in the ball pit, Dee told me that she lived in a collective, a group of people that had bought a row of derelict terraced houses from the council for next to nothing, and how they were working to build a community there, and that there would be room for us all, if I wanted to come and live with her, and she would take care of us. There would be other kids there and plenty of help, even if it was very basic.

There I was, my children's saviour, but it seemed I had been the one who needed rescuing all along.

Do you believe in love? I know I did, then, somehow, even after all I had been through, because it was Grace, my dear friend, the one person I regret leaving behind, who taught me that love doesn't have to be forced, it just is, as easy as breathing. I have lost that certainty. I know that love is an illusion, a story we tell ourselves about life and the reason we crave the company of others. It's a set of hormones and chemicals fizzing in our blood, making us think that this is the one person who will complete us, fill up all those holes and hollows that we didn't know were there, and make us happy. Love is the lie we have been told and sold with every fairy tale and story book, every improbable plot in every romantic film. It is the fiction that keeps us from the despair that is a fact of life.

But then, with Dee, love seemed right, and just, and easy,

and nothing less than miraculous, because it came with a home and the promise of a future. It came on the wings of warmth and smiles that seemed to shine just for me, and the tenderness shown to Aisha and the boys. It came with a companion who could go from playing to showing them how to fix a broken hinge or later, how to work on the various cars and vans owned by the inhabitants of Blossom House. That was what we called it, because of the line of flowering cherry trees that broke up the tarmac pavement out front, shielding us from the busy road noise and the incessant blink, blink of the zebra crossing and the neon glow of the Asian supermarket opposite.

We moved in three scant weeks after meeting Dee, three weeks where she and I stole moments together on the edges of the children's play, sleeping in fits and starts and waking always to reach for each other, as if in the comfort of touch, under cover of darkness, we were feeding each other on some intangible level. Blossom House; six terraced houses all joined up. They had kept the two end houses intact, bookending the central living space with a plan to offer affordable housing to women and families in need. The ground floors of the four central houses had been knocked through to make one vast communal living space comprising a huge lounge area and an equally huge kitchen, and upstairs were four bathrooms and twelve bedrooms, all in various stages of disrepair. Work was progressing on the bathrooms, only one of which had water, and the gardens had all been combined to make a huge space with vegetable patches, raised beds, fruit trees and a play area for the kids. Dee lived in a room above the kitchen. After a meeting with the collective, I moved in with her, and two adjacent rooms were allocated to the kids. The walls needed painting, and there were no carpets, just pitted floorboards covered with paint.

But it was a home. I had found my children a home, so much better than the emergency B&B with its narrow stairs and the two cramped rooms we shared, and the filthy communal kitchen and the bathrooms soiled by other people's waste. Better than anything I could have managed by myself. The whole house smelled of damp and paint and old cooking smells, wafting up from the warm, bright community kitchen where somehow someone was always cooking something, and of joss sticks which reminded me sharply of the Kingdom, and sometimes the odd waft of cigarette smoke and weed. There was often music playing, and on Tuesday nights drumming throbbed through the old walls because we rented the big room out to community groups and the Samba group met then. Thursdays was pregnancy yoga, and we all had to creep around, and try to keep the kids quiet.

"The social knows us," Penny said, that first week when I was explaining my worries about living somewhere new, with group of relative strangers. "Social services too. We had them round when Flora moved in. They know what we're trying to do here. Try not to worry. If you demonstrate that you have no contact with the perpetrator, they should be satisfied."

The surprising kindness of strangers, these women I hardly knew, opening their home to us, helping us to settle in, helping me register the boys with the local school, get the vouchers for school uniforms, school dinners, made me feel guilty and blessed and finally, finally, as if I could breathe out.

"And we've got some friends working in a local charity shop," Pippa added, sitting at the table watching me chop mountains of onions with the speed of long experience. "We get first pickings of the good stuff. Just tell us what you need."

What did I need? Everything. Clothes for the children, and for me, and toiletries, and toys, books to help them with their English, and the time, love and energy needed to help them realise that this life could be as good to them as the one we left behind.

Blossom House and its blossoming inhabitants, and Dee, sweet Dee with her slow, deep smile and her gravelly voice and the way she blushed when I touched her or when I smiled. I had forgotten how to smile like that, or maybe I never knew it, how to let love burn and glow in a look. Certainly, having her there, wanting me, loving me, made everything easier suddenly. Always "yes", and "do what you think best, sweetheart", and "I love you, but they're your children so I can only support you".

Pam, Penny and Pippa were sisters, all of an age between 40 and 50, all blonde. Pam was thin, with greying hair at her roots, steel grey and silver, and the blonde locks more often than not screwed up in a bun. She was thin, painfully so, and walked with a limp and a hitch, steadying herself with a wooden walking stick, grasped in hands made into claws by rheumatoid arthritis. She couldn't really move her neck so she would move her whole body one way or another when looking at people around the table. But she had a sunny disposition and always seemed to be listening hard to whoever was speaking. Pippa was the most glamorous of the three, always the best dressed and well made-up, her golden hair falling like morning sunlight over gardens and driveways. She was a solicitor, working for women like me. She brought in the money that kept Blossom House afloat. She was bigger than Pam and slimmer than Penny, who was rounded and soft, but all three looked similar with their slightly bulbous noses and slightly buck teeth and eyes the colour of the sky on a sunny spring afternoon. All the sisters sounded so similar it was like interacting with three different versions of the same person.

Blossom House had been their idea, three years ago, when Penny had to leave her husband of nineteen years because his

40

alcoholism finally broke her, and Pippa, Molly's mother, had just received a life insurance payment following her husband's suspected suicide three years previously. Pippa and Molly at that time lived in number 1, which had been mostly renovated, where Pippa also had an "office" where she ran her legal business. Molly, just nineteen and doing a degree in politics, did admin for her. Pam also did admin; for Pippa as well as the collective. A born organiser, she kept everything and everyone in check.

"Now, let's go around, say our names, and give one word that describes how we are feeling."

The meetings always started like this. I almost laughed. But everyone said what they needed to.

"Tired," Pippa said, closing a cardboard folder with a snap. She always seemed to be working, either reading documents or tapping on a laptop or closeted in her office.

"Surprised," Dee said, one hand twined in mine.

"Grateful," I said, not looking at anyone, but seeing the general nods and smiles.

"Thoughtful," said Samara, a retired GP, originally from India, who had lost her entire family – husband, son, daughter-in-law and two grandchildren – in a house fire. She had been the first of their "rescue women" and now offered free health advice and antenatal care with a local independent midwife using the big room and one of the rooms in number 1.

"Relieved," said Flora, her Swedish accent musical and light. Flora was small, dark and very slim, with two daughters, Jenna and Elonie, aged 6 and 8, also brown-skinned and mixed race, tall and slender limbed. Flora hardly spoke to anyone. It was Dee who explained her story to me, in her usual way, hushed tones as we shopped or did housework, well, in the days when she still did housework. Flora had met a man on holiday in France, and fallen in love. Within a matter of months she had moved to the UK and married him, and within three years had two small children. He worked long hours and was often away on business. One day she came home to find him there, waiting for her. He informed her that his boyfriend was coming to stay that evening, and that she should move into the spare room, with all her things. Humiliated, she had done so. After two years of trying to tolerate his behaviour, she asked for a divorce and he told her he would take the children. She'd then come into contact with Pippa, whose business was family law, and Pippa had invited her to join the collective.

Waifs and strays, coming and going; she was one of many they had taken in, always women, always with some kind of catastrophe in their wake.

Ah, those meetings! Every decision had to be agreed by consensus, which took forever. It seems so long ago, now, but when I think of them all I can feel the hard wood of the kitchen bench, and the scent of burned toast stings my nostrils. I can see them all, nodding, talking, discussing the business of the community in the same order, every single week. Site issues. Jobs. Activities needed. Activities offered. Blossom was meant to be a learning community, so we were encouraged to share our expertise in the form of 'workshops' to which we could also invite outsiders from the local community groups we were connected to. This way we could apply for grants and funding for renovations and other activities. I remember that week Samara was offering an Indian cooking class and Dee was offering basic bicycle maintenance. I remember how Dee rested her hand on my leg as we talked, and how the weak sun coming through the windows highlighted the line of toast crumbs on the wooden counter.

"And now Amanda," Penny said, who was leading the meeting. "As our newest member, you have to read the articles of membership." A blue cardboard folder, complete with tea stains, was passed to me. "The main thing is that we share the work. You are expected to put in 20 hours a week on community work. Other than that, your time is your own. As you have a child under school age, you aren't required to go out to work, but once Aisha is in school, you are expected to find part-time employment. Until then, the housing benefit you'll get will be your contribution to the collective." I nodded. I was ready to do whatever it took just to stay there. I know Dee was pouring love into me at that point, her attention fixed on me.

Have you felt that, the way that someone can fill you up with their energy just by loving you, by wanting you? It's like a drug, that energy, and it went to my head like wine. Maybe that was when it started. Maybe that was when I started to believe that I needed someone else, someone to fix me, to be the other pillar holding up the temple of my life. I should have questioned why a woman would want to take someone on with five children and nothing to offer. I should have at least wondered.

I volunteered to cook several times a week. It was the one thing I knew I could do, cook for large numbers of people, even if it was more of a challenge because all communal meals were vegan and gluten free. We were expected to provide our own breakfast and lunch and snacks and we had to cook once a week, plus the cooks often needed helpers with the preparation, simply because of the volume of food.

There were discussions of various issues with the house and garden, and a blackboard with a list of jobs was used to share tasks. I signed up to clean the kitchen that week, and to do laundry duty. "Don't worry, I'll show you how we do everything," Dee whispered, as Penny officiously allocated every kind of task to a member of the group. I remember feeling strange, wondering if history was repeating itself. Wondering if I would always find myself learning how other people wanted things done.

"It's OK, I'm used to this sort of thing," I replied, just as Aisha toddled into the kitchen calling, "Umma, Umma," with Molly hot on her heels. I smiled at Molly's bouncing curls, her heart-shaped face, the way her jeans creased across her generous hips. She seemed so very earthy and alive. I cuddled Aisha briefly and sending her off and thinking, can this be true? Because it was too good to be true, really, that I would find myself here, in this place, with these people, who had instantly accepted me. I was divorced from my own family. My sister Karen hated me, sending cold, cruel letters to tell me that our sister had died. I had not dared to go home to visit, knowing it was the first place my husband would look for us. I told none of them where I was. I had borne the grief of losing gentle Jan whose mind never grew older, silently.

Then, a hot flush of shame as Samara noticed the scars and old bruises on my wrists and forearm, and the way I held my mug of coffee – in my right hand but with my left hand supporting my wrist, weak from repeated breaks that never seemed to heal properly. She could see it as if my story was written there in words for all to read. The taste of fear and the worry and the sense that none of it could last, because sooner or later, he would find us.

"A man doesn't lightly let go of his sons," Pippa confirmed later that week, when we had our first official meeting with her as my legal counsel. "We need to be prepared for when he shows up."

Fear tastes of iron and salt, an old, familiar taste, and though there were moments, minutes and hours sometimes stretching into the greater part of a sunny day or evening when I forgot the fear, forgot what it was to be afraid, and even though those moments grew longer and longer as the weeks and months passed, it never left. At night, while Dee slept deeply, I rose to stand at the window and watch the street, and wonder if somewhere, under a different sky, he was doing the same. I knew, without any doubt, without hope, that he was coming for me.

Mars Violet Deep

In sleep, dreams of fire, always fire, orange-yellow lava, sooty red flames, purple-black billows of soot-smoke, houses burning, people burning, fire all around me and no escape. Fear and threat and urgency, hot lances driving into me. In these dreams I am different; proud, a warrior, or a teacher, always alone, always unassailable. No longer fleeing, but fighting, always standing my ground.

When I wake, I am Ash.

Today, something is different. The face in the mirror is the same, but the eyes are different, like an older, wiser version of me is returning my gaze. Still that fleshy roundness, the soft curve under my chin, but are there hollows forming under my cheekbones? Is it working at last?

Twist up the huge waterfall of thick hair, out, turn left, right. I don't know. Something is different.

A message on my phone. Shahid again.

<hey there sis, what's up>

Then one from Abdullah.

<Not heard from you in a while, what's going on?>

So they know then. The news has travelled around Facebook, and they've picked up on it. I should have told Carl not to comment on anything he saw. Shit.

<Nothing. It's all just crap. Don't worry about it.>

Shahid <We're coming home this weekend>

<No need>

Abdullah <are you talking to Shahid?>

<yes>

Shahid <we are coming home. Tell mum>

<will do>

Abdullah <did he tell you we're coming home for the weekend?>

<YES!>

Abdullah <K. Sort this out then. Does Mum know?>

<No! Don't tell her.>

Shahid <course not>

<Stop confusing me. Are you reading each other's texts?>

Shahid <we are now.>

<see you on Friday.>

Two miles to Carl's house; a fast walk, misty morning and birds singing, feet thudding. The tightness across my chest and belly makes it harder to breathe in, elastic cuts into my skin, but I don't want to breathe deeply, don't want my belly to stick out when I take each breath. Stare straight ahead, try to avoid the reflections in the car windows and the house windows as the street winds down back into the village proper, and houses swallow me, old and new and somewhere in between. Carl lives off the park, the swing set and playpark fenced off for months now and haunted by teenagers smoking pot behind the buckled half-pipe. Dark shapes and light; is one of them him, Jadon? He has hunched shoulders, just like that.

No, I don't care, I don't and even if they say something, even if they all take the piss, what's the difference, anyway? What's the difference from being the dirty Paki and them saying no-one will have me cos I'm a fat gyppo and a pikey and I stink, and that takes me back, helter-skelter of memory and dream and the burning hot air of summer breath which is always associated with the voices. Smelly. Bugsy. You got bugs. Don't touch her, or you'll get bugs. She smells. Smelly lezzie.

Oh, I can't forgive her, moving us from one stinking

rotten house to another, that council house that no one else would have, with its broken toilet and the rancid piles of rubbish left by the last tenants. I remember her opening the bin and it was full, a whole wheelie bin full to the brim with old nappies and a trail of fetid brown ooze running out of the cracked base and we could never get rid of the smell. And before that, Blossom House, the one place that felt like home, but she took that from us too...

Carl is waiting in the hallway, his uniform pressed and his shoes polished, proper trousers from a decent shop, not like mine with the hems falling down and the cheap thin fabric.

"Quick," he says, rolling his eyes. "Before she decides she's taking us in the car."

I hold the door, white pvc moulded to look like wood grain, which makes no sense to me, because it's obviously plastic. Why have a door that pretends to be wood, why not just have a wooden door if you want, or a plastic door if you don't, but then maybe it's just like everything else around here, a sign that nothing is real, it's all fake, and it's because everybody fakes everything and everybody lies. Even Carl doesn't tell me what he really does some evenings when I can't get hold of him, but he's definitely lying about his age; I know they don't let you on those sex hook-up sites when you are under 18 but there you go.

Not my business but sometimes, just sometimes, I want to know because there's so much to know these days and I can't find all of it in books. Everyone knows the internet is a quagmire of lies. Books are kinder. Cleaner. Even the mouldy ones with the foxed pages – yes I know what foxed means, small wonder I read it in a book – even they seem cleaner, more authentic, than the flippantly flipping pages flicking left and right and the memes that come again and again as if there are no new stories in the world, no new wisdom, and everyone already knows everything and they laugh at *me* for reading old books. Even Carl doesn't get it. Though I sometimes wish I could share these thoughts with him, the feelings that come, like how it feels when I read *Jane Eyre* for the umpteenth time and just ache for the lonely child in that burning red room, battling the monstrous nature of her own imagination.

"So?"

Carl cocks his head in that American, hey girlfren' way that kind of bugs me because it makes me wonder how much of him is real.

"So what?"

"Tell us about it, stud," he says in his best sickly-sweet Olivia Newton-John voice, and a strange tightness comes, laughter forced out of my constricted chest making me momentarily breathless as he sashays along the rain-pocked pavement and raises a finger to his pursed lips.

"Oh, stop it."

"Then spill. Or I'll keep on doing this until you do."

"It was...nothing. Really. Just nothing. Over and done within a few seconds. I barely felt it, to be honest."

"Oh. So the earth didn't move?"

"Nothing fucking moved except him humping me like a fucking randy dog and me getting up and leaving."

"Right." He kicks at a cracked bit of stone that has fallen out of the wall near the primary school. "Aw, shucks, and I was hoping for details."

"Details. Right. He stuck his prick in me, it hurt a little, he came, I put my knickers on, I left. Oh, he did offer to walk me home."

"How gallant."

49

"Yes, Clark Gable."

"So, what now, Betty Grable?"

He always does this, matches me quote for quote, blow for blow, like we're fencing all the time, like he never lets his guard down. Fencing words, easing the weight growing with every step towards school, and I would bunk off, right now, but it will happen tomorrow or the next day or the next because there is no escaping this. It'll be all over school, and when Carl looks up from his phone he confirms it.

"Everyone?"

He nods, skipping away like a child past the rainbow-painted fencing that keeps the kids in and the paedos out, and I flash back again to a yard a lot like this one, old iron railings thick with years of paint and decay, cratered with the ghosts of burst bubbles of rust, smell of wet iron and the yearning to step through the narrow bars and out into the patch of scrubby green beyond, to run and run and never stop on legs that would never tire, fuelled by lungs that never ran out of breath.

The pointing and whispering starts when we get near school, a tide of uniformed kids sweeping towards the gates, and the comments already pinging on Carl's phone. Not mine. Mine is so old and so crappy I can't get Whatsapp or Messenger or FB or Instagram, I can just call and text. I've seen how they treat each other, and I don't think I'm missing out, it's just another thing for them to have a go at me about.

"How bad?"

Carl shrugs, slipping back into a more masculine stride and putting on that sullen, sneering look he uses as camouflage. Although everyone knows he's gay he tries to blend in.

"The usual. There's no photos except a couple of blurry ones someone must have taken here, sometime, and someone has stuck your head on a naked body..."

The fact that he stops is enough for me to know what that body must be doing. "It's obviously fake so don't worry," he adds.

"Right. Well, better that than being called a frigid virgin. Fuck the lot of them."

"You go girl," he mutters as we approach the steps and start climbing. I press my thumb to the registration screen just inside the door, and he does the same, and in the corridors I can hear them, the words hitting me like blows, because now I'm a dirty fucking cunt and a slapper and I just keep walking through the crowds, jostled and pushed and the smell of boys and farts and body spray and someone's make-up is so strong, and it's like my feet aren't touching the ground any more. I can't feel anything, just this hot coal of shame and defiance all mixed together, because it's my right, it's my choice to do whatever I want with my body and I should have known that it wouldn't make anything any better.

All through physics I want to cry, to run out, but no way is anyone driving me out, and then lunchtime, running the gauntlet of the yard with its enclaves of boys and girls and the taunting laughter, wet air after sudden rain, nowhere to sit, glistening pools reflecting the half-light, half-dark of the sky.

Carl brings me a sandwich. "You have to eat," he says, forcing it into my hand. "I mean it. You don't eat enough."

I bite it and oh, my jaws ache, saliva pooling in my mouth, and I hate myself for loving it, that sweet white bread marshmallow softness, the slick margerine and the crunch of lettuce and yielding fattiness of cheese. I hate

51

myself for eating it, but I can't stop, I can't stop, I want this food and the thick, sick feeling of it sticking to my teeth and my tongue and then suddenly I don't want to swallow but Carl is watching me and I do, washing it down with diet cola and feeling the bubbles hurting my throat, just punishment for my weakness, and my belly is sickeningly full and everything hurts worse than ever. Good. That will teach me to be so weak.

"It's been a busy weekend," Carl laughs. "I met two guys on Grindr. The first, Jake, well, he was like a bloody battering ram..."

"TMI!" I shout as he goes on. "I mean it. Stop."

"But there's more. I met Ethan, the second one, and turns out they know each other. They were texting each other about me! Next thing I know the three of us are getting together at Jake's flat."

"That's disgusting. How old were they?"

"I dunno. 19, 20. Students, both of them."

Such simplicity, meet and greet and let's fuck, and he obviously enjoys it, isn't looking for anything other than that. Suddenly I have an image of him, naked, with a cock in his mouth like the gay porn he's shown me, hairy men all around him, and I am strangely aroused by the thought of it. There must be something wrong with me, sex on my mind all the time, like a boy. Something wrong that I don't like the boys around me, that I didn't feel anything when I let that kid fuck me, I just wanted to know what it felt like. But then the thought of two men together turns me on. Or maybe it's just that in those films they don't feel anything, no dramas, no expectations, just do this, do that, move like this and everyone is satisfied.

The sandwich lies like a stone inside me. In IT, I go

online and order some shoes, then pay my phone bill. Shahid's sent me £50, so there's enough money left to buy other things this week, tampons and senna and toiletries, maybe a bag of bran to mix with water and drink, to make me feel full. Carl nudges me as we walk between classes. "Hold your head high, and fuck them all," he declares. People, masses, boy sweat and girl perfume, sweets and cigarettes.

Biology. The lab smelling faintly of gas and something earthy. Mr Savage takes us through the male reproductive system, and I think that everyone must be looking at me. The pictures are nothing like the sad reality of that kid's pale dick, looking like nothing other than a baby elephant trunk. Why is this all coming back to me now? Make it go away, something twisting inside me like worms, eating its way outwards and everyone will see, maybe the cheese was bad, rancid, maybe there was mould on the bread, maybe something is poisoning me, insects crawling on the lettuce leaves and burrowing into my guts and through my flesh and moving under my skin.

Hot feeling again, dizziness, the sense of everything fading in and out. I look around the classroom, trying to stay focused, and Jarelle, the Muslim girl who wears a regulation school headscarf, looks back at me with sympathy, then raises her eyebrows and tilts her head as if to say, "I know, right?" I twitch my mouth in something like a smile. She doesn't usually acknowledge me but sometimes we bump into each other or have to sit together in PE, and I wonder what she sees, what they all see. I look a lot like her, I think; we could pass for sisters if I wore a scarf like hers. But she is beautiful and slender, and my face is fat and she doesn't have double chins.

I look back at the whiteboard where he's marking out

the life-cycle of the spermatozoa and I draw the pictures he tells us to, labelling the head, the tail, the nucleus, and I even manage to force a laugh with everyone else when he makes his joke about hyaluronic acid and face cream, but really I want to scream and scream and run until there is nothing left of me but pumping legs and a fleshless body, skin over bone and muscle, and fall burned away by my own anger and the fierce burning of this rage. Instead I grip the pen until my fingers hurt, thinking nothing but "fuck this, fuck this, fuck this" until they turn numb and pins and needles come, and suddenly it's the end of the lesson and Jarelle is standing there, looking beautiful but concerned, and she takes the pen out of my hand and jerks her head at the door and says, "Come on."

Permanent Rose

Blossom House. Even years later, I could be caught out by memory and find myself back there. When the trees first blushed pink. When I saw a contrail in a crystal blue sky, or smelled brown rice cooking. When I saw a woman with corded muscles and strong, practical hands with engine oil or dirt under the fingernails, I was there; scrubbing the long pine table in the kitchen or feeling the ghost of Dee's lips and her clever fingers bringing me back to myself.

It wasn't as if I didn't know gentle touch, or love. I had tasted it, briefly, with Grace, in stolen secret moments that felt like dreams. And after, in those last days, I dreamed of Blossom and its many rooms. That I left some part of myself there is without question. But what about what else was left there? Was it there that the catalyst happened, or the seeds were planted, that brought us to this point in time? Cruel cold mornings and my girl-woman daughter stalking the broken-down corridors and haphazard rooms of this place, this house of ours that was so like and yet unlike Blossom, because there, the rooms were filled with people and the voices of children, and laughter, and, yes, tears as well. But somehow the tears were all part of it and even the fear was diluted by the knowledge that there was someone there, always someone there who would hear the cry, the muted nightmare scream, the sobbing and the laughter, and come looking for the source.

Blossom House, yes, it was a haven. That's what they call it, a place where you can retreat, or escape. The word conjures up safety, happiness. Rest. But there's no rest for a mother of five and there was Dee, my sweet Dee as I saw her then, with her simple loving ways, seeming so invested in playing with the children, helping the boys to grow. How was I to know what was real and what wasn't? She worked as a taxi driver, Friday nights, Saturday all day and night, and Monday to Friday doing the school run and the late evenings. This left her ample time to work at Blossom House, which was like a demanding mother-in-law or a dependant wife; always wanting something, always needing something fixing. Dee had appointed herself our handywoman, and to her fell such tasks as building cold frames, erecting garden sheds, fixing plumbing, putting up plasterboard in number six, and maintaining the collection of bicycles that lived in the shed. Dee's taxi and Pippa's old Mini were the main cars in the household, but Molly had recently got herself an Astra with her student finance and Dee spent a lot of time working on it so that it could limp along getting her to and from uni and out to visit her friends in various far-flung places.

"Hey, love." Dee's voice floated to the surface of the sea of memory. Always love, honey, sweetheart. She rarely used my name.

"Yes, love," I replied, back in the past where everything was tainted and painted by an overlaid wash of could have, would have, should have.

Still looking for it, that thread of reason and meaning. The answer. Did it lie in the way Dee wrapped me in a quilt of sweetness each night and woke me with gentle kisses? Did it lie in the way that regardless of it all, regardless of letting her love me, I couldn't really love her back? Or was it because too often I woke in the night and scrambled away from the weight of her arm on my chest, throat closing in panic? Was it the way that sometimes, when she hovered over me making expert work of my body, I had to bite back the sudden fear?

Or was it that I grew complacent, when the summons didn't come that first year, so I allowed myself to relax? There was so much to do. I had to get the family settled, learn how to respond to the needs of the community, and get to know how things worked. I made breakfast in a corner of the big kitchen, porridge and toast, encouraging the boys to eat until the unfamiliar became familiar. They had free school meals, so there was only me and Aisha and sometimes Dee to feed most days. I would sit Aisha on the counter beside me and hand her bits of fruit and vegetables, and when it was my turn to cook for the community, I'd prepare the food early so I could take her to the park after lunch. Dee and I would walk, talking about my past, about the Kingdom, and she'd talk about her childhood in Devon, living with farming parents and how she loved green and growing things. She didn't talk much about her past, but sometimes it seemed to rise up and spill out of her unchecked. Or we'd work in the garden, Aisha digging in the dirt beside me as I pulled weeds and planted seedlings, cleared rubbish or swept the paths.

"Mum."

I looked up from the curtains I was making for Aisha's room. The donated fabric, thick pink and purple cotton that smelled of chemicals and something else, something clean and fresh, clashing with the scent of fresh paint.

Abdullah stood before me, with a bloody nose, a dirty face and a bruise on his cheek. He said nothing. Shahid barrelled into the room beside him as I set aside the sewing and ran to him, my precious boy, what had they done to him?

"What happened?" I tilted his face one way and another as he tried to pull away.

"It was the boys in school." Shahid looked thunderous, a lot like his father, but I pushed the thought away. "They're always picking on us, but usually they don't hit us. I was held back after the lesson, and when I came out there were three of them on him."

"And where were the teachers?"

"No one was around. When I found a teacher they said all four of them would get reported for fighting. But he wasn't fighting, Mum. They jumped him."

For fuck's sake. "Does it hurt much, Ab?"

He shook his head. "No, except when you poke it like that!"

"I'm trying to see if you've broken anything."

"I'm fine!" He wrenched away from me, storming off. Then I saw that Shahid's knuckles were bloodied and dirty.

"Oh, Shahid."

"I had to fight them, OK? Else they won't stop."

"Does this happen much?"

He shrugged. "Yeah, I suppose so."

I hated it, all of it. I thought things were better, that they'd settled in. Certainly they seemed less clingy, more confident in speaking English and understanding the social cues.

Sending him off after his brother I made my way downstairs to the big room, then into the office. Penny was there, working through some papers. "I need to phone the school. Abdullah's come home bloody and bruised."

She shook her head. "Go on. Want me to leave?"

"No, it's OK."

"Well, just remember to mention their duty of care."

"I will, thanks."

I hated that this was my job, my responsibility, having to ring up people with the power to hurt me and my children, and having to defend my children and my choices. My hand shook as I picked up the phone. The call was unsatisfactory, the head of year less than helpful.

"Abdullah is considered as much to blame as the other boys."

"But they jumped him. He didn't even fight back."

58

"Who says that?"

"His brother."

"Yes, well, that hardly makes him an impartial witness."

"I'm telling you now, Abdullah is a quiet boy. He doesn't fight unless he is provoked."

"Mrs Said, as you well know, children behave differently away from their parents. Especially boys. This was just a case of 'boys will be boys'. We haven't taken further action but we will monitor the situation. I suggest you reinforce with your sons our rules about fighting. I'd hate for them to be in trouble this soon after joining us. There are often issues with integrating when you join a class later in the year, but there's only so much we can do.

"I would have thought they might have settled in by now; it's been several months, and they're doing so well with their English. Perhaps a chat with you can help them focus on trying to fit in. Or perhaps have their father have a word?"

"Their father isn't around, and if you'd taken the trouble to read the information I provided, you wouldn't even have suggested that. You have a duty of care to my children, and that encompasses pastoral care when they're in school."

"And we have sixty pupils in year seven alone. Like I said, we are overlooking it this time. You are the only parent to complain. Perhaps you need to cut the apron strings a little."

I hung up. What the fuck?

"Not helpful?" Penny didn't look up from her computer.

"No!" Fuming, I stormed back to the kitchen where, inevitably, Shahid and Abdullah were rifling through our cupboards, Mahmood watching from the table. All three were muttering to each other in Arabic. "English, please," I said automatically. But I didn't know what else to say to them. I helped them make cheese toasties, a great plate of them, and then Molly appeared, trailing Aisha who was laughing and dirty from being in the garden, and Yusuf, clean and neat, clutching an old cassette player.

"Come here, wild child!" I hugged Aisha and she squealed, one of those perfect moments of love. I was struck then with the rightness of this, for her. She was happy. I could not imagine her controlled, subdued, in a culture that valued her only if she was docile, hiding that wild hair forever under a headscarf.

Then Molly noticed. Abdullah's bruises. "What happened?"

Shahid straightened his shoulders. "We got into a fight."

When did my boys get so tall? Almost as tall as Molly already, and Shahid's shoulders were broadening. Turning into men, already and only eleven.

"I spoke to the school."

"Mum!" Shahid shook his head. "It won't help."

"I know. They said I should have a word with you. Remind you about the rules about not fighting."

"So I was supposed to let them beat him up?" His face darkened, as it always did when he got angry or upset. He put some toasties on a plate for Aisha.

"Shah, Shah!"

She jumped up and down and laughed as he picked her up and swung her round.

"Come on you," he took her to the table and sat her down, and the tenderness, oh, the sweet tenderness of him cutting up the sandwiches and telling her to blow on them, and Abdullah watching Molly as she stole a sandwich and teased him gently.

"I thought you were a lover, not a fighter."

He blushed and I laughed.

Laughter came often, those days. I'd forgotten there could be laughter, and joy; the simple pleasure of being with my children and exchanging thoughts without words with other women, over the heads of our children. How I could have been so lucky to have found this kind of haven for all of us?

In bed, with Dee, quiet at last, noises in the street outside but the children gone to their own rooms; Aisha asleep in the little bed I got her from the charity shop on the High street, with its white metal frame.

"I don't know what to do," I confessed. "I never had to deal with this stuff. It was always the men in the family. I don't want them to suffer because their father isn't around."

"Honey," she rubbed my back. I tried not to flinch, reminded myself to relax into it. Even then I still had to think about it sometimes, about being touched. "You know that's bullshit. Single women raise boys all the time."

"But I don't know what to say to them! I don't want them growing up thinking violence is acceptable. But I don't want them to not feel like proper men, either."

Her clever fingers kneaded my back and shoulders, and I leaned into her, the soft fabric of the old t-shirt I wore for bed bunching around my waist. I pulled up the covers.

"Just remember, they're better off without their father. So don't beat yourself up so much. They have teachers and older boys to learn from, and they will. It may be a little different to what they grew up with, but they'll adjust. This is just a little blip. They have to find their feet, and you have to let them."

"I suppose so."

"Look, how about I teach them to fight properly..."

"What?" I pushed her away. "I told you, I don't want them thinking violence is a good—"

"Hold on, hold on, hear me out. You really do like to go off half-cocked, don't you? What I meant was that I did martial arts, kickboxing and karate, when I was a bit younger. Black belt. I'm not a violent person, but it gave me the confidence I needed to not get picked on in school, or on the street for that matter. It changes the way you walk, the way you hold yourself. And then people don't see you as prey. Let's give them something to do, physically, something that gives them confidence, that's all I'm saying. And it would be good for Aisha, too, in a few years."

"OK. If you think it will help."

"Trust me, it will."

"Make sure you teach Aisha too."

"I will, love."

I leaned back on her. It seemed like I was always leaning on her, on her even temper, her money, her easy way with the children. She seemed to always be able to respond to them, whereas when I was tired and low all I saw were the colours of the desert and their father, multiplied by five, looking back at me reproachfully.

Sundays and sunny days, time wheeling, then Mahmood became more withdrawn, f that was possible. "What's wrong?" I asked him after dinner one evening.

He wouldn't meet my eyes. He looked a lot like Abdullah when he smiled, but just like his father when he didn't. I wondered if he realised this. "Nothing. Just school."

"Perhaps I can help, if you tell me about it." I reached for him but he pulled away. "I don't want your help."

I asked Shahid to talk to him. "He's not happy. But he won't talk to me."

"I'll talk to him." He threw down his pen. Homework was a struggle for him and for Abdullah. "At the least he shouldn't be so rude to you all the time."

Soon after, Yusuf came home crying. Again, Shahid the protector, the mediator; he went with his twin to meet both boys from school every day for a week, skipping lessons to do so, to reinforce the message that they had backup.

A wet Wednesday, dealing with the leak in the downstairs

bathroom, holding Aisha while Dee filled the hole with expanding foam.

"There, it's not pretty, but it won't leak now."

"Umma!"

"Shahid, what's wrong."

I turned to see Yusuf, red-faced and crying, and Mahmood storming through to the garden, shouting in Arabic that he hates it here and he wants to go home.

"What did he say?" Dee took Aisha.

"Don't ask."

"OK, well, we're going to watch some cartoons."

"Thanks."

I sat them down at the big kitchen table, and was joined by Shahid almost immediately.

"What's happened?"

"It's Yusuf. He says that a boy in his class stole his toy car." Mahmood still wouldn't meet my eyes.

"When?" I reached to wipe the tears away, but Yusuf shook his head at me, resisting. Then suddenly, he buried his face in my chest.

"Lunchtime. They have long lunchbreaks in that school."

"I know, it's so the kids can go home for lunch."

"Well, there's a boy there who keeps taking Yusuf's stuff, and never gives it back."

Shahid was furious. "You can't let this happen, Umma."

"I know. I'll do something."

The school was unsympathetic.

"Mrs Said, there are children at this school with no toys. The boy in question borrowed the toy because he has nothing at home."

"So when is he giving it back?"

"I don't know. It's not up to us to interfere when the children lend each other things."

"Yusuf didn't lend it to him! The boy pushed him over, took the car, and won't return it."

"These are deprived children, Mrs Said. I suggest you don't let your son bring toys to school."

"So what is he supposed to do for an hour and a half at lunchtime?"

"Play football with the other boys."

"Yusuf doesn't like football."

"I don't know what else to say. Perhaps he should try to get on with the other boys more. I can ask the lunch supervisors to keep an eye out for any trouble."

"No one tells you how to do this," I almost yelled at Dee, who was looking tired, sleepy, as she cuddled Aisha. There was some awful pink and purple cartoon on the television in the little bedroom. I'd forgotten that she worked late last night. There was a big concert at the Arena and she didn't get in until after two.

"It seems like at every turn there's someone telling me that the problem is my children, not the other children, not the system."

"You have to understand, Manda; they have a lot of children to deal with, and a lot of them are from much worse backgrounds."

I hated it when she was so reasonable. She didn't really get it, the lurch in my stomach every time I saw some new bruise or scuff, or tear in the knee of a pair of school trousers. I was living on the edge, wondering what was happening to them out there in the world without me. I was never this anxious before, not about the boys. If there were issues at school, one of the men sorted it out, or the women got together and told the men how to intervene.

I talked to the twins, following them up to their room overlooking the front of the house and the busy street below.

Buses rumbled past, the top deck of the double-decker almost level with the window.

"What's going on with you both?"

Blank looks, and Mahmood, who was never far away, appeared in the doorway and interrupted in Arabic. "I can't believe we left home, our friends, and family, for this."

"Speak English," I said automatically.

"No," he replied, stubbornly in Arabic. "I hate it here; we all do. I want to go home." The sudden flash of temper as he slammed the door.

Abdullah looked out of the window, the darkening of his face the only sign of how he felt. I ached for them, suddenly, for all I couldn't give them.

"I thought we were doing OK?" I reached out for Shahid's hand, to pat it, noticing that it was almost as large as mine. He was always the one I could rely on to open up to me.

"I don't know." Shahid's accent was still strong. "I miss home, Umma, but I don't want to go back. But..."

"Are you unhappy?" He shook his head. His hair needed cutting; I would have to find a barber for them. "Or don't you feel you belong here?"

Shrug. Of course.

"You will make friends, I know you will. Just give it time. You're doing so well, your English is excellent, and..." The emotion in my voice betrayed me. It hurt to see them struggle, and I knew how it was to feel uprooted.

"It's OK Mum," Shahid's hand covered mine. Abdullah got up and gave me an awkward hug. "It's all going to be OK."

Dee taught them, all five of them, to defend themselves, starting a martial arts class that made the boys walk taller and prouder. She worked tirelessly on their English, and at times seemed like a far better mother than me. We worked in the garden together, mud and dirt and green stains from the weeds, the boys running around with a football on the uncultivated part we called the 'lawn' or helping paint the stained breezeblock walls and hammer up fence panels and pick up the rubbish that got thrown in from the alley and gardens behind.

Samara made nettle soup in spring and summer from the crop that always seemed to grow in our little patch of paradise. Flora would sit with me, shy at first, and talk about her kids and mine, discussing parenting issues like bedtimes and routines and discipline and school. Her English was very good, but when I commented on it she laughed and said, "You English, you are so arrogant, as if learning another language is so hard!" It was the first time I remembered that I also spoke another language, but I couldn't bring myself to say it, or to frame the words that bridged the gap between the past and the present. There were so many bridges I could have built then. But it felt good to be with another parent, sharing stories, the small triumphs and the daily disasters.

As time went by, as the small kernel of fear and anxiety inside me gradually uncurled, I found myself missing the things I used to do, my job teaching children English, the extended family, the desert light, Grace's house. It had often felt like a nightmarish time, that life I had before this, but it wasn't, not always. Still, I never thought that I would miss it. I missed the sounds and smells of the *souk*, spices and the sting of chillies, and the call to prayer cutting through the bands of blue in the early morning, before the sun was fully risen, echoing inside me. I missed that sense of there being something greater, some purpose to all of this. I missed praying, which surprised me, the routine and familiarity of those days. Cut loose, I was anchorless, except for the children.

Aisha loved it there. Molly was readily available to play and to distract her. My beautiful daughter; she spent more time outside than inside, and was sleeping better than before. And though the boys took a while to adjust to Blossom House, the new rules and the new companions, there was so much to keep them busy and focused. There was always someone around to answer a question or break up a dispute or pick up one or the other of them when they fell or banged something or scraped something or broke something. Mahmood grew even more intensely private, turning in on himself.

He came home one day to tell me he had joined a local Christian youth group,

"What group?" I demanded, halfway through chopping vegetables for dinner. Mounds of carrots glowed like jewels. The scent of onion and garlic and the green scent of bruised spinach.

"The church two streets away," he said. "Craig in my class goes."

"Okay." I put down the knife and wiped my hands. Should I worry about this? "And you know that these are religious people."

"Yes."

"So you're learning about the Bible and stuff?"

He rolled his eyes. "Yes Mum." Already he had stopped calling me Umma. Perhaps it was the influence of these new friends. "I like it there. They're nice people."

"I didn't realise... what I mean is, are you a Christian now?"

"I'm thinking about it." He was toying with the carrot peel. "Look, don't make a fuss, OK? I only told you because Shahid said I had to."

"Right. You're ten, which means I need to know where you are, so yes, you did need to tell me. I'd better pop over there and check these people out."

"No Mum, there's no need. Mrs Vaughan, our teacher, she goes to that church. It's OK."

I swept the peelings into the bin. Was he doing this to defy me? Or to reject his past? Or just because he wanted some friends of his own? Who was I to say anything?

"OK, well, I guess I never expected you to become a Christian."

"It's no big deal."

"Mahmood, you were raised a Muslim. I thought…"

"I don't get on with the Muslim boys at school," he said quietly. A gift, the first time in a long time that he had shared something with me about his life, his feelings.

"Why not?"

"I just don't, OK! It doesn't matter. You're not Muslim any more, why do I have to be?"

"My son, you don't have to be anything… I just wanted to understand…"

"There's nothing to understand. It's two streets away. Shahid and Abdullah said they would walk me there and back if you had a problem with me going on my own."

"Okay, well, fine. Whatever you want."

He walked off, munching a piece of carrot, mumbling something inaudible.

Mahmood was out a couple of evenings a week and every Sunday, and he started wearing smart clothes and was less angry. I thought it was just typical boy behaviour that he spoke little to me. Or typical of him. Abdullah started getting into a computer game called Warcraft, spending long hours on the house computer and complaining every time someone else wanted to use it. My boys were growing away from me, living their own lives. No sadness at this, just an overriding relief.

Shahid grew strong and sporty and discovered football, and that meant one of us taking him every Saturday and Sunday morning to play with the local under 13s. When it was Dee who took him I relished the time to myself, because she was always at my elbow, like another child, needing a smile and a quick kiss, the touch and clasp of fingers in passing, some acknowledgement, some gesture. Always.

There I am, back cooking in the big kitchen, great pots of vegan curry with melting sweet butternut squash and glowing wedges of carrot and bright green spinach, the creamy coconut milk a poem on the tongue, the scent spicy and earthy and real. Or there, look, in the garden, kneeling to slip seedlings into fresh earth and compost, growing garlic and onions and pumpkins. Or there, climbing the stairs at night to our bedroom, Dee leading me by the hand with that sweet smile of anticipation. She liked to kiss my scars and my stretchmarks and tell me that she honoured the past that had brought me to her. And I liked to believe her. The day the news came that my father had died, she held me for hours as I sobbed out the regret and the lost, the old, distant pain of loss, all soothed by being there, with her, with this new family.

There I am presiding over a communal meal, the long table filled with new friends and the bobbing heads and animated faces of my children. Aisha is on Molly's lap, eating enthusiastically, in a way she never would for me alone. Shahid is laughing at something Elonie has said. The shadow of fear is almost absent, just a faint dark stain in one corner of this room of memory. We are happy.

Khaki

"You don't look right," Jarelle walks steadily beside me, her head swathed in the navy blue scarf making her face stand out. Huge, brown eyes, button lips, and thin, blue school trousers showing hips and a flat belly and thigh gap. I want to be her. It's like time's slowing down, how she places each foot like a dancer, long brown fingers moving as she speaks.

"It's...I..." Am I blushing? Hot shame now, do girls my age talk about these things? How can I know, the last girl I had as a friend was in primary school in that awful place we lived in Bristol, and we had a falling out, didn't we, because suddenly she stopped playing with me. Why was that? Something I did? Something I said?

Scuffing my feet, the tarmac sloughing off greyish stones like layers of skin, how many girls like me have walked across this yard? Cool hand on my arm. Those liquid brown eyes.

"I get like that too," she says, smiling, her voice light. She has assumed one thing, when I meant another. "Come on, we'll sit down."

Hard bench under the yellow bricks of the sports building. "Maybe you should have stayed home," Jarelle sits straight, crosses her legs. Clouds boil overhead, cold air nips like teeth at my fingers and face, I can never look like that, straight and clean edges, stylish in her uniform, she looks years older than me and miles apart.

"The Savage is such an idiot," she says. That invitation to solidarity. Can I trust it? Is this another joke? Are there others waiting for the punchline now, waiting to laugh at me again?

"Yeah."

She tucks an edge of the scarf in unconsciously. "I sometimes wish I'd let my father send me to boarding school after all."

"He was going to?"

She nods. Oh, if my face were as perfect as hers with its sharp cheekbones and tight skin! If I could look like that!

"Yeah, he wanted to send me and my sister off, said it would be better for us, the year I started my GCSEs." One shoulder lifts, perfect shoulder, I know without having to see beneath the school jumper that it would be bony, the collarbone etched in sharp relief, a hollow between it and her neck. I know she had a sister in the year above us who went to Oxford last year.

"And you didn't want to go?"

"Would you? Being locked up together with a load of hormonal girls?" Her laugh is liquid, a waterfall of clear notes, perfectly tuned, or like a breeze that plays harp strings, haphazardly beautiful, as if it can't help itself. "Besides, I'd lose touch with all my friends."

"Oh, I'd do anything to be somewhere different to this." My fingers twist in the edges of my cardigan; the frayed cuffs look chewed and tatty.

"You don't mean that?"

"Have you met my mother?"

She laughs again, and I laugh with her, a rusty, unaccustomed laugh but it feels like it could be nice, for moment, just to pretend that we're two good friends laughing at the world and not needing to worry about whether or not it's real.

Everything is fake, in the end. All the people who say they love you, they don't mean it. Those women, the ones my mother shacked up with, they said they loved her,

71

they said they'd be there, and they're gone. It's a lie, all of it. There's no one, only my mad mother locked up in her studio painting pictures for weird books and wandering about like she's looking into another reality. Am I telling Jarelle about this? Is she really showing sympathy? Should I be telling her this? But yeah, I should, best to tell her now so she can disappear sooner rather than later. Before I start believing she might be actually interested in me because no one is, it never lasts, not once they see how we live. Not once they get to know me, the real me.

"Sounds like a nightmare," Jarelle squints up at the sky and even with her nose wrinkled up like that she looks beautiful, perfect. "My mother never lets up on me, not for a minute, it's always, 'Jarelle, you must learn to cook better than that, you will shame me when you have a husband', or 'Jarelle, no man wants a lazy wife, pick up your clothes!'"

"I never get any peace at home, even when I'm supposed to be doing homework. It's like she's schizo, one minute she's going on and on about my grades, getting to university, the next she's warning me not to walk home with boys and telling me I need to wear loose clothes or no man will want to marry me!"

"Nuts," I say, feeling some part of the stone inside me warm, as if something is loosening, or melting. "Is she very traditional then?"

"She's a Muslim wife and mother. My dad, he works as a consultant surgeon, so he's not always around, and anyway, she's always riding me. Half the time I wish I didn't have to go home after school."

"I don't get that, mostly Mum ignores me," I admit. "But then when she starts talking to me it's like she's trying to be my friend, or something? But she has no clue, no fucking clue what it's like now."

Jarelle looks at her phone. "Friend me on Facebook," she says. "Are you on Instagram?"

Shame, the heat again. Not faint now, the cold air has helped, but the blazing cheeks, the fire inside, burning again. This encounter will flare and then turn to ash like all the others, surely.

"I can't." I show her my phone. "I only have this piece of crap."

"Oh, that sucks," she grins. "They don't get it, do they, parents? I mean, what was it like, the stone age when they were young? Lol!" She flicks through something on her screen. "Oh, I know, I have my old phone. It's a Samsung, it's still working. All you need is a sim. And we can get a pay as you go at Tesco Extra. If you meet me after school you can walk back with me and I can give it to you."

I want to ask why. Why is she trying to be my friend?

"I..."

"No money for a sim? They're like, a fiver, but why don't you see if you can get some cash out of the old girl?" She stands. Sighs. Picks up her bag. "You're doing chemistry, right?"

"Yeah."

"Why? Are you going into medicine, too?"

I want to laugh. My arse and legs are frozen from the cold bench, the wind that has whipped underneath. Standing hurts, stiff muscles. I straighten up like an old woman. "Actually, I want to be a psychologist. Or something."

"Oh?" As we walk back towards the main building, suddenly we're in step, suddenly I have a friend, suddenly this comrade is beside me on the path and I can't feel the

73

burning arrows of looks and comments from the other students, like Jarelle is a superhero and there's some kind of cloak or shield shining from her and wrapping around me. For a moment I don't care about anything other than this, this feeling like I'm not alone.

"Why?" she asks. I don't mind telling her, though it's a risk, everyone already thinks I'm a weirdo, a psycho.

"I want to study dreams," I confess. "Well, how and why we dream, and what our brains are doing."

"Do you dream a lot?"

"All the time. I have nightmares, ever since I was a kid I've had them." Shut up Ash, don't say any more, it's enough, anything more is too much fodder for future cruelty. Carl keeps telling me I have to learn to protect myself, and isn't this just too good to be true? Don't trust, can't trust, whenever I trust it's a mistake; people leave, we move, the ground falls away and there's nothing solid to stand on. Everything disappears, and this will too. But that doesn't mean I can't enjoy it for a while, does it?

"I have weird dreams, sometimes," she replies. "Like, sometimes I'm flying, and then suddenly I'm underwater and I can breathe."

"Yeah, really weird. I mean, I've read loads of books and stuff on dreams, but we don't really understand them. And there's all this other shit that goes on, about sleep and how much you get and whether you need to dream and stuff, and there's all this other stuff about symbols and archetypes and creativity..." Shut up Ash!

"Yeah? But don't you have to do medicine to be a psychiatrist?"

"Psychologist. I've applied for Psychology via UCAS? I guess you're doing medicine?"

"Yeah, Dad thinks I'll get in to St Andrews, which is

where he went, but I don't know. Scotland, you know, it's a long way away from anything. I've applied to three places in London, and to St Andrews, and to Cambridge."

"Cambridge. Wow."

She shrugs. The glass doors swallow us, crowds of navy blue students again, thumb to the screen for afternoon registration. She sits beside me in chemistry, and the girl she usually sits with, Katya, who's from Poland but also wears a headscarf, gives her a look. She grins.

"Kat is wondering why I've abandoned her."

"I don't mind if you want to sit with her." Go now, before I start to enjoy this too much, before I start to care.

"Nah, I wanted to sit with you. It's OK, right?"

"Yeah." Am I supposed to smile now, or is that too much, too childish?

"Right then." She pulls out her chemistry folder, and I do the same, though hers is a bright pink plastic thing with labelled inserts, neat sections and an A4 book with bright white paper attached at one side, and mine's a battered A4 ring binder with poly pockets and bits of paper, and my A4 pad is the cheapest greyish soft paper that tears too easily.

I look through the homework that was due today and she says, "Oh, that was hard, did you get question 4?"

"Yeah, I did." Was it hard? This sort of thing doesn't seem hard to me, but maybe that's because I spent years studying alone either being home-schooled or after school in the university library while my mother did her painting classes and life drawing classes, and there was no one to tell me which books I could and couldn't read, so I read them all. I loved the science textbooks, laws and quantum theory and chemical formulae, and this chemistry we're doing now isn't so difficult. Not that I would tell anyone, won't give them another reason to hate me.

Halfway through the class Jarelle leans over and writes on my pad, *Her voice sounds like snoring.* I stifle a giggle and bow my head so I won't be noticed. I write on her pad, *Or like a long, drawn-out fart* and wonder if I've gone too far, but she grins and almost laughs out loud.

"You never seem to struggle with Chem," she says as we gather our books. "We should study together sometime."

"Yeah, OK."

"What have you got next? I've got Maths."

"Psychology."

"See you after then, by the front gate?"

"Um, yeah." She fist-bumps me, my hand feels awkward doing it. Strange. Watching Jarelle float away I wonder when the bubble will burst. Psychology is two floors down, I have to hurry, but I text Carl along the way.

‹Walking home with a girl from my class after school, ring u later.›

‹WTF?›

‹Explain later›

‹too right bitch›

Stomach growls, cramps all through psychology, and it's an easy session, Freud again and studies on the impact of psychiatry, so it doesn't even distract me, no need to concentrate, write the notes with mind wandering, thinking of Jarelle and of other things and wishing myself thin, thinking of walking home. I think she lives somewhere near the old school site, where the girls' grammar school used to be, before they built this super-school. Will she even be there waiting for me, or will I stand and wait and a gang of them will start laughing and film me and my disappointment and share it online to make me even more of a laughing stock? At least that boy didn't film me, I made sure of it, I made him switch his phone off and leave it outside, and I'm glad because they did that to Shawna in the year below, last year, a gang of the boys. That's is why I don't trust them, I don't trust any of them. Even Carl, the only person I let take pictures of me, who's been my friend since year 9; even he's as bad, because he still watches that stuff, and I know I'm just his little fat friend and I'm there to make him look good and be company for him in between fucks.

"Ash! Ash!"

I look around. Jarelle running towards me, so lightly, nothing moves on her body, nothing sways or bounces; jealousy is green, the books are right, green glass shards slicing into every part of me. If only.

"I thought you were going to walk off for a minute." She isn't even breathless. How can that be?

"I was going to wait the other side of the gate." I nod at the clot of year 11's just inside the large blue iron gates.

"Oh, yeah," she falls into step with me again, shifts her bag on her shoulder. "Maths was hell. I swear to God I'm going to be doing homework in my sleep."

"I know, right," I say, using the same inflection she did earlier. "Like, in Psych he says 'read this book, this chapter that's online', but when I checked it's like fifty pages." Was that the right thing to say, the right way to say it? Don't act like it's easy, the work they make us do, don't let on you're clever, it's not right; wait until I find out just how clever I'm allowed to be, so I can fit in. Please, don't let me lose this thing that we have now, this almost friendship, don't question why she's suddenly hanging around with me.

As we walk, conversation, her voice mostly, spreading like flowers in a meadow, bright warm colours and so easy, so natural, how could I have gone my life without this? Her family were originally from Oman, her mother was a nurse when she met her father, they moved here 20 years ago, they visit Oman once every couple of years.

A pause. A bare spot, waiting for me to fill it.

"Um, my father's from Saudi Arabia," I admit. Why am I telling her this? Because I'm supposed to. This is how it works. She shares something. I share something. This is how the girls in books do it, how friendship happens. "My mother left there when I was two."

"Do you see your father?"

"No. Umm, yeah, so something happened, some legal stuff, and yeah, we moved around a lot, and then my mother...well, he can't see us, no one from his family can."

I'm still waiting for her to turn and run.

"Yeah, one of my cousins had that happen. She married a man she wasn't supposed to, and the family had to step in, something went on. She's not allowed to see him or his family now, and they can't come anywhere near her. It makes me never want to get married."

"Oh, I wouldn't marry anyone! And I'm not having kids!"

"You sound very definite." She laughs.

"I have four brothers."

"Shit, really? Where are they all?"

"They're all older, like, so they left home years ago, well, Yusuf left two years ago, and he's the last, the youngest, he's four years older than me. Shahid and Abdullah, well, they live near Bristol, both of them, Shahid's living with his girlfriend and Abdullah shares a house with them. They run a garage together, MOTs and stuff, and I think they do up old cars and sell them? And Mahmood, he's still at uni, he did a degree in Modern languages and now he's training to be a vicar or something. Yusuf is working for a cruise company, he's musical, so he plays in some bands or quartets or something and travels all around the world. I get postcards, sometimes, or texts. They all text me, like now and then, not often, but yeah."

"Growing up in a houseful of boys!"

"Exactly. Put me off having kids anyway. Spent years just wanting some space and privacy."

"You and me both."

As we cross the road, she links her arm in mine. Heat and hardness and falling into step with her. Awkward. I've never done this before, so aware of her, and our shadows on the ground, outlines of all that we are, so conscious of my body now, wishing myself not to be sweaty, hoping I smell as nice as she does, don't trip, keep the rhythm of the steps and try not to act like this is so new, so very new. When she lets go I miss the feeling, despite the awkwardness.

Her house is where I thought it would be, along a leafy, quiet street with big old houses set far back from the road. Hers has a small driveway, crunchy, yielding gravel, noisy, making me waddle slightly as she releases my arm again and reaches for the key that hangs around her neck. A wide front lawn, edged with neat flower borders, terracotta and stone pots, old and heavy-looking, with shrubs and more flowers. A tall, red brick house, with a perfectly circular arched porch, mosaic tiles on the floor, a rush mat, and an old boot scraper to one side. I know it is a boot scraper. It tells me how old this house is. Big wooden front door, stained glass panels either side and in a half-moon above the door.

"You have to take your shoes off," Jarelle says as she opens the door into a hallway with a thick rug and more tiles. I do so, curling my toes in the bobbly socks that, when I see them in this light, bright hallway, don't quite match, as a woman appears from a door at the end, beyond the sweep of white painted banisters to the right, edging the curved stairway.

"Jarelle..." She gives out a stream of words I don't understand, but some part of me jolts suddenly, as if I should know what she is saying.

"Mum, this is Aisha, a friend from school."

"Salaam alaykum," says Jarelle's mother, and almost without knowing I'm doing it, I respond the way my brothers taught me, "Alaykum Salaam."

More language, a flood of syllables, sibilant and full of liquid sounds.

"No mum, Aisha doesn't speak Arabic. Her mother's English."

"Oh. Well, welcome to our home." She takes both my hands. "Now, can I get you something to drink, to eat?"

"Oh, no... thanks...."

"Mum, we're going upstairs to study. Chemistry, probably. Right, Ash?" She grins. "I'll be down later to help with dinner, yeah?"

And then we are moving up, thick cream carpet and polished wood and smells of spice and dried flowers in the window at the curve of the stairs, a long landing with white wooden doors with high, old-fashioned latches, more stairs, and then Jarelle's room which sits under the eaves, a wide room with wooden beams and white walls and white carpet and a huge bed. A desk sits under one window, under the other is a couch covered in pastel cushions. There are no posters, no knick-knacks, but on one wall is a huge painting of trees with yellow sunlight coming through them, and on the other is some kind of metalwork shape in silver framed against cream fabric. It's not a teenager's room, but it suits her perfectly.

"Sit down," she nods at the couch. "I'll just be a minute." As she disappears through a door to the right I realise she has her own bathroom up here. Those green shards are back, but now they become a great mirror of dark green and scabrous black showing my jealousy and envy for what it is, and I school my face which I know is twisted with bitterness. Oh, to live like this with green leaves on the tree outside dancing and this great space full of light!

"That's better," Jarelle is back, wearing pale cream jeans and an ivory t-shirt, and no headscarf. Hair longer than mine, but the same brown-black colour, lighter at the ends, a sheet of it dancing as she moves.

"What? You knew I had hair under the scarf, didn't you?"

I laugh. Hide my surprise. "This is a great room."

"Yeah? You think so? Mum won't let me have it the way I really want, but yeah, it's good, I suppose, and I'm far away from my parents here."

She crosses the room, bare feet barely seeming to touch the carpet. Her toes are like her hands, slim and graceful, and her feet are slender and shapely. I am too fat and ugly and tainted for this room, carrying the burden of the thoughts and memories I have turned to smoke and ash inside my mind. Everything burns behind me, this is all I know. And this will too, and for a nightmare second, I imagine this room consumed by fire, and afterwards, the carpet melted, the beams blackened and cracked and silvered at the edges where the flames have eaten away all the beauty they once

81

held, all the strength, until they will crumble at the slightest touch.

"Here." She has been rummaging in a drawer. It is a Samsung, yes, last year's model, and she dangles a charger too, and then plugs it in. "You know, I'm sure they sent a free pay as you go sim with my new phone..."

And within minutes I have a phone, plugged in and charging, and a sim with £5 credit on it, and she's helping me set up all kinds of stuff and this hurts. It's too much because anyone would swear she actually likes me, but she can't, why would she, so it must be pity; and what if it is? It's better than nothing. While my new phone is charging we do chemistry, and with my help we finish it and then we do physics and we laugh about doing four A levels because there aren't many of us, and I don't tell her I only signed up to four because I didn't realise you were only supposed to do three, and I would have done five if they'd let me but they wouldn't because there weren't enough hours left or something. I wanted to do English too, just because I knew I could, because I'd read so many books that I thought it must be good for something but they wouldn't let me. One of the teachers said I could do it as a private candidate if my mother would pay and I said yeah, that's not gonna happen and she just gave me that look, the one they all give me. I know I'm not the only poor kid in school, but I guess I should have got pregnant at 15 and left or left at 16 to do beauty therapy in college or something. Like at times I catch them unawares and they look surprised or something and I hate that look, that look is the reason I make deliberate mistakes on my homework sometimes, just so they won't start paying too much attention, but then again they make allowances when they find out she's an artist, because she's a "creative type" so that's allowed.

After homework Jarelle puts on some music and then we talk about school, and then her mother starts calling.

"Shit, got to go help with dinner." Jarelle scoots to the edge of the sofa and I long to move like that.

I get the hint, gather up my things and stuff them in my backpack, noticing how scruffy and dirty it looks set against this room. "I've got to get home, anyway."

"Yeah, your mother will wonder where you are."

I glance at my phone, my old, hateful one. "Not until no dinner appears. I usually cook for her."

"Why? Is she ill or something?"

"No, she's an artist. She paints." As if that's all the explanation she needs, Jarelle shrugs and leads me back down to the hall to put on my shoes.

"Is Aisha staying for dinner?"

"No, Mum. I'll be there in a minute."

Jarelle turns to me. "So now you know where I live. See you tomorrow?"

"Yeah."

"I'll wait by the gate." And on that promise, I'm outside again, on the beach-like gravel drive and then under the trees and only then do I realise it's dark already and it has begun to rain, so I walk fast, and run a little, but it's too tiring, nothing to eat today. Jarelle didn't even notice I didn't eat at lunchtime, but then, she didn't either, so maybe it's normal, maybe I'm just like her. But my legs ache and they're heavier than lead like I've got weights around my ankles, and the rain is getting heavier, so I know I'll be soaked by the time I get in.

A buzz from my pocket. Carl.

I text him my new number from the old phone and he says he'll come round later, but it's already seven o'clock and I know she won't have lit the fire in the kitchen; the place will be freezing and damp when I get in. I try to hurry again, heart pounding, water soaking into my shoes and socks so my feet slip inside on the cheap plastic and I think yeah, but I have a new phone and Jarelle seems to like me and for once I didn't leave school feeling like I've just escaped from some horrible reality show where they lock you up with people you hate just to see what you do.

Lights on downstairs, what's she up to now? The old wooden door creaks and I have to kick it at the bottom to get it open, the damp has swollen it so much. Cold burning through me, my nipples freeze and harden and it hurts, Jesus and all the gods it hurts like someone is driving nails into them. What the fuck?

"There you are." Mum's looking almost sane, though her batik trousers are on backwards, not that she ever notices, she will insist that the pockets go at the back like jeans.

"What's going on?" Is that my voice? Do I sound that sullen, that childish? Maybe I'm hearing myself differently now, after spending some time with Jarelle, maybe it's the cold and the pain in my chest.

"Marcus and Fliss are here, to talk about the new exhibition."

To hear her talk, you'd swear it was at the Tate rather than the village hall. Marcus, he's the one who does weird sculptures out of recycled Hoovers and other bits of household junk and old engine parts and bikes. He likes to visit and rummage around in the junk in the garden. Fliss is his girlfriend; he calls her his "old lady" in a

84

smarmy, pseudo-cool kind of way that makes me want to vomit. They're all so old but he flirts with me and with Mum and she just can't see it, how he makes my flesh crawl. Fliss is funny, but she's so fat she can barely fit on the kitchen chairs and she always sits on the sofa in the living room and never seems to stop talking, even when the other people in the room aren't paying attention but are having a conversation amongst themselves. It's like she doesn't have an off switch.

"I'm going to my room then."

"They brought food, sweetheart, you should join us."

I look through the door. She's lit the fire in there, after all, logs hissing on the hearth and the dry, smoky heat and smell of it. There's hummus and olives and pitta breads, and salad and sticks of celery with peanut butter and some salsa and tortillas and bean dip, and vegetable fingers baked in the oven, now cold and flabby, which is the same thing they always bring. Still my stomach flips and churns and aches and saliva runs in my mouth, but then I think of Jarelle's perfect figure, the way she moves like she's floating through water, and I see Marcus spread-eagled on the couch with his hand on Fliss's bulgy, monstrous leg, and I shake my head. "I'll get something later."

"You could at least try and be sociable," Mum complains, and I want to slap her, because they are looking at me, both of them, with those condescending adult faces. What the fuck do they know about me and my life anyway?

"Hello, Fliss. Hello, Marcus," I say pointedly. "There, happy now?"

"I see Aisha is practising her conversation skills," Marcus says, and I look at Mum, but she just laughs at

85

him and does nothing to defend me. Nice. I walk to the door.

"At least take something with you." Why does she do this? Just cos she's so fucking skinny, why does she keep trying to feed me? Why does she act like a mother, now, in front of her friends, when half the time she doesn't even notice I'm around?

Upstairs, a plate of celery and salsa and hummus on the desk, the scent almost makes me faint. Celery is OK, salsa is tomatoes and stuff... If I don't eat much of the hummus...

Eating is like I imagine sex is supposed to be, all that anticipation, and the pleasure, texture, taste, jaws aching, saliva running, spice and cold and earthy paste textures and crispy clean celery. This is good, I can have this, but it's over too quickly and I just want more, now I've eaten something; more food, more flavour, more texture. I drink a pint of water from the bathroom tap to make myself feel full, and it comes, sickly feeling, stopping me eating, so I drink more. I haven't taken off the chest bindings, the bodyshaper, and I won't, now, because if I do my hated belly will flop out and I'll just be hungry again, so I pick up my book, then toss it aside because I don't want to read horror, and instead pull out *To the Lighthouse* and try to lose myself in that river of words that runs and runs.

The noise of the phone jolts me from a doze.

<So what's hapnin?>

<Nuthin>

Carl, my oldest friend, not even he knows my secret, no one knows the power that comes from being in control.

<Just finished bloody English FFS>

<It's late>

<No shit Sherlock>

\<I'm going to bed\>

\<Alone?\>

\<No, I have the football team here, we're having a party\>

\<Let me know how it goes\>

I text my brothers the new number, then ask Shahid to send me some money to top up the sim. He does it immediately, asking if I need anything else. I hate asking him. I hate him knowing I need something. I just want to get away, please, someone, show me a way out of this, please.

Dropping the phone onto the faded quilt cover, aching and yearning, rising desire for food, it's all I can see and hear and think now, all I can smell, food, saliva pooling in my mouth, why can't I stop this, why do I have to want like this? So weak. Staring at the ceiling, no, do something, sit up, dizzy, aching, is this what my life will be forever?

This room, oh god, how can I bring Jarelle here, with the patchy vinyl flooring and the faded rugs and the dusty drapes covering the pocked walls? Seeing it now, as if for the first time, how dirty and faded everything is, cobwebs on the windowsill, dust and hair balls and fingermarks and suddenly I have to clean it, thinking of her light, stylish room, but it's all too much now, food heavy in my belly, sickly feeling, I just want to eat now, how can I even hope to have a friend like that, I'm such a disgusting fat pig.

Under the wobbly dresser is the bag of stuff that no one knows about, crisps and those apple pies that are pure sugar, and huge bars of chocolate, and I know once I start it won't stop but I want it, the grease and salt and sugar on my tongue, in my mouth, eat and eat, not caring about the crumbs, the stickiness on my fingers, my cheeks, the acid bite of the sugar on my lips, just give it to me, now, more, so good to eat like this, to crunch and chew and taste and swallow, don't stop, daren't stop, one bag of crisps after another, a chocolate bar, wash it down with more water, lots of water, and then more sugar, more fat... and then the feeling, horrible bloated sick and full feeling, the voices downstairs, no-one to see or notice, lock the bathroom door...

The first time I did this it hurt so much. I scratched the inside of my throat with my fingernails and it took forever. But after I read a thread on the Anaforever group on Facebook, using Carl's phone of course, I realised it doesn't have to be so hard, because the trick is to drink water before, and during, and after, so it comes up easy, and now I barely have to try, just wiggle my fingertips in the back of my mouth and it starts, the sweet agony of it erupting from inside me, all that food, retching and heaving over and over again until my stomach burns, my throat burns, acid coats my teeth. Shaking and weak, heart pounding, but it feels so good. Brush my teeth, twice, then drink another pint of water, take the last of the Senna tablets. Clean the toilet bowl, check for splashes. Look in the mirror, now, yes, I can smile now, I did it. I'm strong again. I am in control.

I feel empty and sore.

Good.

Stagger back to my room, legs unsteady, breathing shallow and heart pounding, aching and so tired, so tired now, just lie down on the quilt, wrap it around me, tears leaking out. They come every time. Tears and sobs because I did it again, I couldn't stop myself, but it will be OK, I've purged, I can rest now and not think, just drift as if I weigh nothing, next to nothing, lighter than gravity, just floating into dream where I can forget it all, how fat I am, how I hate this, hate being like this, how I hate her for making me like this, hate her, it's not fair, just let me float, let me drift away and forget everything that weighs me down, this body, this life, just set me free.

Please, someone. Set me free.

Sage Green

The charcoal moved over the page, catching the shaft of sunlight through the steamy window. I sat in cafés a lot, scribbling and sometimes sketching. My favourite café, staffed by improbably thin young students all in black. The hot smell of coffee and frying. The woman next to me was eating eggs florentine, thick yellow hollandaise oozing over her plate. Despite my obvious concentration, she seemed compelled to talk. I don't mind. It happened a lot. I toyed with the thickly varnished pine surface, leaving charcoal smudges.

She asked, "Where are you from?"

I couldn't answer, because there was no answer. "I live here," I said, thinking of the stories I never told. I couldn't say, "I was made in many places, forged by fires of time and love and loss and pain and fear and yes, shaped by the needs of others and the weight of little hands and little bodies always clinging, always wanting. The space here, now, fills with the pleasure of being alone, unwanted by anyone." She asked, "What do you do?" and I answered, "I do this. I sit in cafés and watch people."

She looked uncomfortable, turned back to her paper, the headlines and the horrors obviously easier to digest. Sometimes I said, "I'm a painter," and they looked awkward because if I was any good they would know me, surely, but sometimes I sat in a café where they had my work on the walls and that meant I was legitimate. But you could see on their faces they would never buy it because no one buys art unless they're rich; money is to be spent on necessary things, or on things that make you look good, and it's a niche thing, the class of people who buy art, real art, and put it on their walls. I never thought I would end up being part of something like that, or that I would be good at anything other than having children, so I don't even know how to talk about it. I looked at the well-meaning woman, with her helmet of neatly styled, dyed hair, the make-up that doesn't quite cover the creases and lines of life in her face. All those stories, hers and mine, and we would never know each other because even then, even then, years on and sons grown and a daughter on the cusp of adulthood, I still don't understand what makes people tick.

It didn't start in Blossom House – not this life and this constant sense of dislocation that dogs me now, even though I am more settled and more established than I have ever been – but the painting did. A class run by a local art student, funding from some charity or other. I wouldn't have gone, but Penny thought I needed to do something other than cleaning and staring off into the distance. I wanted to write, to tell stories, but at the creative writing class I held the pen and stared at the paper, too many words or not enough. The well of pain inside me could not be uncapped by words.

"Let's start with the basics." Janillo, the young art student, a bright, large woman with imposing eyebrows. We stood in the big room. It was light and bright from the wide windows and a scent of summer on the air. Aisha had started in the local nursery and Molly was picking her up. Eight of us, in front of battered easels. All women. I was the only one not wearing a veil.

Janillo showed us how to pin our thick paper to the easel, then set a simple arrangement of driftwood and stones on a table in the centre of our circle.

The weight of the charcoal in my hand, that dusty dryness. Years of time and life concentrated in this fragile stick. The wood, twisted and shaped, greyed and pitted. The two pieces of wood speaking to each other, and something else, speaking through me about the pure form caught in that sweeping, curled shape.

"Yes," Janillo said when I roused from wherever I had been to regard the work. "You've captured that well. I love the shading and the shadow. You have a good eye, Amanda."

Warmth. Pride. Wonder. Then the rushing of guilt, that I had switched off, for just an hour or so, had forgotten the children and the housework and whatever tasks were waiting for me. I had forgotten the pain and the angst and the memories and the fear. For that brief timeslip, there was only me and the picture. "I don't know where it came from," I admitted.

"It came from you," she replied. "So bold. I'm looking forward to seeing what you do with other media."

We tried watercolours, pastels, pencil, pen and ink. But it was the oils that seduced me. Thick, sensuous and malleable, they could be carved and caressed into shapes and textures. They caught the light and captured it, harnessing it to the page.

I realised that paint doesn't ask much of you. Shape and colour and form are easy when your mind is as alive as mine is with fear and regret and dreams and memories, and the simultaneous desire to hold on to the past and to run away from it. For months I painted deserts, landscape after landscape, until Janillo complained she was running out of burnt umber and burnt sienna and brown madder and jaune brilliant and Naples yellow deep and Indian yellow and cadmium yellow pale and terra rosa. Then, slowly, figures appeared, stick thin and black, wavering figures swathed in shadow. And then finally flowers, and buildings, and one day I painted the garden outside the kitchen window, in spring when the new green came on the spindly elder tree that climbed up the old yellow brick wall, and that was the end of the deserts. But sometimes, when the sun hits a stucco wall at just the right angle, or when dust motes dance in the shaft of light through a bedroom window, my fingers itch to paint the million and one moods of the desert dunes and rocks and evoke once again the heat and the space of it all.

Once Aisha started nursery school, painting became my occupation as well as my hobby. I had always thought it would be words that drew me, that I would write books crafted from long strings of linguistic jewels beaded with all the feelings and impressions I had garnered. But words seemed to fly away from me in those days, and I thought in colour and shape, in the abstract rather than the specific. People were jumbles of triangles and circles and oblongs, five pointed stars joining up the lines on a face, or they were visual metaphors – apple-cheeked, emerald-eyed, bird women and horse-women and women whose bodies swayed like elephants in ponderous dance, and I painted them all, sometimes as they were, sometimes as what they seemed to be, and sometimes a morphing of the two.

Penny helped me to apply for a grant from a women's arts council, which paid for me to make some prints, and cards, and buy a table and canopy, and I sold my pictures at markets and craft fairs, Dee taking me in the taxi and picking me up, sometimes staying to help out, bringing me cups of tea in plastic cups as I sat at my table and smiled and talked in ways that still seemed so difficult, Aisha more often than not playing on a picnic blanket beside me. It didn't matter that I wasn't making much money, because I still had my housing benefit and my income support and I still had Blossom House and the kids had this great family to belong to and it seemed, just for a while, that I was making up for everything I had taken them away from.

Having an occupation raised my status in the household as well, which meant that I didn't have to go out and find other work. The women treated me differently then, as if I was morphing out of my fleeing victim status and into something else, something like the woman I was meant to become. I modelled myself on them, on Pam and Penny and their liveliness, on their confidence and their seeming unerring belief that they could do anything, *be* anything, simply by putting their minds to it. Pam had signed up to do an MBA, with funding provided by the government, and Penny was single-handedly turning Blossom House into a hub of community activities. I learned a lot – how to make reusable sanitary pads, how to cook jambalaya and dhal fry, how to recycle plastic bottles into vases. How to paint.

Time marching on, years turning, dirty streets clogged with gold and brown and red leaves, blushing spring sunsets, summer in the garden, the lushness of green and growing things. Watching the boys settle, watching Aisha suddenly sprout long limbs, losing the baby face and baby chubbiness, bouncing in from nursery in her little school uniform of a blue skirt and yellow polo shirt in winter, yellow gingham dress in summer. Jenna and Elonie went to the same school, so Flora passed their clothes down to Aisha, though the dresses were a little large for her and the shoes were never any good.

Dark winter morning, I woke early, as if in response to a call, or a threat. I used to wake like this in the Kingdom, but there, it was never cold except when the air conditioning was turned up too high. And never cold like this, biting my nose, numbing the hand outside the blankets. I nudged Dee, who was snoring gently.

"Mmm... what?"

"Dee, the boiler's gone out again."

"Mmm?"

"The boiler? Everyone will be getting up soon. It's freezing."

She grunted and complained, rolling over and almost falling out of bed, then cursing. "Bloody hell it's brass monkeys!"

"I told you." I whispered. "And keep your voice down."

"Why is it always me who has to fix things?" She dragged on jeans and a sweatshirt, padding barefoot out of the room. I watched the shadows and the glow of the streetlight, listened to the traffic outside, heard the call of a crow, rough and lonely. I woke, as I used to, fully alert to something, to the sense of something coming. I swung myself out of bed, stumbling to the bathroom, then threw on my clothes, A muffled thud and then I heard the kettle being filled.

"All done," Dee said as I entered the draughty kitchen, the cold tiles biting at my toes. I started making porridge, with lots of brown sugar and cinnamon, the boys' favourite, then heard the wail from upstairs.

"Mum! Mum!"

I couldn't stop stirring or the porridge might catch. "Dee, will you...?"

"Yeah, I'll go," Dee stumped out of the room. We didn't talk as much those days. Most days she slumped in her chair after work and read the paper. Most days she didn't help so much with the kids.

I made coffee, and a big pot of tea, hearing floorboards creak and doors opening and shutting. The house was moving. Jenna and Elonie appeared, then Flora, their piping voices shattering the early morning quiet. Soon after, Shahid with his messy hair.

"Morning, Mum." I noticed that the girls hugged Flora, but Shahid didn't hug me. Was it a boy thing? Scent of apples from the washing up liquid, of cinnamon and hot oats, coffee and soap, voices filling this space, the heat of the stove. Would I spend my life like this, cooking huge pots of food?

My boys arrived, one by one, collected orange juice and porridge, then disappeared into the sitting room at the far end of the house to watch TV. Dee brought Aisha, set her at the table, washed and dressed in a bright yellow dress and blue leggings. Only her hair needed plaiting. We ate porridge. Aisha chattered away over her food as I helped her to eat. I let out my breath. This was it, the life I wanted for them. I smiled at Dee, who smiled back as she folded her paper in two and propped it against the teapot to read it.

Pippa, sitting beside me, murmured in my ear. "We need to talk."

The bottom can drop out of the world, just like that. One moment, you can be sitting, savouring the small pleasures. The next fear rises like a smoke-faced demon with angry jaws wide, advancing towards you inexorably, dream-real and terrible. I left Aisha in the kitchen with Dee, who simply grunted, as always unaware of the undercurrents of life. Perhaps that's why I liked her. She had no real sense of the horror I carry, just lived as if that day was the only day.

The office was cold, dusty and dim. The eco-bulbs took a while to brighten as I sat in one of the chairs Pippa used for her clients. She was drawn-looking, pale and tired, but she looked me right in the eye. "I had a phone call yesterday, from a lawyer representing a Mohammed Said. Asking if you and your children lived here."

That swooping, diving feeling, that sense of an ending, of the world shifting, quicksand where there once was solid ground, and the fear, tasting like blood and ashes.

"What did you say?"

"I said that there was no one of that description here. I told him we are a charity and that many people might visit this house, so that you might have visited, but that you were not resident here."

"But we are. And we have benefits. So there are records."

"Which cannot be released without a court order."

Rushing like a river in my ears, no sense of what to do next. Pippa wore the weight of her status, her authority, her stature in the real-world of "out there" beyond the borders of Blossom House where people lived in their little boxes and the nuclear family still ruled. Inside the house she seemed larger and more real than the rest of us, and when she saw clients she wore a business suit and heels and I felt like a child watching a grown up at work. There were charity meetings and meetings with other groups. She always busy in her little office with papers and her laptop and her phone, her energy spilling out like magic smoke through the doorways and down the corridors and through each room, firing us all up to keep working, keep playing. No one was allowed to work more than five hours a day, and no one had to work when they are ill. She set the tone of the whole community.

"What should we do?"

"For the time being, nothing. As I said, there are records, but you are not on the electoral roll. The council tax records should be sealed, and your children's schools cannot release their information either. But you should be aware, there may be people watching the house, the kids."

"It's been three years. Would he even recognise them?"

"I think so. They can't have changed that much." She pulled out her laptop. "You need to start proceedings for a restraining order, so that he can't access the children. And be ready, social services will get involved too. And you need to look at proceedings for a divorce."

"You think he'll go for custody?"

"Why else is he trying to find you?"

I nodded. My boys, all of them, only just seeming to settle in this new place, and Aisha, whose English was flawless.

What might he do to them? What might he do to her, my little girl?

"He can't have them," I fought a sudden rush of tears. "He can't."

"Amanda, your best bet is to start the legal process now. We have your records, we have photographs. We can start proceedings to get your medical records released, the ones from Saudi Arabia."

I never talked about the Kingdom, never talked about my life there. I couldn't think back to the person I was, then, the sheer strength of will it took simply to survive.

"Is there anyone who can be a witness to what happened?"

"There was only my friend, Grace, and she never saw it happen, only the aftermath. And I... I can't involve her. There's his family, but they wouldn't be witnesses for me."

"They knew what was happening?"

"Some of it. But it won't matter. He won't be doing this alone. They will be behind it."

"I see." She typed for a while, lightning fingers on the laptop keys. "OK, well I can file with the court this week, to prevent him coming near you and the children. I also think you should start divorce proceedings."

"But that would mean contacting him."

"Yes, it would, but I think it won't be long until he contacts you. I did warn you to be pre-emptive."

No, I wanted to say. I wanted to pack up my children and run, again, but there was nowhere to go, and I couldn't do it to them. Pippa seemed confident, assured, still typing. "In cases like this it's highly unlikely the court will grant access, or custody. At least, not in my experience."

I had to believe in her. I had to believe that she knew best. Or else my children's lives would be nothing more than a nightmare of fear and flight, insecurity and impermanence. I never planned all of this, it just happened, but I took it as fate, as the hand I was being dealt by some higher power, and I did my best. Surely that had to count for something?

Blossom House. It seemed idyllic, but there was always something to do, and the roof leaked in the rain, and the bathrooms took forever to sort out so there was always someone hanging about, desperate, because one or the other toilet was blocked or didn't flush. The radiators were unreliable, leaving some rooms frigid while others were uncontrollably hot, steamy as the damp oozed out of the walls. At night, after that the first contact, I spent hours sitting up at the window, hiding behind the curtains, watching the street, unable to sleep for the noise and light. After ten years behind frosted glass and heavy curtains, veiled from all but my children and close family, the wide clear glass frightened me, as if restless spirits prowled outside, always watching.

I had spent ten years with little thought for anything other than survival, and it took those three years for me to blossom myself, for the seeds of the woman I could have been, should have been, to flourish and put out leaves and then, finally, to bloom. The paintings that I started to sell, at local craft fairs mostly, and for less than the cost of the materials, sometimes, were the blossoms that came at the end of the long winter. Every one seemed to contain the essence of the one that came before, a streak of colour in a sunrise, or the exact same veined beech leaf, or a fox-faced flower poking amber and red out of a hedgerow. I painted everything that was inside me, that I could not name, all of the feelings and thoughts I could have, should have had in those years when I was reduced to less than nothing, and it seemed that there were endless landscapes, intensely, frighteningly beautiful that emerged from the brush and knife, my hands barely keeping up with the demands of the vision. As if I had to paint it all, now, before it was too late.

Charcoal Black

Burning forests, swathes of flame and heat haze, riding above like a bird, scanning the horizon for somewhere to land. Heat so fierce it burns the breath out of my lungs, melts the flesh from my bones. I wake screaming with the vision, the feeling, the scent of my own hair burning.

Just another dream I won't tell anyone about. A nightmare land that calls me back, time after time. Mum's weird friends think that dreams mean something, but what does it mean to dream of fire and desert, heat and drought, night after night? What does it mean to see myself on fire?

Aching, spilling out of bed to grab my dressing gown in the cold room, run across the landing, use the toilet. Dare I step onto the scales? I want to, but I don't, because it will set the tone for the day, make it a good day or a bad one. No use. I have to look, watch the digital figures change, dread and nausea, shivering, thinking about the heat and wishing, for a while, that I could simply burn this house down and be done with it. At least I would be warm.

No change.

No change? How can there be no fucking change? I've hardly eaten for days, have walked and exercised, how can I still weigh the same? I pull at the flab of my belly, looking down over the mounds of my breasts. It's not fair! I am doing everything I can and I'm still not thin.

There's a noise outside, the roaring of Shahid's car, a 9-year-old Fiat he's done something to, to make the exhaust louder. He still acts like a teenager. The smile comes out of nowhere. If he's here in the car that means he's brought Abdullah, which means I won't be stuck, alone in the house, with her. The water in the shower is lukewarm. I don't bother washing my hair, it'll take too long to dry. Instead I plait it and twist it into a bun, apply makeup, dash back to room and put on my jeans and the binder and a sweatshirt. The ache inside me, I want to eat something, but what can I eat that won't make me fat? There is nothing. Not the cabbage soup again, all it did was give me wind, bloating my belly. Morning sunlight, casting a shard of light across the rug. Socks, trainers, and then I run downstairs.

"There she is!" Shahid grins up at me, standing at the end of the plank that covers the hole in the floor. Abdullah is picking his way across it. "What took you so long, shorty!"

Shahid hugs me. He smells of aftershave, and engine oil, and cigarettes. It's the first time someone has touched me since.... No, don't think about it. The past is just that. Past.

"Gonna help me with these?"

Abdullah is bringing in bags of shopping. I take some, feeling the strain in my arms. In the kitchen, Shahid rolls up his shirt sleeves. "Right, you put away while I start cleaning up."

"Have a coffee first?"

"Coffee after we've cleaned the kitchen," he yells as I run back to get more bags. Abdullah unloads tools, a workbench. "What's that for?"

"Going to fix this hole in the floor," he says, smiling. "Go help Shahid. Sooner we get started sooner we can take you out for lunch. Where's Mum?"

"Dunno." The house feels alive suddenly, full of them. Shahid puts the radio on, his bulk filling half the kitchen it seems. "Go and see if she's up," he orders as soon as I have put the food away, the cleaning stuff. "And take that bag of loo roll upstairs."

101

Outside her room I can smell cigarettes. "Mum!" I yell through the door. "The twins are home."

"I'm coming down," that voice, thin and reedy, her Welsh accent still strong. I wish she'd just stay there, rotting in that room until she turns into one of her own spooky, weird paintings. But then she's there, wearing jeans and a tie-dye top, a cigarette in one hand, her phone in the other. In the jumble and noise she somehow gets herself a coffee and a place to sit at the kitchen table while Shahid cleans the room in no time at all, empties the bins, sweeps the floor.

"Make your brothers a cuppa," she orders as I try to slink from the room. It smells different, of grapefruit-scented cleaner and boy. I had forgotten this feeling, and how she always speaks to me differently when they're around. Like she suddenly has to be a parent again, instead of ignoring me like she usually does.

"Make it yourself." The words escape before I realise. Shahid spins round. "Ash..."

"No, don't," I never defy him, not like this. "She just got up and made a drink and sat down. I've been putting food away, you've been cleaning. How come she gets to order me around?"

He shakes his head. "I'll get my own cuppa."

A stab of guilt, as I leave the kitchen. I should have been nicer to him. I catch what she says. "You spoil her, every time you come here. She's impossible once you leave."

Crouched over the hole in the hallway floor, Abdullah is slimmer, shorter and somehow less vital than Shahid. In fact, they look very little like each other, except they have the same eyes, the same hair.

"Need any help?"

102

"Naw, this won't take too long." He's resting a floorboard in place, checking the fit. "I should have done it months ago."

"Well, none of us knew Terri would do one, did we?" I sit on the bottom step of the stairs. Outside, the wind makes the branches of the trees dance. The glass window above the front door is filled with it, green shadows and light. It reminds me of the trees in my dream, burning.

"Didn't we?" He sighs, reaching for a nail. "Don't they always?"

"What do you mean?"

"I mean our mother seems to have a special gift for picking women who don't hang around."

I shrug. "So? It's not like it matters. You don't live here anymore."

"No, but you do."

I don't want him to look at me like that, he knows me too well. All of them do, these brothers of mine. They've been there since I was born, and the best thing about them moving out was having no one to notice my changing moods and feelings, always, always written all over my betraying face. My stomach clenches, head spinning. So tired now, hunger chewing at my insides already. And how will I do this, now, how will I not eat with them around?

As if he's reading my thoughts, Abdullah gives me a critical look. "We'll all go out for lunch later, OK? I think Shahid is going to fix that broken window on the stairs first, and I'll finish this."

Yellow floorboards soon fill the hole as I watch. Voices in the kitchen, I don't want to know what they're talking about. It's enough that they're here.

Carl.

<my brothers are here. U comin over?>

<Which ones>

<Twins>

<Might catch you l8r>

<use your words>

<yes miss>

Maybe we're friends because we're the only people we know who get each other's references. There's a black and white marathon on the Film Channel later. We were going to watch it together. Jarelle mentioned doing something too but I don't think she's the type to like old movies.

<Be over later> I type rapidly. <One of them will drop me off>

<Don't be late, mate>

I send a couple of emoticons, feeling torn. I go to Carl's to get out of this house, to get away from her and her weird friends and the constant feeling that she's waiting for me to do something. I am waiting, but I don't know for what. For life to change, for time to pass, for me to be old enough to finally get out of here and start living. Time seems to slow down between these walls, the old paint and paper and the layers of dirt. Great gaps of time, of empty hours. I envy my brothers, suddenly, who seem to be able to do anything they set their minds to. They have lives, goals, something. I don't know what it is I am waiting for, but it has to happen soon. I can't stay here, like this, for another year, just waiting to go to uni. I just can't.

I take my book upstairs and watch Shahid knock out the broken pane of glass and fit a new one, and read about Virginia Woolf putting stones into her pockets and walking into the river while he bangs and mutters and swears. Familiar sounds: music and Abdullah's voice calling that he's putting the kettle on again, and Mum making them toast and warning Shahid to be careful with the broken glass. As if I was six again, or seven, busy sounds and homey smells and I wish I was six again and could crawl onto her lap, or Shahid's, or Abdullah's, and read story books and play silly games and not have to think about all of it, all of this. I don't want to open up my laptop and look at Facebook, don't want to see what people are saying about me. Not that anyone messages me other than my brothers and Carl. It's not like I have friends.

The sun shifts round, then we are being bundled into the car, Shahid driving, Abdullah beside me in the back seat. "You're getting skinny," he says, poking me in the ribs. "But don't worry, we'll fatten you up."

"Shut up!" I hiss. "Stop taking the piss."

"Actually, Aisha, I think your brother's right," Mum chimes in. I can see her looking at me in the mirror on the visor. "You should eat better."

"What do you care? It's not like you do much cooking these days."

"You're almost an adult, I shouldn't have to cook for you."

"No, you shouldn't, and you don't, so don't start acting like you care if I eat or not."

She gives Shahid a look: *see what I have to put up with?* I slide down in the seat and take out my phone. What's the point of even trying to talk to her? It's always the same, the comments, the remarks, especially when there's someone else around.

At dinner, a pub chain, I order the chicken salad, and a pint of water. I eat slowly, while Shahid devours a huge steak that turns my stomach, Abdullah has chilli, and she, of course, has to make a scene asking if the veg is cooked in butter and if the vegetable burger is vegan. Every fucking time. She picks at her food and interrogates the twins, which is a relief because it takes the heat off me.

"So, how are things with Stacey?"

Why does she have to say her name in that way? Fucking hell, she's so annoying. And stop watching me, fuck's sake, stop watching me eat.

"Great Mum. She's at her parents' this weekend."

"And you, got a girlfriend yet?"

"Nope," Abdullah grins. "Last thing I want or need. Waste of time and money. I'd rather save up."

"Yeah, we're, uh, thinking of buying somewhere, if we can," Shahid says. He rubs his eyebrows, just like Mum does when she's worried. "It's... well, I guess I should tell you, Stacey's pregnant."

"What?"

"It's only eight weeks, Mum, but we wanted you to know."

"Shit, Shahid, what have you done? I thought you knew better than that!"

"Just hold on, Mum," he says, setting down his cutlery deliberately. Oh shit, his temper is rising. "Stop assuming it wasn't planned. It was. We decided a few months ago we wanted to start a family."

"But..." She is stabbing at her chips, huge and flabby on the plate. It makes me feel sick. I can't eat any more. I drink the water, deliberately. A baby. My brother is going to be a father.

"But nothing. Yeah, I know we aren't married but that's not my thing, OK?"

"I..."

"I know you find it hard to imagine, but Stacey finished her degree last year and she's got a good job. She'll get maternity leave. She wants her kids now, while we're both still young."

Silence. I take the chance to get up and head for the loo. The food comes back up easily, too easily, quickly and explosively. I wipe the toilet seat, then wash the mucus and vomit from my hands and check myself in the mirror. No splashes, just the red eyes, teary, and flushed cheeks that I always get when I do this. Wipe my face, breathe deeply against the pounding of my heart, repair my eyeliner. There are shadows under my eyes. I check the loo, flush it again just as someone else walks in. I wash my hands again, and then leave.

"Well, that went well." Shahid sighs as I sit down. Mum is outside having a cigarette.

"What did you expect?" Has he forgotten what she is really like.

"I thought she might at least be happy about it?"

Abdullah laughs. "Come on, bro, can you see her as the doting grandmother? Because I can't!"

I chuckle. "No, me neither." I sip some more water. I can't see myself as an aunt, either. Will they want me to babysit? "So, is that why you came over and started sorting the house out?"

He nods. "I couldn't bring Stace and the baby there in that state. It's not safe. Besides, she flatly refuses to come here with me until I do." He takes my hand, turning it over and looking at my fingers, then my palm. "And to be honest, sis, I should have done it years ago. You shouldn't be living like that."

A stab of feeling. It should matter that he cares. But it's easier to think that no one does.

"That fucking Terri," Abdullah growls. "What a waster."

"She wasn't," I retort. "She was nice. It was Mum's fault, as always. She drove her away."

"What do you mean?" Shahid rolls a cigarette. "Fuck, I'm going to miss smoking. But Stacey wants me to quit. So I'm going to. Soon."

"It was Mum," I repeat, keeping my eye on her as she stands outside, smoking and looking into some other place only she can see. "Terri tried, she really did, but Mum just treated her like dirt. Mum just expected her to always be doing stuff, fixing the house up. And then Mum would disappear and paint and leave Terri just sitting there in front of the telly. Plus, she wouldn't let Terri eat meat in the house, and Terri pretty much only eats meat, as far as I can tell."

"Shit." Shahid stands. "Right, I'm going out for a fag. And to face the music. Wish me luck."

"No point," Abdullah shrugs. "It's gonna work out, one way or another."

"You said it," Shahid laughs. With that I realise that he's actually fine about everything, and that perhaps this is a good thing, because at least the house will get sorted now. Just in time for me to leave. If only I could go now, go and live with my brothers maybe. But no, they know me too well. Why can't I just go somewhere where no one knows me, where I can be me, not whatever it is they keep expecting me to be?

Abdullah turns to me. "What was all that about on Facebook?"

I shrug. "Nothing. It wasn't me. I don't even go on Facebook much, except when I'm with Carl."

"Are you all right?"

It's weird him asking me this. It was always Shahid who

talked to me, who listened to me the best. "Yeah, I'm fine. Honest. It was nothing. Just school stuff, you know. Please don't go on about it. You know how kids are."

He nods, letting it go. We sit for a while, him on his phone, me reading my book, and it feels good.

Watching films, sitting in Carl's bedroom with the lights off and his 40 inch TV and his perfectly arranged shelves and the pristine rug, and the sadness hits me. Shahid's having a baby. That means his life will be somewhere else, about someone else now. Not just my brother, but a father, a partner.

"I never want children," I say to Carl as he lounges, half on my lap, eating popcorn. The film, a black and white version of *Pride and Prejudice*, features Greer Garson in improbably wide dresses and a similarly unfeasibly ugly Mary Bennett in glasses.

"Well I might," he replies. "Maybe. One day."

"And how exactly will you do that, given that you're gay?"

He sits up, pummelling a pillow to get it into the right shape, then slumps against the headboard.

"It's not that hard. Find a willing woman with a womb, of course."

"Right. Well, don't ask me. I mean it. I never want kids."

"Why not?"

"Because they tie you down. Think about it. In relationships, it's always the woman, the mother, who gets saddled with the kids, while the other one buggers off. I don't want to get tied down like that."

"Ash, you're seventeen years old. You think like that now, because you haven't lived yet. You want freedom. Things might change."

"I doubt it." I tell him about Shahid and Stacey, and the baby. As the film unfolds towards its inevitable conclusion, I think about what a lie marriage is, for women in any case. Some man declares undying love, and then suddenly you're changing nappies and doing night feeds while he still gets to go and work and carry on with his life.

I walk the two miles home in the dark, let myself into the house, and hear the sounds of my brothers in the spare room, listening to music and talking, and I think, nothing is ever going to be the same.

Nothing.

Amber

See them all now, the past played through a camera lens. Moving shapes and shadows, sepia and amber with time and memory's kind filters, which block out the worst of everything, leaving only the memories we choose to keep, to frame, to revisit time and again. Like the dreams of houses that haunted me. Room upon room, always searching for something, always trying to find a way to keep my children safe. As if the answers were there, somewhere, buried in the twisting, endless corridors of mind and consciousness, if only I knew how to find them.

The letter came on a Wednesday, and Pippa found me bending over the piles of laundry in the laundry room we set up in number six, in what would be the kitchen, one day. Piles of cotton sheets in my hands, fresh from the machine, the smell, soap and fabric conditioner and the heat, steam and closeness. Sweating under the jeans and t-shirt that hung less loosely from my frame. Finally I was eating properly and resting properly, and the hungry ghosts of fear had left me alone for so long.

"A letter," Pippa said, and I sensed immediately something wrong.

"What?"

"It's from that firm of solicitors."

I took the envelope and saw the name and address stamped on the back, embossed, imprinted. And then I knew.

Cool floor, tile against my cheek, concerned voices above me, Pippa calling for help and opening the back door, and all I could think is, I'm not pregnant. Why did I faint?

Helping hands, lifting me up, supporting my senseless limbs to the couch in the big room, cool water and a cool flannel, and then little Molly taking my pulse and Pippa's voice, loud and yet somehow distant. "She's had a shock."

Struggling to sit up. "The letter. Give me the letter."

Thick pages, creamy paper like linen. I knew they would throw money at it, at this, that they'd stop at nothing to steal everything that was precious to me. Tasting acid in my mouth, and fear twisting inside me again. A long-forgotten fear but how could I have forgotten what he's capable of, and the ache in my wrist that never really goes away.

Was it then it started? Let me pull it out of the deepest pit of memory. Because I was happy, for a while, if you can call it happiness, or I was happy enough, and there were days when it was more than enough, but there were also wakeful nights when I wondered if I was capable of loving anyone and if someday, someone would realise that this was just too good to be true, too convenient.

They brought me hot, sweet tea and fussed about as the contents of the letter are read and discussed. It all seemed to be happening far away, or through a veil.

"What happened?" Dee rushing in, pale and frightened. Of course, Pippa called the cab office and she came straight home, but I couldn't feel her, not even when she held all of me against her hard, little body and tried to reassure me.

"It's OK, love," she whispered, over and over, but it wasn't, it never would be because *he had found us*. Years of it, the beatings and the fear. It took everything I had to run from him. Aisha was the catalyst, but it took everything just to survive. I should have known it couldn't last. I didn't deserve to be happy. Her confusion, the pain as I withdrew from her. She seemed distant, unreal, uni-dimensional, a poorly-written description in a cheap book, nothing that could matter to me, not faced with the rich thick paper and the powerful words that pinned me to the page and proscribed my fate once again.

"I can't do this," I sighed, barely making the words come out. "I just can't."

"You have to." Pippa's fierce look tells Dee to let go. She set me in a chair. Another cup of tea appeared. The universal restorative. I should be doing something. What was it?

"Dee, go and get Samara, then see about Aisha. She needs fetching from nursery."

"OK."

I didn't feel her go. There was nothing to feel. The fear was back. There was nothing else.

"Right, let's take a look," Pippa sat beside me, pulling the letter towards her. "Drink that tea. And pull yourself together. You can't afford to be weak, not now. That's what he wants, don't you see? If you fall apart now, he wins."

Where was it, the steel and strength that got me away from the horror? I didn't know. I lost it somehow, along with the steel bands that bounded my self-space so that I could survive. I'd grown weak, and soft, and stupid.

"Just as we thought," she sighed. "Custody. He says he wants you to return with the children to the family home, and that if you don't, he'll take the children. Suitable environment...extended family... Blah blah blah. The usual."

I looked at the letter, the names of the family members, the petitioner. Echoes from a long feverish dream. My arms, too heavy to lift, my hands shaking as I tried to grip the paper. Dee returning with Aisha, my wild child, her plaits half undone, bouncing and jumping through the kitchen, beaming as she hurtled herself into my arms.

"I can't," I said, pushing her off. "Dee, take her, please?"

"Come on baby," Dee almost dragged Aisha off me and immediately I regretted it, a bitter cold ache where her warm little body was, why push her away, she's my baby, it's not her fault, none of this is her fault, sweet little girl.

"I don't know what to do."

Penny, bustling in, looked from me to Pippa and back again. "I was just going to start the dinner."

"Go ahead," Pippa picked up the letter and papers. "Come on, Amanda, let's go to my office. We can decide how to reply. And you can get yourself together before the boys come home. You don't want them to see you like this."

I followed her out. In the garden, Dee was making a fire with Aisha in the little fire pit, a pile of garden waste ready to burn. Poor child, she was always cold, even in her thick coat and bobble hat, and the gloves she kept losing. A rush of gratitude that Dee was there, that Pippa was there, that the dinner would be made, that I was not alone, but despair kept it all at bay. Despair, fear, the taste of blood in my mouth, only a memory but more powerful than anything I could see and feel then.

"What do I tell the children," I asked as Pippa outlined the next stages of the legal proceedings.

"The truth. They will have to meet with the solicitors, with social services. The older ones will get a chance to say whether or not they want to live with him."

"No!"

"Yes, Amanda. That's how it goes."

Fever dreams, that night, almost every night afterwards, the terror of losing my children, of them going back to their father. Nightmares I thought would pass, of pain and near-death, of being trapped.

Dee knew she was losing me from that day. Maybe that was the beginning of the end for her too. Maybe I pushed her away by having to focus my attention on legal papers and discussions and court attendance and petitions for restraining orders and orders to stop him taking the children out of the country and orders to stop visitation at all, even supervised, because he posed a risk. Maybe it was my fault. I just couldn't get her to understand. No one seemed to believe just how bad it would be, could be; even when the boys themselves looked panicked and fearful at the mention of his name. Dee grew more resentful that all my time and energy went on dealing with the situation. What was left went to the kids.

I had to tell them, of course, sitting with Pippa in the big communal room, explaining carefully what was happening, and I remember thinking, *oh, Dee's not here, she should be here for this.*

During all the weeks of legal wrangling, applying for emergency injunctions, dealing with social workers and meeting with solicitors, she grew gradually more distant too, unable to rise and take ownership of the thing we shared, to carry the burden herself for a while. Soon, it seemed, she was never there. There were later nights when she said she was working, and sometimes she was not home in the mornings when I got up. I never asked for an explanation, but the boys did, wondering where she was when they wanted her to fix a bike or help tinker with Molly's car, or play football on a Sunday morning.

Maybe too much of my time and energy went on convincing social workers and police and solicitors that the photos taken of my injuries were real, and working with Pippa to petition my medical records from the Kingdom, trying to recall the exact details of the day he played Russian roulette with my children around the kitchen table, drunk and high and laughing as he held a pistol to their heads. None of it seemed real to anyone, and the social workers were even more sceptical when they saw how we lived at Blossom House. There were more investigations into the children and reports from school, and then Flora's kids were investigated. For a while it seemed as if our very existence was tentative simply because of the way we lived. It didn't help that the boys, teenagers now, were sharing a room and suddenly began kicking off at school a lot more and staying out with their mates later and later.

I should have tried harder. I should have sat down with Dee and tried to pull us closer together; done something about the distance I could see growing. But it seemed the least important thing, and that makes it my fault. I just didn't have the time and energy to take care of her too, to constantly think about her feelings. Some weeks I'd wonder when I'd last felt it, that closeness, and a part of me would question why I wasn't missing her, and why I wasn't really doing anything about the significant looks and the pregnant silences when she wasn't home for communal meals more than once or twice a week. And the months had passed swiftly into years, and nothing said meant nothing changed.

And then the day that the telephone call came.

Painting in the sunny communal room. The cookery class was long gone, leaving behind the sharp-sweet smell of garlic and basil. Long slanting sunlight. I was working on a commission from a local business; a painting of their premises for their fiftieth anniversary, my first serious commission. Thick charcoal outlines, deep shadows, catching the shapes of the old windows and the glint of light on the glass. I was lost in it, in my few hours of freedom. Dee was picking Aisha up from nursery, then Yusuf from primary school. The older boys would walk themselves home.

"Mrs Said?"

"Yes?"

"We were wondering whether you had sent someone new to pick up Aisha."

"What?"

"Aisha. She was approached by a man today to take her home, but Mrs Johnson checked the contacts form and you haven't authorised anyone else to pick her up other than yourself and Miss Collins."

"That's right." I set down the stick of charcoal and brushed at my right hand, holding the phone in between my ear and shoulder. "Miss Collins should be picking her up."

"She hasn't arrived. Aisha is still with us."

"Right. OK, I'll be there to pick her up as soon as possible."
Fuming, heart pounding. "And no, there is no one else
authorised to pick her up. Please ensure that she never leaves
school premises with anyone else."

"You can be assured of that."

"Thank you."

The ringing in my ears, almost dizzy with fear and worry.
A call to Yusuf's school, he was still there. Then Dee's mobile,
fingers shaking as I tried to hit the numbers. No answer. The
cab company said she wasn't working when I rang through.
Yes they will send another cab to take me to the school. I
rushed to Yusuf's school first. He was there, waiting patiently
in the front office.

"Where's Dee, Mum?"

"I don't know. Come on, the cab is waiting. Are you OK?
Did anyone else try to take you home?" Confusion, he
remembered less and less, of course, of how things had been,
though I didn't know what the older boys talk about with
him when they are alone. "No, Mum. When no one came the
teacher said to wait here."

"Good boy. Now let's get going."

Aisha was sitting in her blue and yellow dress sorting
through dolls' clothes in the play area, surrounded by other,
larger children.

"Mummy!" She leapt up, her bouncing run punctuated by
skips and little jumps, her face lighting up, the widest smile,
and my heart ached as I swallowed all the other feelings,
trying to show her only a loving mother's smile. "Baby girl," I
called, gathering her into my arms and swinging her around.
"Sorry I was late. Did you have a good time in nursery?"

"I did." The feel of her small, warm hand in mine as she
walked with me to the pegs to collect her bag, shocking pink,
and her coat. "We were making a fashion show!"

"Sounds amazing." I filled my voice with enthusiasm, then hurried back to the waiting cab.

"Where's Dee?" Aisha asked as soon as she saw the familiar shape and livery.

"Oh, she couldn't come love," I made my voice light. "Let's get you home now. Jump in next to your brother and then we can see what's for tea!"

Once she was in bed I asked the boys if they'd seen anyone hanging around their schools when they went in or when they went out?

"No, Mum," Shahid assured me. Mahmood shook his head. Yusuf did too. My youngest boy, he still constantly looked to his brothers for confirmation on how to act.

"You're sure? No strangers? No one familiar?"

"Nothing, Mum," Abdullah this time. "Really."

I didn't say anything when Dee came home, apologising, saying she hadn't realised she was picking the kids up. Not then. Anger simmered, somewhere beneath the renewed fear, but I couldn't waste it on her. She had lied to me. If she was playing away, then so be it. There was no point wondering, no point challenging. There was nothing I could do to change it, to make her want me more. I simply asked her to keep an eye out for strangers.

"It would be like him to snatch them," I said. "Either him or one of his family or friends."

"I don't like this, Amanda. I don't like being questioned by social services and I certainly don't like the thought that someone might be following me."

"And you think I like it? You think I want to live in fear like this?" I turned on her, after half an hour of vigilantly shutting windows and doors and begging everyone in the house to be extra careful about locking doors. "I thought we were safe."

Burnt Umber

In the books I used to read, like those Enid Blyton school stories and Noel Streatfield, and the ones written during the war, teachers are powerful, absolute in their authority. In those books, children are children right up until they undergo some magical transformation, having passed the requisite exams and graduated to university, work, or marriage. As if the school is some alternate reality, protected by a great force field of tradition and learning that creates the exact conditions needed for that alchemical reaction of making girls into feminine women, boys into manly, responsible men.

As if anyone is like that, really.

The best thing about school is that I can get away from her.

It's like all she wants is for me to be something she wasn't, something more, something better. As if she knows all the answers before I even ask the questions, just like in school where you can't ask questions, you can't deviate or else you're in trouble because that's disrupting the lesson and we have to follow the curriculum and no one tells you why.

And I look into her eyes and there's all that weight on me, her waiting and wanting something, something; what the fuck is it? Some part of me to appear, miraculously, and fulfil her fantasies of the perfect daughter? But I never asked for any of it, did I?

Oh yes, like those girls in the books she gave me, the ones I loved so much when I was little, when I thought life could be like that. When I thought books could be real and that I could be like the girls who rebel against authority but come good in the end, as if somehow virtue and honour would emerge at the right time, pin themselves onto the chest of the heroine and prove her to be made of 'the right stuff'.

But there's no right stuff in me. There is nothing. She's waiting for something that's never coming, something that can never exist.

I know how that feels. It seemed every time I made a friend, settled in, we moved, and they never stayed in touch. It's like no one ever really cared about me. Not enough to want to keep me in their life. Just like our absent father and the family we used to have. How bad could it have been, anyway? Mahmood, when he would still talk to me, before I grew breasts and got almost as tall as him, said that we had a huge family once, uncles and aunts and grandparents and cousins, and that there was a big house and plenty of money. I don't remember any of it.

I remember Blossom House, which was full of women, and I remember other children there, and Dee always somewhere around. But I don't remember anything from before, when we lived under a white hot sun and ate dates and almonds and where the only person who stuck out was my mother. At least, that's what Mahmood said.

Voices below. One of her friends, no doubt. Maybe it's Claire, the fat one who always shows up moaning about her girlfriend. Hours and hours of it. 'She doesn't do the dishes, she doesn't listen to me, she expects me to cook every night, she expects me to pay all the bills.' Same fucking song over and over again.

Just leave her, I want to say, every time I wander through one of these conversations. But *she*, my sainted fucking mother, just nods and talks crap, oh, it must be so difficult for you, no, it's not fair, poor you.

What's wrong with these women? Is that really all there is in life?

Edge of the bed, mattress creaking under the quilt.

Her voice. Terri's name. Right. Terri. The last one in the long line of failures, the pathetic specimens she drags in and sets up home with. As if she is going to find some fictional happily-ever-after and it's all just another set of lies and empty promises because they always leave.

Cerulean Blue

When I remember Dee, I remember how the birdsong danced through the open windows on the first warm days of spring, and the sound of Pam in the kitchen below, singing as she made her breakfast porridge. I remember Dee's sweetness, the heat and cool of her body, and how I traced the muscles in her arms and the corded veins of her hands and how just thinking of those hands on me could make me melt. And I remember, how could I not, that she always stole the covers and left me shivering on the edge of the bed, and how she never once said thank you for the meals I made her. How quick she was to complain if her favourite jeans weren't dry when she wanted them. How we argued over disciplining the boys, because she wanted to use harsher sanctions than I ever would and she thought I shouldn't try so hard with them, try to compensate for what had happened to them. But it didn't matter, none of it mattered, because she said she loved me every morning and every night. She sent me texts during the day saying, *You are my world*. For a while it was so good I started to forget how bad it could be.

Friday afternoon, one of those bright blue autumn days when the sky is so deep, so perfectly blue that it makes you ache, walking back from school with Aisha, kicking through the soggy leaves, most plastered to the pavements after endless days of rain. The air cold but my body warm inside a long coat I picked up in the charity shop and Aisha chattering at the top of her piping voice, running across the grass when she saw one of her schoolfriends. The mother, we had a nodding acquaintance from the school gates, looking awkward, then venturing a smile.

"Mum, Mum, can Dorothy come to our house?" Aisha bouncing, she never seemed to walk, but jumped and bounced, forward or back or on the spot, or skipped or rocked when sitting, as if staying still was just too difficult.

I looked at the mother. "Hi, I'm Amanda. Seems like our girls are friends."

"Yes, Dorothy talks about Aisha. They play together in school."

"Same for Aisha."

I leaned up against the fence, noticing she had her eye on a smaller child, maybe about two years old. Aisha was much taller than Dorothy, with long limbs, while Dorothy was a round dumpling of a child in a pink quilted coat and white tights.

Aisha's wrists stuck out too far from the sleeves of her duffle coat. "I think I'm going to have to get her another coat, that one's getting too short," I said. Another trip around the shops looking for something. Dee would offer to pay, of course, and I would accept, but there was always something. I wished it could be me paying for everything.

The other mother – milky-white face, dyed-blonde hair, high ponytail – was desperately trying not to make conversation. I could tell she didn't want to let Dorothy come to our house. I wondered why. Was it that she's heard about Blossom House, and that it's a community? Or was it that she knew about me and Dee?

"Mum, look at me!" Aisha, fearless, at the top of the climbing frame, feet set apart, arms in the air as if flying, or sailing. Firmly at the helm of her own life, while I couldn't even make conversation with another child's mother.

Aisha clamouring for a doughnut at the kiosk in the park. "Not now honey, it's almost time to go home. Dee will be getting dinner ready."

A rare afternoon when she wasn't working, or "otherwise engaged". They came around less and less. I didn't ask

123

questions. Blossom House was home, and Flora and I spent a lot of time sharing parenting stories and looking after each other's kids, and if there was an acre of space between me and Dee in bed at night, neither of us mentioned it.

Years passing, winters and springs and wet summers and the children growing. The boys as tall as me and their voices growing deeper; stubble on Shahid's chin that he kept rubbing, as if to check if it would come off.

"Can't I go to Dorothy's house, then, Mum, Mum, Mum, can I go to Dorothy's house!" The two children stood close together, stage-whispers and giggles. But Dorothy's mother was heading off, calling the child away.

My mobile rang. "Hey, honey."

"How long do you want this pie in for? And what number?" I tried not to sigh. Surely she cooked for herself before me? "Two hundred, for about 40 minutes. We'll head home soon."

"OK. Abdullah's in trouble again. Apparently, he refused to play cricket because there were girls on his team."

"Oh, shit." Not again. There was always something, one or other of them. Yusuf was behind in his reading and writing. The teacher had mentioned remedial classes. She thought he was unteachable. I thought he was simply not enjoying school. Mostly he liked to sit in the garden with Flora's battered old guitar and pick out songs, or run around with his brothers., or listen to music in his room. He just wasn't that bothered by school. Shahid was always fighting, someone or other. Mahmood didn't get into trouble, but Dee badgered me that he shouldn't be spending all his time alone in his room, or out with his new friends from the Church down the road. She was right to complain. He barely spoke to any of us, and his attitude towards me and her was less than tolerable.

Trudging up the hill, dragging Aisha as she whined and cried. "I want to go to Dorothy's house. Why can't I go to Dorothy's house? Mum, Mum, I want to go to Dorothy's house."

I stopped, yanking at her arm so she faced me as I bent down. "Because you can't, Aisha, because Dorothy's mummy is not a very nice person and doesn't like us. So you can't go there because she hasn't invited us." My voice was high and hard and harsh, and I hated speaking to her like this, but I couldn't help it. "Some people are just not nice, and it seems Dorothy's mother is one of those. There's nothing I can do about it so just stop whining, OK?"

She cried in earnest then, great sobs, refusing to move, and I noticed a yellow stain on her white socks.

Fuck. What kind of mother had I become?

"Oh, don't cry honey," I said, gathering her in to me. She was too heavy, at seven, to carry, but I hugged her close and we stumbled slowly home together, her sobs turning into hiccups as the guilt once more settled onto me like a sheen of oil.

"It's not your fault. You can't help the way that people are."

But she remained pale and cool and distant, and didn't respond to my hugs until she had been bathed and settled into bed with a DVD on the sickeningly pink portable player, with jammy dodgers on a plate and a glass of pink milk.

"I'm sorry, Mummy," she murmured as I cuddled down with her.

"What for sweetheart?"

"I wet my pants."

"I know. But it happens sometimes, especially when you're upset."

"OK." Her voice was small, achingly restrained. Oh, I didn't want this world to break her spirit, to squash everything wild and strong about her, but what could I do?

125

"Perhaps I'll speak to Dorothy's mother tomorrow, see if she will let Dorothy come to the café with us after school one day. Would you like that?"

She nodded, long curling brown lashes already lowering, flickering onto her soft, coffee-coloured cheeks. I wanted to weep, but I didn't know how; tears left me long ago and there was only this burning anger at the injustice of it all.

In bed, slamming my hand into the thin mattress as Dee peeled off her clothes. Always in the same order, always slow and deliberate. "I can't stand it. The bloody bitch. I can get that they don't like me, or us, for some reason, but why take it out on the children? You could see they wanted to play together."

"Don't let it get to you." That makes me even angrier. Oh, if it were so easy! I turned my back on her as she climbed into bed and seethed silently.

Did I use her? Perhaps, like a bandage for all those deep wounds, or like a drug that would make me forget, from time to time, but when I realised he was coming after me, all I could feel was pain and terror and I was glad, in the end, that she'd moved on already, had found another harbour for her heart's longing, because it was easier then to just run, to leave.

Cold, wet autumn day, leaving the dentist with Yusuf, whose teeth had never been right, watching the streets and the cars and vans and wondering if *he* was there or someone sent by him to find us. The fear never went away, even though Pippa was confident about the court case. Across the road I saw Dee, just walking into Mothercare with a woman in her thirties, heavily pregnant, pushing a pushchair with a 3-year-old in it. A tall slim woman, and stylish in a slightly alternative way, wearing a dress over jeans and little boots, and her long dark

126

hair swept back by a headband. Dee looked at her the way she used to look at me, as if the sun had just come up for the first time, and I felt the shift in every part of me, from certainty to uncertainty.

The walk home was a blur. "Mama, my face hurts."

"I know son."

"I'm hungry."

"I'll get you something soft."

He was growing too, and just as with his brothers I felt like I hardly knew him. What was his inner landscape? How did the world look through his eyes? Had he seen Dee too?

I got Yusuf settled with a DVD and some lukewarm soup, and ran into Pippa in the kitchen.

When I told her, she just nodded. "That's Dee. She's always attracted to women with children."

"What? You aren't surprised?"

"Not really." A whole world of meaning behind two small words, a vindication and a condemnation all neatly packaged in one statement.

"So she's done this before."

"Yes."

We were sitting in her office, the tears long dried on my face, leaving my cheeks stiff and cold. It wasn't a huge surprise. Sooner or later I knew there'd be proof of the transfer of her affections. Nothing lasted, after all, and Dee was the smallest of my worries.

"This is for you." Pippa held out some letters. New paperwork had come from the court, and with it is a visitation order.

"They really can't do this, can they," I asked, gesturing to the papers. The conversation, spiralling around the same issue, leaves a heavy dread in its wake.

"They're suggesting that the children need to see their

father so that they can make a clear decision about whether or not they want to live with him."

"But that's ridiculous! Don't they know what he did, to me, to them? Social services can't allow this! I was told if I let him see them they'd take them away! And now they're allowing visitation."

"That's what the court has suggested. Supervised visitation until they make the custody decision. Apparently, he's a reformed man and, well, someone's spent a lot of money on a good barrister."

"You can't honestly think I would let him see them."

"You might not have much choice in the matter."

"What are you going to do about Dee?" Pippa asked. We were packing, pulling out the old cases and adding two large laundry bags with the kids' bedding and toys, and bin bags full of their clothes and mine, rushing, rushing, fearful I might forget something. I put my painting gear into a large banana box and wrapped quilts around my stacks of canvases.

"Nothing," I retorted, intent on my task. The old, familiar feeling was back, the extraneous parts of life disappearing to leave only a single purpose. "She's not even here. So there's nothing to say, is there?" I slammed toys and bits of kitchen gear into a bag.

"I guess not."

Pippa arranged for us to go to a safe house in a little town in North Wales, but even she didn't know the address. Escape Route was a project managed by a network of women's charities and only four people at any one time knew the address of each house. Pippa called them when she saw the turn being taken by the legal proceedings and my state of mind. She could see I was going to run.

"I can continue to act on your behalf while you're gone," she assured me. "I don't think you should do this, I really don't. But if this is what you want, just make sure you disappear for a bit. Don't let them find you, at least until I can take this emergency protection order to the court. The money we've given you should last a while, and the volunteers will make sure you're OK."

Words spinning, over and over, an endless loop. How could they? It's not fair, my children, they can't do that to my children. Don't let him find us. The powerless feeling; he was coming for me.

"As for Dee..." I almost cried, but told myself to be strong. Nothing lasts. "I still can't believe it."

Pippa rolled up bedding and stuffed it into a black bag. "She... Look, unless she's told you herself I can't say much. It's not my story to tell." She stood there, in her charcoal suit with its narrow skirt and silver buttons, and I wished that she had told me every story there was to know or remember way before it had got to this point. Had they all been laughing at me, then, these women who knew her well?

"How many other women?"

Pippa sighed. I wondered, was it the fact that we were two women that makes her look so uncomfortable? Or that she should have warned me beforehand that this was Dee's M.O. "Since we've known her, there have been two, neither of which ended well. And now you. She... Hmm... Dee doesn't cope well with stress, or with anything that disturbs her equilibrium, or takes the attention away from her. She's a lovely person, but not good with responsibility. I think she just wants to belong to a family but... Oh, it's not my place to say."

Sun on the dusty window and light and dark against the walls, sadness at the thought of leaving this place, these walls. This home. But we could come back. Maybe Pippa could sort this legal thing and we could come back. Even as I thought it, a dark hollowed out place inside me swallowed even that hope.

"Are you sure you won't tell her?"

"No." I looked around for more things to pack. We still had mercifully few possessions. "What is there to say?"

"You can always come back," Pippa's soft voice made the lie gentle. "When it's safe. You belong here, with us. With or without Dee, you and the children can always come back."

I hugged her, both of us a little surprised at the contact. "Thank you."

"The children, you should keep an eye on them," she added. "This is the kind of thing that causes problems, especially with the boys the age that they are. Uprooting them, changing schools..."

"Again."

"Yes, again, well you know it's not ideal."

"I know, but that visitation order..."

"You know I can't advise you to defy a court order. It's your choice though. You could stay here, and see what happens."

"I can't see him again. I can't." Dread and the old, shaking fear, a trapped animal desperate enough to chew off its own leg to be free of the trap.

"I also suggest seeing a GP as soon as you are settled. Your anxiety is through the roof. I told you should get someone to look into PTSD."

"So they can say I'm an unfit mother? No."

"Amanda, there's no shame in it."

"You know what they're like! I won't be labelled like that. Social Services would have a field day. It would play right into his hands.

Pam rushed in, tense and flustered, blonde hair flying out of its ponytail, panting.

130

"Here. I got these from the store room." She'd brought three rucksacks, old and worn and frayed in places, but still functional. "I can pack some of the boys' things into these, and they can carry them." A driver is coming for us, apparently, late in the evening. "Penny is making sandwiches."

I almost laughed, such a prosaic response. I would have laughed if the dread and fear and the betrayal had not taken me and turned me to stone. As Pam rushed off again, I turned to Pippa and say, "Tell me, how did Dee end up here in the first place?"

It was the question I should have asked Dee years previously, but there never seemed to be the right time, and each time I broached it she just shrugged.

"Well, that I can tell you, because it's in the book."

There was a book of Blossom House stories they'd written and had published, a year or so before I arrived, another grant for another arts project. I'd never read it. Other women's stories were another burden.

Pippa busied herself folding clothes. "Dee was in a relationship with a woman called Charlie, who lived with her son. They had a smallholding, of sorts, clinging to the side of a steep hill in a village in Devon, with horses and a vegetable plot and chickens and dogs, and it was a strange arrangement, because Charlie's mother, who was certifiable by all accounts, lived nearby and would turn up at all hours of the day or night and start cooking and moving furniture around. Sometimes she would bring over hordes of friends and demand Charlie cook for them, or turn up in the middle of the night needed to be driven to the other end of the country. Apparently, Charlie was a lovely woman, but every girlfriend had been driven off by the mother.

"Dee stuck it out for a few years, but when the son hit puberty he shot up to be six foot odd and about four foot wide, and started laying into his mother on a regular basis, and when Dee tried to put a stop to it he laid into her too while the grandmother looked on and said that's what you get for being gay.

"She tried reporting it to the police but because the mother-in-law wasn't living in the house it wasn't classed as domestic abuse, and the boy was still a minor. The police passed her my details when she asked for legal help, because I'd helped set up a rape crisis centre in the area. They knew me and what I do. I helped her to get away and she came to live with us here.

"Like I said, it's not my story, and she should really tell you herself, but from what I can tell, her own mother neglected her, terribly. If I'm honest, I think she's spent most of her life looking for someone to mother her."

"Why didn't you warn me?"

Pippa shrugged. "I wanted to believe it was different this time. And if it wasn't, I thought at least you and the children would be happy here."

The words replayed on a mental loop all through the long, night-dark drive in the mini-bus that scooped us all up, bag and baggage, and whisked us away under cover of darkness to an unknown future. Memories attached themselves to that same loop. All those times Dee had nestled into me, wanting her hair stroked, wanting to be held on my lap like one of the kids. All the meals I cooked for her. When did I move from lover to mother-figure? Somewhere along the line I became the one managing the finances and doing the shopping. I planned meals and managed the kids timetables and their commitments, and she just went along with it all. Yes, I took all the responsibility for the hard stuff, the boring stuff. Dentists and sickness and nightmares and bed wetting and laundry and parents' evenings and all of it, while she just had fun with the kids when it suited her.

The boys, young men then, with the beginnings of beards and grown taller and leaner, were sullen and reluctant to talk through the long journey. Yusuf, still too young to be equal to his brothers, complained the loudest when they tried to leave him behind. "Mum, my, it's not fair. Make them wait for me." I watched them mooch off to the toilet at the services, suffered their complaining about the sandwiches and the cans of cheap soda. Aisha, woken from uneasy sleep, was tired and tearful; whining constantly about being taken away from Blossom House.

"It won't be for long, sweetie, just until Pippa sorts things out."

"But why, Mum? Why?"

I had explained it to the boys, and of course, they resisted. They questioned my actions, a new thing. Still they came along, and I was glad of it, that they haven't refused to leave. They remembered, well, at least, Shahid and Abdullah and Mahmood did. Mahmood was the most vocal, the most challenging. "We can't just run away. We should stay. Maybe we should see him."

"No." I was firm, and he didn't like that either. Too much like his father. But Aisha had no memories of the Kingdom and no clue about what happened there, and she fretted and complained until she fell again into a restless sleep as the road wound away and the night deepened. Deep dark, roadside lights like glowing jewels on a thread, the twists and turns of this new path, like a story that everyone knows and no one tells anymore.

Was it that moment that changed things? Was it that point that drove the wedge between me and my daughter, made my boys less trusting of me, because I turned my back on their grownup playmate and dragged them away from the home they'd come to love? Would Dee miss us at all? Would I miss her? Would Aisha forgive me for leaving?

Empty questions, but I couldn't help wondering, later, was it that which turned my daughter away from me and brought about the new horror, that greatest of horrors when I'd thought that the past, and the nightmares, were finally behind us? Where I sat remembering, in the overgrown garden, Victorian planting long gone wild, the sun filtered through the massive bay tree and dappled the tangled grass. I felt like a child waiting for gnomes and fairies to appear from the edges of the bramble-clotted terrace or swing down from the spreading azaleas. Uneven steps down to the sunken garden with its long-ago-lawn, lichen-kissed grey slabs, buried paths and forgotten arbours and grottos, and the sagging red brick walls with ivy sprouting from vines as thick as my wrist.

I painted that garden a hundred times: painted in weeping girls on the bench under the lilac tree; princely lovers half in and half out of the shadows near the monstrous rhododendrons; hybrid half-animals stalking the flower bed where corseted ladies once bent to sample this bloom or that. Look, there lay the browned, dead stalks of old Christmas wreaths, their ribbons still bright and fresh amongst the washed out grey and brown holly and ivy fronds. There were the buried statues and animal carvings now eaten up by weeds. From one angle it looked romantic, from another, just a garden full of too much mess, too much work for one woman whose sons had stepped off into the world and whose daughter, though she was still there, seemed more and more lost each day.

The fear returned, cold and sharp and bitter. It had a shape now, an image that kept appearing in my paintings almost against my will. But every week I found myself ordering more and more Ivory Black because she was there, this figure, in the corner of every landscape, hiding in leaf-shadows or rising from the bole of a mossy tree, moving more and more into the centre, and there was nothing I can do to stop it.

Blue Black

This is what it's like, burning dreams and hot flesh, secret smells and sounds, touching and testing and searching, the dark caverns of hidden red flesh canyons. Heat and cold, hot skin, cold air, pumping muscles now, stretching and aching and reaching, curling and pulling through the muscle strain, arms lifted to the sky, then down to the floor, ridges of the floorboards against my palms, and back up again. This is how it is.

Change the music, bring up the tempo, legs moving, lifting this body, this heavy weight, running in place, no progression, just intercession, this is my body, fleshy unwanted shape, and if I work, if I work, if I exercise like this, like this, then I can change it. I can make myself into something else, something unlike me, unlike her, unlike any of them. Thinner, stronger, prettier, better.

Arms burning, lifting the stack of books over and over, then the heavy file, hard floor pressing against my tailbone, hold the file against my chest, sit-up after sit-up, I can do 100 today, 100, driving up and through, breath short, the pain intense, thump of shoulder blades against the wood, head spinning, ears ringing.

Lie flat, panting. Sweat cooling, smell of myself, like earth, like unknown nature, rotting undergrowth, mysteries of deep forests. Phone beeps, ignore it, there is only this, the music; get up, move, faster now, lunge and reach, lunge and reach, reach, up, kick, one, two, one two, one two, endlessly, like she showed me, Dee, way back when, these kicks and these punches. I tie weights around my ankles, legs almost too heavy to lift, push through, Ash, push through, breath catching, pain in my chest, guts clenching, the stitch in my side unbearable.

Breathe.

The endorphins now, we learned about these in biology, and it is a sweet, sweet rush, like the pure pleasure of not eating, mind kicking into overdrive, sudden flush, like pleasure, like arousal, laughing as I plank for four minutes, then one hand, then the other, it hurts, pain like nothing else, but I can't stop, this is the only way, force my flesh into submission, this is how to do it.

This is control.

Turquoise

The boys all left, but that's the way of it, that's what you sign up to as a mother, they have to go so that they can come back. And Aisha, shut away from me, a closed book. Did I neglect her, somehow? I remember playing with her, with Dee, in the sunlit garden at Blossom House, and afterwards playing endless games with her in that awful place in North Wales where we waited out one long miserable autumn and winter and the boys bounced off the walls with boredom and frustration because I wouldn't even send them to school. There was a home school network, and weekdays we'd meet in the museum or the library or at the leisure centre, and Pippa's charity friends sent us money because I couldn't claim benefits.

I got a job, yes, a memory of cleaning fluids and fabric freshener, cleaning the caravans in a caravan park and then cleaning chalets, and I took Aisha along with me or sometimes left her with Abdullah. He was the only one I could trust to look after her properly. Shahid was always getting distracted, out with his mates from the park, smoking weed, or sitting playing on the cheap games console I bought him, his mind wandering off one way or another. Mahmood at fourteen was so serious, so very serious, spending every spare evening and weekend he could working, doing gardens and odd jobs and studying, or going to church, and he flatly refused to be responsible for her.

Too many memories, hangover dreams and the bitterness in my gut from drinking wine alone late at night. I shouldn't drink, it makes me maudlin, and there was a painting to finish. Good light, this was always the brightest room in the house. I looked at the easel and thought about how to create the texture of a peony in the foreground, and suddenly realised, yes, there she is, the dark figure, captured as a reflection in the bulging dew drop on a blade of grass curling over towards the left hand corner of the painting. When did I paint her? I didn't know. I never knew, those days, but she was there, always, in one place or another, just a shroud, a death mask, a spectral shape that you didn't see unless you knew to look for her, and I wondered which part of myself kept painting her in when I wasn't looking.

With the windows open I could hear the street noise, distant and faint, cars and buses and the occasional voice, and the bin-lorry and clanking of recycling being thrown into the back. It reminded me of Blossom House and the way the noise from the street seemed to fade away when we were in that huge, high-walled garden; how on lazy afternoons, while the kids were in school, Dee and I would lie there making love and dreaming dreams aloud. And then I remembered what happened afterwards, what happened to Blossom House and Pam and Pippa and Penny and I wanted to tear out the memories and scour the regret from my heart and soul, because it was all my fault.

My wrist ached, the one he broke, over and over again, as I mixed red on the palette and spread it onto the canvas, watching the light. Yes, I will add carmine red here, and a touch of red ochre, and a smear of yellow to make the texture right. Other things ached, too, my hips and back, a heaviness deep down inside my belly, though it couldn't be that time, not any more, I hadn't bled for over a year, but the sharp scent of the linseed oil reminded me of blood somehow. It was early for menopause, Fliss said, and it wasn't like I could ask my mother, though there had been a thousand different questions I had longed to ask her, that I still wished I could ask; but with her dead there was no one else. I thought she was menopausal at this age, but I couldn't be sure. And my sisters wouldn't be able to tell me, Karen because we never spoke, not after Mum's funeral, where she poured scorn and disgust onto me and my children. And Jan, sweet thing, because she was never very good at understanding stuff like that, and because she died just after I came back from the Kingdom.

Dad went just after Jan, as if he'd lost any reason to live, and maybe he had, because he never got to see the boys grow up and he never got to know Aisha. She was a funny little thing, at seven, at eight, all arms and legs and energy, and she was always jumping and bouncing, rocking back and forth on the sofa bouncing her head off the cushions at the back, jumping on beds and chairs, even after I got her a trampoline, just a cheap one, after North Wales, when Escape Route found us a place in Bristol. It was a council house in an area where my children didn't stand out as the only coloured kids in the village. She'd bounce all evening on the trampoline until it got too dark to see, and then come in and bounce on her bed. She wouldn't sleep; she was terrible at going to bed, wouldn't sleep without me, even at seven she refused to go into her own bed, and wouldn't let me go far away, even following me to the toilet. I should have understood it, really.

Switch to golds, for sunlight on the underside of leaves. Switch to happier memories, stay away from the smoke and ashes and the imagined smell of burnt plastic and wood and paper because that's where the madness lies, and I can't go there again.

Mindfulness, they call it, anchoring yourself in the now, but I remembered when the now was so terrible I wanted to fly away, when he broke my body so many times and I wanted to disappear. But there were always the children, and who else would protect them if I couldn't? Even though Dee betrayed me in the end, even though she proved that love never lasts, still I thought of her sometimes when the wood pigeon spills its sad song into the leaves outside my window. I remembered how she was the first one to touch me tenderly and to remind me that not all touch hurts, that love can be gentle as rose petals, and that pleasure is really such a simple thing.

It makes no sense, knowing what I know; unless it really was just that Aisha loved Dee, and missed her too much. Maybe that's what did it, maybe that's the root and seed of this thing. Or maybe it was Blossom House, losing that sense of home and family. Maybe I should never have taken her away, but if I hadn't, if we'd stayed, he would have had access to them, and we'd have been there when...

Blue. Sky blue and reflections in dew droplets, the colours I missed for so long, the wetness and the green. It took me years to get to that point, years to be able to sit and think of it all without losing my grip and seeing reality wing away on the backs of the black crows that picked at my eyeballs and rent my flesh while I slept. The thoughts and the feelings that came at the worst times and reminded me I should go to the doctor or go back on the meds. But those meds, they made me different, somehow, and I couldn't create the same way when I was on them. Better to pour it all into my painting, this act of creation that no one blames me for.

The commission was for seasons, three paintings of each, twelve in all, for a book. I told Ash about it, but she barely noticed, just pushed past me and disappeared into her room. They would be exhibited first and that meant they might sell, good money, enough to keep us going for a long time. The client said she liked my intensity, the claustrophobic feel of being so close to nature. This was the last of the summer series, reds and golds of August, and next would be the sweet slow decay of autumn. I could feel it already, greens and browns and then dusty reds and oranges and sunlit golds, and wet rain weeping from half naked trees, and mist under hedges or lying in layers on morning fields. Once I started it was hard to stop, but I used to stop, every day, for school pick up and shopping, parents' evening and cooking dinner.

There were paintings from that time, lots of paintings of bright scenes, in playschool colours, as if I was trying to create the world my children needed myself. Big shapes and bright reds and oranges and yellows and sky blues and greens like cake icing and pinks deeper and richer than they ought to be. In them, the dark figure, the woman in her black shroud, appeared diminished. She was two-dimensional, a cartoon on a book cover in the corner of a jolly family room, or one of many people sitting looking to the front of a jolly red bus.

When Pippa called to say that the court proceedings against Muhammed were progressing, that there were emergency protection orders in place and that soon he would have no access to the children, not ever, and that it was time to move on so that I could go back into the system again so that everything was above board, it felt as if the sky had opened up, letting in natural light for the first time in months. She told me that Escape Route would find us somewhere to settle for a while before we moved back to Blossom House, let the boys do their exams and then once it was all over, once the legal stuff was finished with, we could go home.

I knew I was overcompensating, trying too hard, letting them all run wilder than they should, not focusing on what normal people would think was important. I didn't push any of them in school. I didn't make them clean or do other stuff. I just got on with it and tried to keep them happy.

"Is this it?"

Shahid, too tall suddenly, sixteen and manly with it,

dropped the large rucksack onto the cracked concrete of the front path.

I ushered Aisha out of the taxi, juggling the large suitcase with its half-detached handle. Why was everything I owned old and broken?

"Yes, this is it."

I knew it wouldn't be glamorous, but I thought they were supposed to leave places clean for new tenants. It was truly awful. Someone else's rotting rubbish filled the overgrown front garden and spilled out of the wheelie-bin. The sick, foul smell of stale urine and decomposing nappies turned my stomach.

"Come on, it's nothing we can't fix," The light tone of my words could not cover the disgust. "Everybody in."

A long narrow corridor, horrible black and white linoleum and pale, patchy walls. On the right, a living room, with a large, old brown sofa and dark grey cord carpet, and patches on the walls where pictures used to hang. Broken blinds at the window. The smell of damp and dust and unchanged air, and a faint, stale public toilet odour.

At the end of the corridor, stairs, an understairs cupboard, and the door into the kitchen, white cupboards that sagged, a stainless steel sink under a grimy window. A dirty looking washing machine, a small, battered under-counter fridge, space for a table and chairs. A rime of dirt covered every surface.

"Don't worry, nothing that a little cleaning up won't fix!"

"Mum, are we really going to live here?" Yusuf in his high voice – at 11 he still had the voice and body of a boy.

"Shut up, Yus!" Shahid with his big brother face on, bringing in the last of the bags. He looked furious.

The thin windows rattled in their panes as buses and lorries roared past on the dual carriageway behind the small

143

back garden. If you could call it that: overgrown lawn and covered in rubbish. Straggly hedges and brambles filled the borders, and a washing line sagged, attached to a rusty pole.

"Mum, mum, where is my room? Mum!" Aisha, of course, she could never master 'inside voice.'

"We'll see love. Let's get settled."

She dashed off, hair bouncing, twisting away from my comforting arm. "Shah, Ab, wait for me! Let me see! Let me choose!"

Dirty carpets, filthy windows. Every room we entered was grimy, the paint chipped, smelling unpleasant. Upstairs, three bedrooms – two doubles and a single. I took the small room, set down my own bag, and tried not to collapse. Really? This was our safe house?

"Mum, this place is disgusting." Mahmood scowled as he brought up rucksacks and cases, and the box of Alisha's toys. I wondered suddenly when was the last time I had seen him smile. When was the last time he said something pleasant to me? "And there's no beds. Where are we supposed to sleep?"

"It's going to be fine," I insisted. "We'll get some beds and some paint and we'll sort it out. We just have to rough it for a while, OK?"

I could see it was not OK. Shahid and Abdullah reverted to muttering in Arabic, which they knew I hated, but Shahid was at least jollying the others along. Always the peacemaker. Ash had that thunderous look about her, shoulders rigid, eyes narrowed. We all knew what it could be like when she lost her temper, and a storm was brewing. "Come on Ash," he tried to deflect the worst of his sister's impending wrath. "Let's get your room sorted."

I got on the phone to the housing office straight away, finding a payphone in the community centre at the end of the road. "There's nothing here," I explained to the woman at the other end. "No furniture. I have five children. We have nothing to sleep on."

"Mrs Said, we will have your emergency payment soon, and the furniture will be delivered next week."

"What are my children supposed to sleep on until then?"

An interim payment was arranged. The bored and patronising tone of the woman at the benefits office enraged me.

An ache in my legs, my back, the weight of it all pressing down. Every step on the return journey an effort. Mahmood and Yusuf had unpacked the kettle, the mugs, the few dishes we had collected over the last year. Mismatched pieces, odd bits of kitchen gear. It all seemed pitiful.

Rather than drag them all back out to town, I left Aisha with Shahid, taking a sulky Abdullah with me to carry things, and got the bus to pick up the payment, buy air mattresses and new pillows, food, some cleaning spray and cloths and bleach, and a bean bag for the living room. At the charity furniture recycling shop, having proved I was on benefits, I paid for a sofa and chair, and a set of bunk beds, balking at the delivery fee. "It's not a very nice colour Mum," Abdullah bounced on the brown and cream sofa.

"It's fine," I insisted. It was the best I could afford – the cheapest in the shop. But with six of us we couldn't sit on the floor for long, and there would be fights over the bean bag until more seats arrived.

Another bumpy bus ride home, stinking of other people, stale air. We dragged the bags up the path, the noise level from the open windows a siren, warning of rocks ahead. Aisha was crying, which sounded more like screaming and Yusuf looked sullen, while Shahid stood in the kitchen shouting.

"What's going on?"

"It's him!" Aisha threw herself at me. "He's mean!"

"She was turning the cooker on and off!" Shahid gestured to the gas hob. "She had all four burners on high. I only turned my back for a minute. Yusuf was supposed to be playing with her."

His whine made me want to slap him. "For fuck's sake, Shahid, you're sixteen years old! I should be able to leave you in charge for a couple of hours." I turned to Aisha. "And you, don't touch that cooker unless I'm around, do you hear?"

She howled, running upstairs, and I felt myself start to lose control, frustration and fatigue draining my will. "Here." I thrust the last of the money at Shahid. "Go over the chip shop. There's one at the end of the road. I can't be bothered to cook. Get what you can with that."

Hot, salty, vinegary chips, greasy sausage and fish, flabby pie pastry and sweet fizzy drinks. They ate, scattered over the sofa and floor, arguing about the TV. I gave the kitchen cupboards and surfaces a wipe down, then stood at the kitchen window, watching the traffic pass and not bothering to eat, drinking tea and finishing the unpacking of kitchen things. I left their clothes in their cases, nothing to unpack them into yet.

Thoughts running again, looping up and down, and sinking lower each time. I'm too tired for this, tired and old and worn down with running and fighting and trying, just trying, every day. Always something, always one of them complaining, or all of them, never quiet, never calm, never accepting, and Aisha, it seems like she's the worst. Nothing is ever good enough. Mum, I don't like this bread. Mum, I wanted rice pops not cornflakes. Mum, Mum, Mum.

I could hear her still, her voice rising, a spiral of indignation. "But *I* wanted the battered sausage! I didn't want pie."

"You asked for pie," Abdullah. They were all so tired. It took a lot to get him annoyed.

"I didn't."

"You did!"

"I DIDN'T!"

"Just shut up both of you." Mahmood. Yes, of course it was him, stomping out with his chip wrappers, stuffing them into the plastic bag that held the cleaning bits and pieces. "I'm going to my room."

"Take the pump, sort out the mattresses, will you?"

That dark look, who am I to think I can order him around? He never said it, just stood there, sullen, and I know he would ignore me if he could, just slouch upstairs and "forget".

"I mean it, Mahmood, I'm too tired to do everything myself. Get the mattresses out of the boxes and pump them up. There are three doubles. One for each room."

"You mean I have to sleep on the same bed as Yusuf?"

"Yes. Just temporarily."

"That's disgusting."

"And it's how it is," I took the toiletries and cleaning spray through to the bathroom, which was white, with horrible dark green lino and a stained white bath and sagging shower head. No shower curtain. Great. Another thing we needed.

Darkness. Aisha cried herself to sleep in the little room that we shared. Mahmood was refusing to sleep with Yusuf, and had claimed the bean bag as his bed.

Shahid appeared in the kitchen where I stood again at the window. "Mum, why are we here? I thought we'd be going back home?"

"We can't, not yet," I sighed. "It's just not the right time. Your father can find us there."

"He can find us here, too. He can find us anywhere. Can't you see what a fucking mess this is? What it's doing to us?"

147

"Don't use that language with me." When did I become my mother, parroting her phrases? "And it doesn't matter now. He can't *legally* see you, the courts have finally sorted that. Pippa has managed to squash the visitation order. But we have to make sure he doesn't know where we are for a while. She told me he's still in the country, and she warned me not to go back there. He's been seen hanging around the street. We have to stay here. It's the only way to keep you all safe."

"Sorry, but you just don't see it. Mahmood hates it, Aisha is miserable, Yusuf just doesn't talk, and none of us have any friends. Again. We just want to go home. Why are you doing this to us?"

"I'm just trying to keep you safe."

"Is this safe? I'd rather be back home with Dee and the others."

"Dee doesn't live there anymore," I sighed. "You may as well know. She found someone else, before we even moved out. She's got herself another family now."

Silence. I knew it must hurt him, but I couldn't carry all of it, all the time, all on my own.

"Look, I'm knackered. I can't do anything else tonight. Just trust me, OK? We can make this work."

"But what if we don't want to," he muttered, low enough that I could pretend I hadn't heard.

I knew it was hard for them, but I had to run, couldn't live any more thinking that one day one of them might not come home. Or that I would wake to find him standing over me, Aisha in his arms. Or worse, wake to find her gone from her bed.

I painted the walls with bright colours and I painted the floorboards and we played games where we pretended to be camping until I could afford more furniture, and we made fun of the old sofa with the sagging springs that slowly swallowed you whole the longer you sat on it. I strung charity shop curtains up to make tents and pirate ships, and even the boys, sullen teenagers as they were, except for Yusuf who was 11 and still liked to have Mummy-cuddles sometimes when his brothers weren't looking, took part in the fantasy world I created. I overcompensated with gifts, cheap toys and lots of books and posters and board games that we played for hours until the rows and tears rolled inevitably through our little family.

I let Aisha sleep in with me still and made light of it when her new school complained that she was soiling herself and far too old to need changing twice a day. I just washed her clothes and bought more underwear and tights and skirts and never let her feel that there was something wrong with her. I didn't stop her bouncing on all the beds or complain when she crayoned her name, misspelled, on the back of the sofa. When they all started school again, I took her on playdates with classmates, when I would rather have been painting, and when it was our turn for playdates I always took them to soft play so no one would see our terrible house and the kids wouldn't tell their parents they weren't allowed in the garden because it wasn't safe. I made sure they were fed, clothed. I nagged about homework. I mediated the fights. I couldn't let myself feel, just boxed up the memories and the pain like I did before, shut it away and got on with the business of living.

I met Terri on one of those playdates. She was there with her sister, Chloe, stern-faced mother of Cassie, who was Aisha's current best friend. They had one of those houses in Clifton that were usually broken up into student lets because they were so huge, but there they were; Chloe and Cassie and little Daniel who was just 18 months old. Terri was drinking coffee in the kitchen. She had a cheeky smile, a long face and eyebrows that just wouldn't stay still. She was a large woman, muscled and heavy and very wide, but she moved easily with it, rising to shake my hand. Hands again, it was her hand, which was surprisingly slim given her bulk, that first caused the tingle, as she held on just a little too long and one corner of her mouth lifted as she raised her eyebrows at me.

"A pleasure to meet you, Amanda," she said as Chloe made introductions. "I'm Terri. The nice sister."

Aisha had already run off into the conservatory off the kitchen, yelling to Cassie that they had to play dollies, skipping and jumping, and I felt awkward. I knew it wasn't good form just to "dump and run" but I wasn't that fond of Chloe who was arrogant and superior, one of those intensive, over-achieving mothers. It was the first Saturday in ages where I wouldn't have Aisha hanging around my neck and demanding my attention every other minute, and couldn't help but want to dash out of there.

"Hi, Terri. Nice to meet you too. Thanks for this, Chloe, are you still OK to have her until after lunch? I can come back earlier if you like."

"It's fine, we're going to Café Rosa for lunch, so take as long as you like." I winced. Café Rosa was the most expensive of the yummy mummy cafés, and we hadn't been there yet. I hoped Aisha wouldn't start demanding to go there after this.

"OK, I'll be back at about 1 or 1.30."

Terri stood again, setting down her cup on the long, deeply stained and highly polished oak table. She had an earthy, slightly flowery scent, like moss after rain, and I could feel her presence like a pressure. "I'll be going too, see you next week."

At the door she ushered me through first. "You've got quite a handful there," she said as we walked down the steps. "Very lively. She'll be good for Cassie. I'm always telling Chloe she needs to get out of herself, run around more."

"Oh, Aisha never sits still!" We walked down the path towards the bus stop and I realised she was still beside me. Then she stopped at a blue car and said, "Can I offer you a lift anywhere?" I shrugged and said yes, because it was quicker and easier than the bus, and before I knew it she'd dropped me at the cheap stationery shop in town and I was standing there with her phone number clutched in my hand and wondering what had happened.

I don't know if time and experience make us better people, but they certainly make us better at reading others and seeing them for what they are. I may have been wanting, and needy, I may still have been in love with the idea of love, which is essentially how we get sold on the whole thing; romance, love, marriage, and putting up with people treating us badly. But Terri; Terri was the queen of hearts and she knew exactly how to capture mine, pouring attention into the painful cracks and fissures, into the spaces and gaps where there had once been Blossom House, and friends that were like family.

Although we didn't live in Clifton, the Saturday morning dance class I enrolled Aisha in was there. Two buses, fusty bus seat smell and letting Aisha press the bell. I liked it there; the energy and the atmosphere were different, somehow, with the big old houses and the students and the trendy cafes. Here and there were odd little boutique shops that seem too impossibly specialist to stay open. Yusuf got into Warhammer, obsessed with plastic figures and rule books, and Mahmood was happy enough to take him to the Games Workshop on a Saturday for all-day free gaming as it was just across the road from his church. Both Abdullah and Shahid were working paper rounds and garden maintenance; clearing up rubbish, cleaning paths, mowing lawns and trimming hedges. Shahid worked in a local garage some weekends, and I encouraged it because it got them out of the house. Anything that got all of us out of that house was a good thing. None of the boys liked high school, and Aisha went to a primary just under two miles away, which meant another ride on the bus. I painted while they were at school, time a river in flood, washing away those precious hours until I had to step back onto the hamster wheel again. Each day rolled into the next, like colours bleeding from one frame to another, with cleaning and trying to make house into a home, with living. Surviving. We were all still mourning Blossom House and its ghost wouldn't quite let us settle, as if we were the restless ones.

I never meant to be a gypsy, to have my children move from place to place. It wasn't as if I planned it. I knew, deep down, that it wasn't good for them, instilling at the very least a deep distrust of anything that seemed permanent and settled and, at worst, a fundamental insecurity, a knowledge that nothing lasts and everything ends. Maybe these were important life lessons, but I knew they weren't ready for them.

Only time would tell whether this would be the making of them. At least Bristol was big enough to allow us to disappear. Though the house was rough there were things to do and lots of different parts of the city to visit, and now that they were earning the twins and Mahmood were out and about a lot more. But I liked Clifton and its leafy greenness. The magnolia trees in the Spring weren't too much like cherry blossom, and the dance class was quite firm about asking mums to leave because it distracted the children. So, Saturday mornings I had two hours to kill in Clifton. I spent them reading and nursing two expensive cups of tea in a little café across the road, sketching out ideas for paintings and sometimes just watching the world go by. There was a church hall nearby, and on one of my first visits I stumbled across a charity jumble sale. Someone seemed to have donated their entire book collection, because there was a collection of books from various women's presses. I came away with two carrier bags of feminist books and lesbian fiction for a fiver.

I hadn't really put a label on myself until that point. I'm not sure that I did even then. There had been the children's father. There had been my saving Grace, my best friend through the years I lived in Riyadh. I never told anyone about her, and how close we were. Not that we ever spoke of it. Stolen time, and the only tenderness I knew. And Dee. To tell the truth I didn't even think about the fact that Dee was a woman. She was just Dee.

Those books. They were like drugs,. The feminist non-fiction brought my consciousness back to life, got me thinking about the world and my place in it. The books spoke to me, words that framed my own experiences, gave me a language to express myself, a lens through which to see clearly. They connected me to other women – poets and playwrights, artists and authors, and made me see myself as something more than just this hamster-wheel mother riddled with self-doubt and the constant feeling that I could never quite get it right.

And the romance novels? They were an anodyne, sugar-sweet oblivion-coated fantasy, and so easy to read, so satisfying, they made up for the fact that I could never justify buying a cake with my cup of tea, or one of the delicious-smelling breakfast muffins that other patrons were served each Saturday morning. I schooled myself not to care and simply to lose myself in the books.

And then Terri walked in. She had a swagger, Terri did. A large woman, one of the largest women I've ever met, but she walked as if she owned the street, the ground, the air around her. Some big women act as if they feel guilty for taking up so much space in the world, but never Terri. Spring was passing; the green on the trees was darker, the magnolia blooms long gone and only a few yellowed petals caught in the corner of windowsills and gutters to remind us. I was idling the morning away reading a romance about a woman painter, and wondering whether I should actually bring some paints with me and spend the two hours working rather than reading.

The last dregs of my cup of tea were cold; I was eking them out for another 15 minutes until the hour turned and I could order a second cup which would give me an excuse to sit here for another hour and allay the disdainful glances of the waif-like, black-clad waitresses.

And then Terri, smiling, standing over me.

"Hello!"

"Oh, hi, Terri."

"You remember me then?"

"How are you?"

Bright, cheeky smile, so bright I didn't give enough attention to the tension around her mouth, the hardness in her eyes. I'd just finished a passage about the heroine, who was cold and aloof due to past tragedy, and the initial melting of the edges of her iceberg heart.

"You never called me."

"I know. I've been busy. The kids, you know."

"I don't see them now." She looked around as if I might have left them somewhere, or tucked them under the tables and chairs out of the way.

"They're all doing various hobbies or working. And Aisha is in dance class."

"Ah, the Stage Academy. Chloe tried Cassie there but she wouldn't stay without her mum."

"To be honest, I'm amazed that Aisha will. But I think the fact that she gets to jump up and down a lot and watch herself in the mirror swayed it."

154

We both chuckled, and, was it there, in that moment of solidarity, that it started?

"Can I get you another?" She nodded at my cup.

"Oh. Yes please." I said yes because the £3.20 for that cup of tea would buy Aisha a magazine on the way home and keep her quiet for maybe another half an hour when I got in. I said yes because she asked, and because of the twinkle in her eyes, and because adult company was a rarity, at least adult company where I could potentially have a real conversation. The front garden at the house was ours, but the back garden opened onto a communal courtyard garden for all the flats and houses that surround it, half covered in dark, new tarmac, and occupied by a line of covered sheds for the bins and a long row of rotary washing lines. My only other adult conversation was with the other mothers as we put our washing out on fine days. I always had too many clothes to just use the single washing line in our own garden. These discussions were either tense, as we silently fought our claims for the limited drying space, or focused on boyfriends/husbands/lack thereof, or on what had happened in the soaps the previous night.

Terri brought tea for me, and coffee for herself, and told me she had ordered me a toasted teacake.

"How do you know I like toasted teacakes," I asked as she lowered her bulk onto one of the wooden chairs.

"How do you know you don't?"

Her eyes were a kind of blue-grey, almost uniform in colour, with just the odd inclusion; a darker blue line radiating out from the centre of the right eye, like the shadow on a sundial, and a couple of gold flecks in the left. Mismatched eyes, and a quirky smile that emerged slowly, a teasing eruption, drawing my attention and making me want it, and want to make it happen.

"What are you reading?"

Ah. The book. I let her lift it and read the back, flick through the pages. I accepted her knowing smile. I laughed a little as we talked about books, and about these kinds of stories, and pretended I knew about famous lesbian kisses on TV and when she tilted her head to one side I found myself nodding without thought, accepting the question, confirming it. White china cups and sweet tea and the thick salty-sweet flavour of teacake, crisp edges and chewy soft centre and bursting jewels of dried fruit. My jaws ached. Saliva flowed. Warmth flooding my limbs, reaching the parts of me I had left shut off, like abandoned rooms in a house grown too large for its occupants once love has fled.

"So what do you do with yourself when Aisha's in school?"

"I paint."

"Oh? I know a few artists. What do you paint?"

"Landscapes, mostly. But I work on a kind of hyper-realistic magical realism focus, focusing in or focusing out. Oh, it's hard to describe."

Nodding. "Would I have seen any of your work?"

"I used to sell prints at car boot sales and craft fairs, but not since we moved here, not really. I've done the odd commission but nothing major. I'm just working out how to get better at this, you know? I didn't even know I could paint and now I'm thinking about whether to do another course or something."

It felt good to talk to someone about painting, about something other than the kids. The surge and urge of it all, the way it ate up time and how sometimes when I came out of the immersion zone it was as if the entire world had changed and I didn't really know who I was.

"I get like that when I'm working," she admits.

"What do you do?"

"I have a garage I'm trying to get off the ground, though

it's hard as people are still funny about female mechanics. For my bread and butter I write technical manuals for engineers, for vehicles," she said. "It's not very glamorous. But I lose myself in the complexity of what I'm writing about, and whole days slip by."

"What do you do to relax?"

"I ride my motorbike. Or tinker with it. I just get on and go for a ride. Buy a cup of tea somewhere, drink it, then ride home. There's something magical about riding a bike."

Perhaps it was then, as her face lit up, that I fell, that I let the attraction in. Perhaps I was just lonely, there'd been no one since Dee, and perhaps I just didn't want to spend every day alone or refereeing the kids, because it gets you down, over time, the endless repetition of cleaning, cooking, shopping, ironing, mediating, reminding, carrying that mental load, never feeling like it's quite good enough. Sometimes it was a battle to manage all of them, sometimes they ran themselves and sometimes Shahid would bring me a cup of tea and ask how I was, or Abdullah would fetch the washing in without asking, and I would swell with love and pride that they were good boys, really. Other days I'd run out of cutlery and find mountains of dishes in the boys' rooms, and mouldering laundry, and I'd want to scream. But I had no friends, really, and even though I wanted to be self-sufficient, unwilling to connect again and risk more loss, there's a yearning in all of us to be known, to be wanted. To taste some kind of sweetness and to share something that the books call love. Not that I believed in love. But I could pretend that I did. And I liked the respect, the admiration that came with telling Terri I was a painter. And when she came to visit and admired my work, it was easy to pretend that I was what she thought I was.

People assume that I'm middle-class, because I've lived

abroad, because I paint. They make up a history for me, apply their own values. When they meet me at the galleries or art fairs, they think I am something I'm not. Terri did. When I told her we were in temporary accommodation, fleeing an abusive husband, she wrote her own back story for my life and I let her. It was easier. She was a rescuer, and she liked a challenge. In her eyes I was a newly-fledged lesbian and it was her job to show me the ropes.

It was a Wednesday. She'd taken an afternoon off, something to do with a completed commission and time to relax before starting a new project. A pale grey day with bright sky and no promise of rain, cold air and inside the house, condensation on the windows from laundry I didn't dare put out. That's what I remember most, that sharp clean laundry smell, *jardin des fleurs* fabric conditioner mixing with the linseed oil smell as I painted swathes of blue-grey cloud and storm-tossed leaves. Darkness inside me; but this was as far as I dared to go, the black figure on the canvas had appeared in the cloud shadows of her own volition. I had stopped to make a cup of tea and do the breakfast dishes, caked-on Weetabix and bloated, swollen cereal hoops in souring pools of milk, toast crumbs and crusts and orange-juice scented plastic cups.

A knock at the door, drying my hands on a greying tea-towel.

"Hi."

Terri, large and strong and somehow bright, brighter than the day, than the sun behind the clouds, than the laundry scent. I wanted to paint her, as yellow flowers, that bright pale yellow of primroses, with their fat leaves.

"I brought coffee cake," she lifted a box. "You said to come over one afternoon."

"I did."

I let her in, embarrassed at the house, suddenly. She was my first proper visitor and it felt strange to be inviting someone else into my home. She waved away my apologies. Filling the cheap white plastic kettle, finding the nicest mugs, small talk and then talk about the kids, always, and how is work, and the kettle singing and bubbling.

"So," she said, as we drank tea in the kitchen, relief flooding me that I'd cleaned up and not just left everything until the evening. I couldn't take my eyes away from her face, the way her mouth moved. And that smile. Such a smile, full of warmth and promise.

"So."

"Well, we've covered your boys, their exams, Aisha's progress in dance class, and the weather, of course."

"Of course."

"So, now what shall we talk about?"

In the slanting sun I became suddenly hot. "Books?"

She laughed. "Fine, OK. What's your favourite book?"

"*Jane Eyre*," I reply. "What's yours?"

"*Motorcycle News*."

"Really? You don't read books."

"Oh, not so much anymore, who has time?"

"I do. When I'm not painting."

"You mentioned you paint." She leaned forward, her face seeming to fill the whole of my vision. Eyes so compelling, that sideways smile. Charming and disarming. Terri's speciality.

That frisson, that electricity, the connection, it's like a drug. You know you shouldn't, that it will be a short-term fix, a brief high before reality strikes again and you have to come back to earth; you'll be left shaking and craving more, and you'll hate yourself for your own weakness and the power it has over you. Still, you reach for it, forgetting the pain that will come after, losing yourself in the rush and flush of it all, not caring about later, just about now, right now, and how good it feels to say yes.

We barely made it to the living room. The curtains were closed, as usual, a habit from living in the Kingdom that I still hadn't broken. Shadows and shade. Her body, the bulk and weight of it, the yielding softness and the underlying power of strong muscle. Her hands, surprisingly slender, with long fingers. Light touches that woke every part of me and made me forget for long moments that I was ever raped, ever beaten and hurt and brutalised. Confidence and tenderness, nothing like the needy child that Dee was, wanting nurturing, Terri was commanding, gentle. She kissed my scars with lips and tongue, and then she knelt between my legs, spreading them wide, drawing me to the edge of the sofa, and her mouth made a poem of every part of me, and I cried, sobbing and smiling and sinking back into a white haze of nothing. Nothing and everything and who knew it could be like this? Who knew love could be white hot and icefield cold, brilliant and beautiful? Her broken voice, whispering that she honoured me, honoured my body and the place where I brought forth life, and I wondered if this was a pinnacle moment of my life when pleasure would finally overtake the pain I had carried for so long.

Now, I think that maybe it was my fault, that it was me all along, not just for saying yes then, to Terri, or even to Dee years before. Is it that women know each other's bodies so well, that they can play them like instruments, a symphony of touch and taste and heat and cold, and the pressure, the sweet, heart-aching pleasure of soft flesh against soft flesh? Not that much of me was or is soft, just that wrinkled belly skin where my children once curled secretly and at peace, almost safe, the ones that made it and the ones that didn't.

But there's a harmony in it, curves against curves, a shape both alien and familiar, in the bright melodic line of skin on skin and the crashing chorus of what comes after, melodic and complete.

Now, I think "yes" comes without volition, in the wanting and the waiting, and in the desperate yearning to be loved. Some of us are not designed to be alone. We feel unbalanced when uncoupled. Some of us crave love like food and water, we yearn for the feelings we imagine we see in a lover's eye, for the whispered midnight promises, for the potential future that lies dormant in the happily ever after, if only we can find it.

I think that what's happened, this thing that haunts me, was my fault, because I took my eyes off the ball. I made love my priority, and just expected my children to accept it. I let myself believe the lie because just once, just once, I wanted all those stories in all those books to be true.

Now I know that I should never have believed that women would treat me any better than a man had.

Scarlet

Cramps, razor blades slicing inside me, and pressure, urgency, roll me out of bed in the cold dark, bruising my knee in the fall to the floor, scrabbling through the discarded crisp packets and wrappers and crumbs as I run to the toilet, the sudden explosion, cramping pain, acid burning pain, more pain, like vomiting but from the other end, and that stink, I need to remember that stink, that rotten smell, that's the smell of someone who can't control themselves, the just reward for weakness.

Cold hard plastic pressing in to my hated flesh, mouldy smell of the bathroom underneath the sewer stink, and the dream comes back to me now, a rush like wings or a plane flying low, a dream of weight, that was it, weight pressing me down, hot and heavy, burning weight and the smell of singed hair and burning plastic. I was trapped, yes, trapped and the burning turned into the sharp slicing pain and that was what woke me up.

Wasted empty feeling, hollow, welcome it, shower away the smell and brush teeth, extra mouthwash. Ana.com says it happens, bad breath. Sign of success and a reminder that we are all rotting inside. Once all the fat is gone I will be clean, pure, strong, smelling clean and fresh with none of these dark sticky odours and hairs in secret places. Ana says even your periods stop, after a while. How much longer to wait before it happens? How much more of this? But this is forever, this is how I control myself.

"Ash, lovely, are you OK?"

Why does she have to be there all the time, always asking, always in my way, never leaving me alone? Why is she always there? Leave me alone for fuck's sake, leave me in peace, stop asking me for this or that or to do this or that or if I'm OK? What the fuck is it to do with you anyway, all you care about is your stupid friends and my brothers and your paintings, just painting all the time, day and night and watching this fucking house fall apart around us, and there's never any money but you think you can fix it all just by acting like you give a shit when you don't, not really. Five kids and you just disappear into your fucking studio and paint so why don't you do that now and leave me alone!

"Fine, Mum. Fine." Infuse my voice with brightness, but I want to yell at her, *fuck off, just fuck off and don't come back. Stop looking at me in that way, expectant, searching. Stop hoping that we're going to be like friends all of a sudden cos it's not going to happen and I'm not going to let you in no matter how hard you try, just fuck off and find yourself another girlfriend and then leave me alone again because it's better that way.*

‹Mornings suck›

Jarelle. New feeling – not quite happiness, because it's not to be trusted, any of it, not really.

‹Got Mum nagging, fucking hate mornings.›

She sends a selfie on snapchat, with bunny ears and a pig snout. I laugh. The sound feels strange in the echoing bathroom. Or is it that it's been so very long since I laughed out loud?

‹PMSL›

Squeeze into clothes again, the chest binder feels even more uncomfortable today, how long before it all goes, all of it, the extra flesh I never asked for? I just want it gone. Messages from Jarelle, pictures of her breakfast, shares of music she likes, running to keep up it feels like, answer the messages, stay in touch, stay upbeat. I don't know half the music she likes but I say I do, I don't know the stuff she watches on Netflix but I won't let on, don't let on, don't let them see what a freak I am. So hungry, insides aching empty and why can't my muscles be hollow and the fat disappear? Why can't I hide these curves and lumps and the putrid flesh that wobbles between my thighs, making them press together, I can't even cross my legs like Jarelle does, like all the girls do. Every step feels like thunder, a weight hammering down on my feet into the floorboards, the hallway tiles, the cracked concrete path, thud, thud, pound, pound, if only I was losing pounds not carrying this weight shifting from one foot to the other. How did I get this monstrous, this grotesque? Size twelve, may as well be size 20, so huge, Jarelle's got to be a six, maybe even a four.

<Yo>

IM from Carl, with pictures of his face close up and distorted.

<The dragon is taking me to school. Want a lift?>

<Nah, m k, walking is my religion>

<pmsl>

Suddenly there are gifs and pictures and this whole world of stuff and I'm going to have to figure out how to do all of this, walking and looking and fielding messages from Jarelle and Carl, and then Jarelle's friend Nina asks to connect, and I only know Nina from those awful PHSE classes they still make us take even though we're doing A levels. And then Kat too, and the pictures and messages flying back and forth and before I know it I'm at the school gate and Jarelle is there, with Kat.

"Morning."

She gives me a weird look. What's wrong with that?

"Hey," Kat gives me that upwards nod with the raised

eyebrows and I don't know why but I'm wondering whether this is a new thing, or has it always been something people did to say hello, or is it like in Jane Austen's time when people bowed and curtseyed. Awkwardness as I walk between the two of them in their perfectly wrapped headscarves and their stylish uniforms. I am bloated, at least twice their size, what makes me this way, not fair, it's not fucking fair, and the cramps in my stomach remind me of what happened yesterday, and then I make up my mind that I just won't eat for the rest of the week and maybe that will help, maybe I can lose half a stone in a week, that would help, that would show them all, yes, if I lose at least six pounds this week, then I can let myself eat on the weekend, let myself have something nice.

Ash taste in my mouth suddenly, last night's dream, rushing back, roaring flames around me, watching walls burning to the ground, and outside, a ring of people – my brothers, my mother, a man in a black suit I know is my father, Carl, Jarelle – all there, all laughing, all watching me burn.

"What's up, Ash?" Don't say anything, don't let Jarelle and Kat see me like this.

"It's Flo visiting," Jarelle says to Kat.

I don't correct her. I don't know what their exchanged looks mean, this is just too hard because I didn't grow up with girls like this, I don't know anything it seems, not about people and talking or anything important, because I learned everything from books and my brothers and all I've gathered from being out here in the real world is that it's nothing like anything in any of the books I've read, because the mean girls don't get punished or redeemed and the boys get away with everything and it's always the fat girls who are lazy and deceitful in those books, and cruel and vain and shallow, and that's not me, that's not who I want to be. Waves of faintness, the aching, burning pain in my guts, the hollow gnawing of my empty stomach, the sore feeling in my throat, the blisters on my gums from stomach acid, but I have to do it, have to do it now so I can shrink, so I can fit in, so no one notices me.

Then Kat links her arm in mine. "We'll cheer you up. Let's all go for Starbucks after school. That new barista..."

"You know it!"

Their voices, their words, I nod, bemused, thinking about how I will afford it, but there's my allowance, she does give me that, the £22 a week the government gives her for having a kid, but half the time she spends it anyway on food and stuff instead of transferring it to me. I can go and get some money out, I suppose. It should have gone in today, I should check, but don't say anything, don't let them know. I could message Shahid, but he has enough on his plate now, and he's going to be a dad soon. I can't keep asking him for money.

"So what are we doing on the weekend?"

Kat pulls me along with her, bony arm tight against mine, and the sick feeling rises, flesh, thick and gristly, that's all I am, too much flesh taking up too much space and listening to their conversation and wondering what I will ever have to offer girls like them.

Swallow it, that nausea, and smile, paint on the smile and the brightness, and listen, listen hard to how they speak and how they laugh, copy how they walk and how they talk about boys.

Crowded corridors, and that horrible smell of school, floor polish and people and perfume, though we're not supposed to wear it, and boys and sweat, Kat laughing

166

about a joke her sister played on some boy she's in college with, setting him up on a date and sending this fat girl from her class instead, and how he reacted. Is that what I am? The fat girl joke? Try not to think. Jarelle walks with me to physics and smiles when she hands in her homework, and the hunger recedes when I look at her, because she is so beautiful, so perfect, not a blemish on her skin, and her eyes, so like mine, it makes me think that yes, one day, I can look like that. I can be like that.

Through quick, brutal rain showers we run and laugh, dusting off water from our shoulders inside the coffee shop with its steamed-up windows and crowds of damp, depressed shoppers with their bags of stuff.

"Ash, what are you having?"

This is it, this is one of those moments, hot coffee smell and that screaming hiss of the beast that makes the coffee, the bangs and crashes, how can anyone find this restful or relaxing with all this noise, like being inside some kind of industrial monster?

Jarelle is fishing for her wallet. "Skinny soy caramel latte with an extra shot," and I just want to be her, that self-assuredness, I want to pick it up and lay it over me like a cloak, watch it cover and meld into every part of me, so I can move through the world the way she does. My mouth waters at the sudden smell of toasting cheese and the huge cabinet of cakes and muffins and cookies and crisps. "Same, without the caramel," I hear myself saying, fishing for my own purse.

"I've got these," Jarelle says. "You get them next time. Oh, Kat, look, it's Tanya." I look too, at a woman she's pointing to.

"What's up?"

We wait for our drinks, watching the moves of the

barista, a well-practised dance, move, lift, select, place, fill, swirl...

"Tanya. Over there." A Muslim woman in the full gear, obviously pregnant.

"What's wrong?"

"Tanya was in our year at school. Don't you remember her?" Kat is watching the barista now through narrowed eyes. Shifting slightly to see past the vast swell of her headscarf – what is under it, surely that's not all hair – I see the woman sitting opposite a man with a beard and a suit, pleasant enough, but he looks old, thirty-five at least.

"Kat, she wouldn't recognise her now, would she?" Jarelle picks up the tray and nods towards a table in the window.

Strange, narrow chairs in half circles, squeeze my hips in, watching how Kat sits, knees together, ankles crossed to one side, and she barely takes up half the chair, but this hateful flesh, spreading to touch the edges as I sit, how must I look to them, monstrous and obese. Oh, how I want to carve up my own skin and shave my bones to fit. When I was little I remember sitting beside my mother in chairs like this, side by side, both of us together, always, and it seemed that she was never far away, and we slipped into small spaces that others couldn't, and now I'm almost too fat for this chair, and the smell of the caramel in Jarelle's drink makes me almost dizzy with wanting, but I sip mine and savour the bitterness of the coffee, and before long there's a ringing in my ears from the caffeine and the churning burn in my stomach but it's better than feeling full.

"She left just after GCSEs, remember?"

I drag myself back to the conversation.

"I think so, wasn't she the really bright one?"

168

Eager nods, savouring the gossip. "Yeah, her parents took her on holiday to Pakistan – a family wedding. Only when she got there, she found out it was her wedding!"

"I still say she's better off," Kat murmurs. "I mean, yeah, she had 12 As and A stars but look what she's got now? It's where we're all headed. So what if she went for it earlier?"

"What, you'd want that? Babies and a husband?" I can't help but say it.

"No, not right now, yeah, I get what you say, but what's the difference? So we have a few more years? That's where we're heading."

"Not me." Jarelle tucks a fold of her headscarf in more tightly. "No matter what my mother says."

"I can't imagine it." Is that my voice? Have I said the right thing?

"No, me neither," Jarelle widens her eyes meaningfully at Kat. "And neither can you. She can't be happy."

I watch her. She looks like any other woman in *hijab*, and there is something so familiar about her, something about that shape, and then it's like I am dreaming, the steamy air and the noise all floating and disappearing and my head spins and the room seems far away and Kat and Jarelle seem so very small, all of a sudden, or is it that I have grown big, like Alice, or am I floating away now...

Voices. Hard surface. Hands on my face, calling my name. Ash, Ash, that's what I am, a pillar of ash held together by dreams and wishes and waiting to dissolve into the rain and be washed away, rushing through drains into dark sewers and cast out into the flow of rivers until finally, in the sea, falling, just falling, to be lost in the endless depths.

169

"...I don't know, she looked a bit off..."

"...never seen someone faint like that..."

"...call an ambulance?"

No, no, don't do that, please, no fuss, not that. I struggle out of a mire of wet cinders with a burnt taste in my mouth. "No, I'm ok." Force the world into focus, feel my feet on the floor, the edges of the chair where I am slumped. Pull my body upright. Is it possible to feel so heavy and yet so light at the same time?

Oh, what have I done? They are looking at me strangely.

"Sorry!" I try to laugh. "I've been on that diet, you know?"

"The five and two?"

"Yeah."

"So it's a fasting day?"

"Yeah. I just got a bit faint. It's OK though. I'm fine now.

"Well, at least let's get a lift home. Do you want me to call your mum?"

"No! I mean, no, she doesn't drive."

The room swims back into focus, the sounds, the smells, Jarelle's beautiful face, concern making a little frown line between her brows, and even that is just so cute. How can anyone be so pretty?

"I know..." Kat pulls out her phone. "My cousin's friend, Avad, he's got a car. He's home from Uni this weekend... I'll give him a call."

She gets up to go outside.

"Want me to get you something to eat?" Jarelle murmurs. Her closeness, that sweet coconut and fruit scent of her, makes my head swim again.

"No, honest, it's OK. I just..."

"I know, right? Dieting is hell. But you're doing it, yeah?

Like, it's like this for all of us? And you can eat what you like tomorrow."

"Yeah." Oh, if only you knew, you with your perfect body and that beautiful face, and no diet is going to make me look like you, make my body move like yours, like oil on water.

"It's OK, Avad is on his way. He'll be about ten minutes."

Finish the coffee, bitter and sickly, breathing, trying to take deep breaths but the binder and the bodyshaper squeeze every part of me and I want to run away, panic, I can't do this, everything aches and burns and hurts and somehow it's unfair, really, so unfair, and why do I feel so sick all the time, I don't know, so sick, I don't want this feeling any more, maybe I should eat...

Avad beeps outside. He has an Audi, black, with chrome wheels and leather seats, and warns us not to put our wet coats on the leather,

"Is she OK?" I can see him watching me in the mirror, dark eyes, beautiful skin, something about him is a little familiar. Jarelle in the back with me, Kat in the front. I want to lay my head on Jarelle's lap and have her stroke my hair. I want something, I don't know what, someone to touch me, to make me feel real again, because I still feel like I'm floating, or falling, or something, and the swaying movement of the car only makes me feel sicker and fainter. Is that my voice giving directions? So remote, so far away, childlike.

"No, don't get out," I say when he pulls up at the gate. "It's pissing down. I'm fine now."

Jarelle catches my arm as I slide out of the door. "Catch you later, yeah? Sure you don't want me to come in?"

"Nah, I'm fine."

171

"Tomorrow, yeah? We'll do our physics and then go into town?"

"Yeah, I'll come to yours."

"OK. See you."

"Later."

"Later," Kat says too, and as I force myself to walk normally up the path, I wonder if I've blown it, but I don't know what's happening, I feel awful, and I can't imagine it, spending all day with Jarelle, not when I feel so sick and so tired and everything seems to hurt like this. The front door resists, as always, until I kick the bottom and it springs out of its frame, but the house is quiet. Mum is out, it seems, no tell-tale light or the smell of her paints or the weird goddess music she plays "to get into the flow". Instead, there's an emptiness, not like silence, more like quiet breathing, and I can't wait to get upstairs and take off the binder and the bodyshaper and just put on pajamas and go to bed and sleep. Maybe I will feel better in the morning.

Dampish bedding, plug in my phone, messages from Carl, I answer, from Jarelle, from Kat, suddenly she's my friend too and we have a group chat for the three of us, then some friend requests from friends of hers and as I drift off I have images of them all, these girls, and the one in black, in the coffee shop, the hard round bulge of her belly showing, and her eyes, which were black and distant and it's her figure I see standing over me, saying, "Why wait, this is what we're all heading for, anyway," and the dream sweeps me up and casts me down, down into the waiting clouds of grey-black ash and

I

Am

Gone.

Winsor Red Deep

Like blood, the paint on the canvas clotted and darkened as it dried. A shadow across the window reminded me that the light was fading, and nothing had changed. Not the feelings that assaulted me every time I lifted my head from the painting, not the emptiness in the house, not the lack of messages or phonecalls or visitors with news.

Nothing.

I used to want to fade away, to dissolve and disappear, but then I had children and being a mother makes you more real, more grounded, it steals your dreams but it gives you the reality of little people you *have* to love and who have to love you back.

At least, until they don't. Until puberty forces that necessary wedge between you and them, and the world steals them away, casting them adrift on the sea of adulthood, and they return from time to time, so much flotsam washed up on the beaches of home. Outside the ancient oak tree with its belly-like bowl and the hollow place inside loomed up. I spent too much time at the window, watching, waiting, and the tree watched with me. And remembered.

Terri was a joker, in public, all affability and bonhomie. She charmed the boys from the very first day, making dinner in our jumble of a kitchen, filling the house with good smells. She made spaghetti bolognaise, and it was delicious, and there were mountains of it, mouth-watering food that even picky Yusuf dived into. She made them laugh with stories of her travels on the bike, and her antics with the horses, and talked with warm admiration of my work, and it felt strange, like I was playing a part, an actor in someone else's life, because she assumed a pose of total respect for me and it made the boys sit up and take notice. In between she flirted with me, winks and nods and whispered comments, sighing "I want you" into my ear as she passed with the dirty dishes, stroking my back with a finger that left a trail of fire along every centimetre touched, flicking her tongue over her lips whilst raising her eyebrow, smiling with satisfaction when I reacted. She brought my body alive like no one had, no one since Grace, sweet, impossible Grace, my friend, secret lover, the woman who kept me alive in the death-knell nightmare time that became my life in the Kingdom. I had thought, when I left, that I would live a life of fear and flight, always running, always missing her, but like the other memories, she faded with time and the intensity paled to a wash of faint remembering. But then Terri, who possessed me, brought it all back, and there it was, the yearning and the returning and for a long time it was all I could think of.

Day after day of it, she kept on turning up, saying she couldn't stay away, that she just wanted to spend time with me. Cooking in my messy kitchen, making magic happen, transforming the dregs and oddments of pasta and spices and vegetables and tired fruit in the dusty fruit bowl into a feast – pesto pasta bake and home-made garlic bread, and apple turnovers with ice cream. Terri standing outside under the rusting rotary lines, smoking, staring into the distance or into some other place only she understood. Terri drawing my legs and feet onto her lap on the sofa, watching old movies. Who can blame me for thinking that maybe I could do this, because every word out of her mouth seemed to make me feel good and the fact that I had five kids didn't bother her and it just felt so good, to have someone who was there just for me.

"Is she your girlfriend now?"

Mahmood, not as tall as Shahid, slender and wiry looking, but his brows heavy and stern. He looked most like his father, out of all of them. Yusuf in the garden with Terri, kicking a football, her showing him ball control. She moved well despite her bulk. Don't react to his tone, I thought, because he reminds me too much of Muhammed, that taunting, disrespectful voice.

"Yes, I suppose so."

"It's disgusting."

"I beg your pardon?"

"Look, it's one thing to put up with it when we lived at Blossom House," he slouched against the doorframe. "It wasn't so obvious there, with that house full of women. And you didn't flaunt it, not like now." The smell of washing up liquid and an underlying smell of damp washing left too long without drying. I knew I should get the pile on the table out on the line. It was the first fine day for a while. But he was in my way and for a moment there was a stab of fear.

"Put up with what? Terri's a nice person. She brings us stuff, she buys us all food. She plays with Aisha, she gives you lifts to places. I don't have any other friends here."

"None of us has any friends here. You've done nothing but spoil everything since we moved to this country. I thought you had family here." You. As if he is not connected to me. "At least at Blossom we thought we were settled, and we had friends and familiar people around. I still don't understand why we had to move!"

"Because your father was going for visitation, for custody. And because we thought he was going to abduct Aisha from school." I picked up the basket, hinting that I wanted to go out into the garden. He remained in the doorway. That look, did he learn it or was it inherited, a genetic predisposition to arrogant disdain?

"And why would seeing him be such a bad thing? Maybe he's changed."

I slammed the washing basket down in frustration. "Do you really have to ask me that?"

"Yes! I know he was an arse, and yeah, he treated you badly, but he's our father."

"And he almost killed you."

"I don't remember that. At least having him around would be normal. What you are, what you do... it's immoral."

He shoved himself upright, the arrogance palpable. I backed away a little.

"Mum, Mum, I can't find my trainers." Aisha barrelled past her brother, whose thunderous look did not soften.

"By the back door. Are you going out to play with Yusuf and Terri?"

"Mmhmm." She skipped off, bouncing and whispering, "mmhmm, going to play... Mmhmm, going to play..."

"You can't just keep doing this," dark voice, accented still. Hand on my arm, gripping as I tried to pass.

"Who I choose to spend my time with is none of your business. You're my son, and still a child."

"I'm almost sixteen."

"And I am still your mother." I barged past him. "And I shouldn't have to be doing everything in this house, but here I am, washing *your* clothes and cooking *your* food."

"Not for much longer." He muttered. I used to hate that when his father did it, the menacing muttering and threatening statements.

Fresh air, Terri laughing, sweating as Aisha kicked the ball and she ran after it. Her eyes met mine, happy, knowing. "Right kids, time to work. Let's help Mum do the laundry."

Yusuf and Aisha looked mutinous, but followed her and helped, catching her enthusiasm. I glanced back at the house, at the ominous shadow of my third son at the kitchen window, watching us.

Terri's displays of respect for me made the children behave differently, other than Mahmood, and when she was there the dishes were always done and dried and put away, the floors swept, the communal rooms kept tidy. We played games, Aisha, Terri and me, and Terri taught her some martial arts, which reminded the boys of Blossom House and of Dee, and they talked more, all of them, Aisha warming to her more and more each day. Terry even got her to help in the garden, and some days it was more about the family than just me and her, but then at night, behind closed doors, long sleepless nights that seemed to pass between one heaving, gasping breath and another, pleasure a spiral galaxy, never ending, wondrous, our spirits lifting out of our bodies to join in some otherworldly realm where for a time there were no words and no past and no future. Just now.

What is love but an agreement to put each other first? To spend time and energy on and with each other? A tacit agreement, perhaps, and my mistake was believing what I thought her to be, trusting what I assumed to be the foundations of her decisions, her feelings, her actions. And if I was sometimes uncomfortable, if she took more of my time and attention than I wanted her to, if I felt unhappy about her disciplining the children, it all disappeared when she kissed me, the softest, most sensual of kisses that woke my body's deepest responses. I had never before felt such arousal. I was haunted by the way she kissed, a kiss like floodwaters overwhelming the riverbanks and spilling through into every part of me, desire like tidal waves, like boiling cauldrons of undersea volcanoes, there are no metaphors for it, and if I painted it there would be swirls of impossible colours and unheard-of shapes, that was how new it was for me.

Lying in bed in the morning, grey light slipping around the edges of the curtains, sleep heavy mind and body, the bed so comfortable I felt as if I could never move again. Half awake, a dream playing against the cinema screen of my eyelids, watching it, aware that I'm dreaming whilst still awake, the sound of Terri dressing, soft whispers of cloth against skin, small movements around the room, creak of floorboards as she quietly went about the business of the morning.

"Sleep," she whispered, "there's no need for you to get up. I can look after myself." And then the familiar sound of someone pottering about the kitchen, making tea, and in that half-awake, half-asleep, post-coital haze of barely aware, I remembered how it had been with Dee, in Blossom House, and how she had made me tea and cherished me in the beginning, and how that changed so quickly to me mothering her. And there was Terri, with a cup of tea and a gentle smile and all I could see and feel was her. And I thought, yes, I have this, this one day, and if this is all I have then let it be so.

But she did it again. And again, weeks and months of it, always the same, that urgent longing, billowing steam-clouds of want. And on a cold Maundy Thursday evening, crisp, acid-white wine in mismatched glasses, we sat in my bedroom on the sway-backed futon and listened to her favourite song by Barclay James Harvest while the kids watched DVDs in the sitting room, and she told me she loved me. She told me she didn't want to love me, that she had been hurt and let down by other women, and that she was tired of trying, of losing and of the deep sadness, but that she couldn't help but love me. And I fell in love with her broken heart and vowed to love it and every part of her in such a way that she would never feel sad again. It made me feel powerful, suddenly, as if I could believe what she said about me being a survivor, a saviour, and there I was, the strong one, saving her.

No one had ever said they needed me before, not like that, and I had never thought that love would make me feel powerful. And she didn't seem afraid of my history, of the fractured fragments of the past that escaped my control and aired themselves at the tail end of late night drinking sessions. Oh if only I had known then what it would lead to, losing myself in love. I saw the best version of myself reflected in those beautiful blue eyes, and I forgot to worry about the future and the shadow and the threat that still stalked me. And if I was painting less, because evenings and weekends she wanted me with her, and weekdays there was always so much to do – shopping, cleaning, laundry, cooking for when she got home from work – then I didn't mind because every minute with her was like coming home and being with her, just sitting and watching TV or listening to her music and her stories of her past, made me happy. She moved in, bag and baggage, just as June reached its apex, almost without discussion, just a natural progression.

Terri bought new furniture, masterfully constructing flat-pack shelves and cupboards, aligning new sofas and chairs. She painted rooms, with real paint, in nice colours, paying attention to the edges and the finish, matching curtains and new bedding and cushions. She moved her desk into the dining room so she could work from home some days, and I moved my painting gear in there too so we could be together more. She took on the rubbish-filled front garden, and dragged me and the boys out on weekends to clear and plant and cut and mow and scrub the concrete. She took me to garden centres and bought ornaments in the shape of angels and Buddhas and fairies, so many fairies, because fairies were her thing, and she liked them everywhere, and soon there were fairy prints on the walls, and fairy coasters protecting the new table in the kitchen and the coffee table in the lounge. Sexy fairies hung over our bed, magical fairy trees looked down on me as I climbed the stairs. She started inviting friends over for regular weekly drinking sessions, and took me out on weekends to a pub with painfully loud, terrible music and drag queens, and I didn't mind because she stood beside me, an arm hooked around my waist, and told everyone I was her partner, and it felt good. And if she was a little more possessive as time went on, that was OK too. It felt good to be wanted.

Flash-forward, days and weeks and months. Terri at the bar, buying drinks, ordering me doubles because she thought I was too uptight, flashing lights making my head spin and the pounding music, too loud to talk, too loud to think, making me want to paint the freeze-frame strobe scenes.

Terri in the kitchen, smoking by the back door, her bulk filling the frame, blocking the light, and me at the counter, chopping and cooking and cleaning, always cleaning, somehow, and it reminded me of the past, sometimes, when I sliced into big, deep red tomatoes and watched the juices run out, or when I made chicken and rice, what Aisha called *yellow chicken,* the one dish the boys all adored, because it was a childhood staple, and the spices reminded me of a past that seemed like a half-forgotten dream.

Terri at night, claiming my body, passion as possession, mouth devouring, fingers, long and firm and clever teasing the skin that had longed to be touched with love, whispered words, and my responses, my skin on hers, my heat and her cool softness, acres of her to map and trace and tease and remember.

And if I slept deeper, with her, if sleep came without dreams, leaving me to wake half-numb and hung over, surely it was a good thing, that I was sleeping better than I ever? And if we drank more, went out more, if I found myself late at night eating Indian food and drinking cheap wine, then it was just normal life, wasn't it, the life I could have had, should have had, those ten years I spent in the Kingdom?

And if she got firmer and more authoritarian with the kids, especially with Aisha, then that was OK too, because it was a relief not to have to do it all alone any more, to be able to sit back and not bear all that burden of responsibility myself. It was a relief when she enforced Aisha's bed time, and built a cabin bed for her so that we could have privacy at night in the room she shared with us. She helped Shahid and Abdullah find apprenticeships, and then enforced them paying rent, and set curfews and yes, if sometimes I felt she was too harsh, if the shouting and arguments got too much, at least it kept the boys in line during the hard times when they resisted everything.

Terri drew me into her friendship circle. Cally, a tall, overly made-up lesbian who talked so loudly it made my ears hurt. Chris, a friend from her schooldays, and her partner Nic. Chris drank too much and Terri matched her, and Nic would sit beside me and laugh at their antics, even when Chris was being lewd and inappropriate with strangers on the dancefloor. We went to bars, or hung out at home, strangers became friends filling my walls and spaces, me being the hostess, providing clean glasses and chilled wine and olives and crudités and dips spread out on the kitchen table, keeping people's glasses filled, clearing up constantly, listening to stories of past lovers and their friends I didn't know, until it seemed they were simply retelling the same stories every week.

Aisha running in and out, eating garlic bread and looking confused as they teased her, unsure if this was a good thing, looking to me for reassurance, and the scent of Cally's perfume mixing with the garlic smell and the bitter salty olive taste and the wine, bottles and bottles in the recycling bag the next morning, Terri denying any hangover as she roared off on the bike. The boys playing their music and videogames, or out with the friends they finally made, the twins almost men, doing apprenticeships and going to college, working part time on weekends. Mahmood closeted in his room studying, Yusuf playing his guitar and violin and the second-hand electric piano Terri 'found' for him. His music was everything, choir and orchestra in school, his spare time spent in the local youth orchestra and playing in a folk band.

We weren't truly happy, but it was a kind of contentment. We were waiting for something to happen, for the time to be right to go back to Blossom House and take up the reins of our old lives.

The inheritance came out of the blue.

The note, from my sister Karen, was short and to the point.

"This is the final disbursement of your inheritance. I have been scrupulous in listing every asset and the particulars of the sale. The fact that our father left *you* the money from his house amazes me, given that you estranged yourself from your family for so long, and denied him any possibility of a relationship with his grandchildren. But he would not be dissuaded. So you and your children will be comfortable now.

He is buried with our mother, if you are interested, and with Jan, who as you know died of cardiac problems. Although I tried to care for him when he was sick, I couldn't give him what he needed, what he desperately wanted – his family.

This is the last you will hear from me. When people ask, I tell them I am an orphan and that my sister is dead, and if people ask about you, I say that you may as well be dead too. Whatever you say, however you try to change the past, all we know is that you abandoned your family and no one here has any affection for you now. This was your choice. I only hope that you don't live to regret it."

Nothing unexpected in that. She's always resented me, the baby of the family, and we were never close. But family is family, an old, familiar cardigan, hanging in folds on the back of the kitchen door, a little house in a little town with those awful patterned carpets, the Anaglypta walls, the Sunday dinners and the afternoon teas and the long stuffy days shut in with mum and Jan, cleaning and cooking, and watching terrible telly and wishing, longing for some other life.

"You're still married," Terri warned me as I sat, staring at the huge amount of money. "Before you do anything with that, you need to get divorced. A financial clean break. You don't want him coming after that."

And so it was that after almost two years, two years when the gap in my life left by Blossom House was at least filled with happy memories, I made contact with Pippa. I knew she'd help me to finish what we started. And I was ready to face my past, the husband who had abused me and threatened the lives of my children, and to insist on the divorce that I should have been granted years ago. With Terri at my side, I was ready to fight. The future she promised was worth the fear. I wanted it all, this real life, this normality, the thing everyone else seemed to have, two parents and a home and just life, life without fear.

"Do it," Terri said. "I don't want your past hanging over us, holding us back. You belong to me now."

I thought of Blossom House, and wondered if we could think of going back there. When I mentioned it to Terri, she was non-committal, said she would consider it. In my mind, she would come with us. We would all make a life together there, and our days as wanderers would be over.

I know that it wasn't really my fault. I know that I didn't do it. But when the cherry-blossom falls, pale petals floating on the first warm air of spring, I still think of the line of trees in front of Blossom House, and the ashes flying and landing like the petals in spring, and my heart breaks because none of it would have happened if it wasn't for me. Blossom House would still be there, and Penny would still be alive, and little Jenna, if it wasn't for me. I know how it feels to lose a child, before its time, but how much worse must it have been for Flora, who had already fought so hard for freedom, to lose the one of the two most precious parts of her world?

Paint, paint it all away, the darkness and the light, paint it away and let me think of something else, not that, not of all that pain and the anger and the loss and the sorrow. Bring me cerulean blue for the surreal dream sky and Winsor Green for the leaves, and terra verte for the grass and paint me a landscape of memory and loss. Indanthrene Blue for the pool of sadness beneath a dead tree canted sideways, death amongst the impossibly vivid life of the forest as the leaves turn Indian Yellow and Cadmium Orange and Quinacridone Red. Death in life this one would be called, this painting of summer's end and then I thought about how it was with Pippa and how hard I tried not to feel her anger and how I just couldn't avoid it.

Let it be me, the one that was lost. Let time roll back like clouds after a storm, let the wind and rain scour away the smoke and ash, the bitterness and the pain. And one day, maybe, in some other place, some other plane, Penny and Jenna will still be playing in the bright rooms, running in the garden of Blossom House, laughing and smiling. And maybe they will forgive us, forgive me for what I'd done. Maybe their ghosts linger beside their loved ones, beside Pippa and Pam, beside Flora, whispering, "It's OK, you can forgive them." Maybe they'll say it one day, the women I loved like family. "We forgive you."

Goodness knows, I will never forgive myself.

"Is that it?"

"Yes."

Terri slid the car into one of the designated residents' parking spaces, while Aisha barely looked up from her tablet. Some game or other, annoying beeping and a shrill female voice, American. Still, it had kept her occupied during the drive. Yusuf had his headphones on, as always, looking as if he's seeing the music rather than hearing it. Still I hoped that he was happy to be back, even if only for a visit.

Almost before the car stopped, Aisha was out, racing along the pavement to the big front door that lead directly into the community room.

"Mum, Mum, come on," she beckoned, and then the door opened, spilling out the familiar scent of rice and vegetables cooking, and there was Pippa, older but still the same, and Penny wrapping Aisha in a hug, and Pam telling us to "hurry up inside, kettle's on". Yusuf followed us sulkily. He didn't want to come, but I couldn't leave him home with Mahmood, who flatly refused to be responsible for his younger siblings.

Jumble of people and voices, Terri lumbering in last, smiles and hugs and handshakes. Too many words, questions, "How was your journey?", "Would you like tea?" "Have you seen the renovations?" Too much to take in, just a flood of love and warmth. How could I have forgotten how good it can feel to be welcomed home?

Aisha danced through the crowd of adults. "Come on Yus, let's go in the garden." He followed her, taller now, thinner than his brothers, less precocious physically despite his apparent musical genius.

"She's still the same..." Pam laughed, a tray of mugs, teapot, coffee pot appearing while we were settled on sofas and chairs.

A young girl, thirteen maybe, ran through the room and out into the garden, blonde ponytail dancing.

185

"That's not Jenna is it?" Not that young woman, all long limbs and grace?

"Yes, it is." Flora, sweet Flora, older, a little heavier, but her hug was warm and she hugged Terri too. I had forgotten how much they hugged. For a moment, a pang of regret that we wouldn't be coming here to live again, but I swallowed it. I couldn't change the fact that despite everything, none of the children wanted to move again. And Terri had vetoed the suggestion. We were there at last. And we could come back whenever we wanted to.

"I can't believe how much she's grown! Where's Elonie?"

"She has dancing class," Flora passed me a mug of tea, made just the way I like it, strong with just a touch of milk, and the years slipped way, and were home, here amongst the posters advertising women's groups and pregnancy yoga and mindfulness and baby massage and English classes. And the only thing that was different was that it was Terri's hand on my knee, not Dee's, and the room was brighter, with a new, pale wood laminate floor and new windows facing the street.

"It's so good to see you all," I beamed around at them

"You too," Pam and Penny chimed in.

"I can't believe it's your ten-year anniversary," I added. "And the house is looking so good."

"Yes, we're all ready for the party tonight." Penny gestured at the balloons and banners. I knew without having to see it that the kitchen would already be full of food and drink and that tonight the garden would be strung with fairy-lights and filled with music and laughter.

"And where's Samara?"

"She's out with one of our other residents, fetching more goodies from some volunteers."

More catching up, how are the boys, nods and words of approval and praise.

"They'll be here later," I assured Pippa, who was most concerned. "Well, at least, Shahid and Abdullah will. They passed their driving tests on their birthday, with a little help from Terri."

More nods, smiles. Yes, bring her into this, make her feel valued. I know how she can be if she feels excluded. "And Shahid has bought a little car."

"And what is Mahmood doing?"

Terri grunted. "He's just doing his exams. That's why he wanted to stay home."

More discussion, what Elonie was studying for GCSEs, how well Jenna was doing with her singing. Oh, I could have stayed there forever, wrapped in this circle of friendship. I had forgotten how it could feel, like visiting family who are truly pleased to see you, good feelings of hot tea, sticky cake and melting chocolate chip cookies, caring voices, total acceptance. With Terri's friends I always felt a little on edge, like I had to be on best behaviour, I realised as I sank into the warmth of it all.

They dispersed, eventually. Terri stumped off to help in the garden, leaving Pippa and me alone at last.

"Here," she said, pushing an envelope towards me. I draw out the thin piece of paper. Just a single sheet with the stamp of the court on the top. *Decree Absolute.*

"That's it? It's over? Really?"

"Really." She laughed, such a rare laugh, but I could only cry, sudden, hot tears. It had been so long, always there in the background, always coming back to me, legal papers and court orders and questions. I could never breathe out, fully, knowing I was still attached to the past by a legal thread. It was finally, finally done.

"It's over, Amanda." She laid her hand on my arm, right on the bad break, the scar that would never fully heal. "You're free."

Yes, I thought, yes. At last.

"And here."

The larger packet was the legal paperwork for the custody case, the order banning him or his family from any contact with us. I signed where she told me to, initialled page after page.

"However did you do it?"

"To be honest, I thought we wouldn't, but you had many friends in the Kingdom, once we were able to contact them. And an unexpected ally from within his family."

"Who?"

"One of his sisters. They did her deposition by video link, like yours. It was very compelling."

I cried again. Always, always, the women in my life surprised me.

"Well, that's that." Pippa sat back. "The children are safe."

"Oh, Pippa, how can I ever repay you." I just had to hug her. There were no words strong and deep enough for that feeling.

"Just...live. Be happy." Her voice was fierce. "Get out there and move on. Don't look back."

"That I can do," I smiled.

As we both stood, she added, "And Amanda, please, don't get married again!"

I laughed out loud, and something trapped inside me was released, flying up and away on ghostly wings. "No, never again." And we strolled to the garden, arm in arm, to join the others.

It was everything a party should be. The twins arrived in Shahid's car, a ratty Clio with dirty seats, bringing more food and booze and big grins, seeming to fill up half the garden with their presence. We milled around with volunteers, residents, and friends, eating vegan barbecue and drinking too-sweet wine.

"I can't believe this is Abdullah!" Pam exclaimed, reaching up to ruffle his hair. He had filled out a lot.

"You haven't changed a bit," he flattered her.

"Oi, stop flirting with the ladies," Shahid joined his twin. "Everyone knows I'm the better looking one."

Pam laughed, and little Elonie, who was nearby, gave both boys a look of adoration. The smell of woodsmoke from the bonfire, the thick, savoury smell of cooking food, the cool air of evening, and the music and voices of friends. I found a chair near where a couple of guitarists and a djembe player were setting up, watched avidly by Aisha.

"It's lovely," Terri joined me, choosing to squat down rather than risk one of the rickety garden chairs with her bulk. "But I couldn't live here love."

I kept my voice calm, schooled my expression, and glanced quickly at Aisha, wondering if she had overhead. She didn't like it when I was overly emotional. And I had to accept that she couldn't understand what this place had meant to me. "Why not?"

"I'm too private. It's all very well, living with a bunch of people, but they're your friends, not mine. And I need my own space, my own four walls. I'm not cut out for all this communal stuff." She lit a cigarette, inhaled, and blew the smoke out of the side of her mouth.

"I don't know what to say. I was hoping you would at least consider it...? They're lovely people, you can see that."

"It just won't work for me babe. I want my own bathroom, my own kitchen. And I don't want to share you with half a dozen other people."

You already do, I wanted to say. Instead, I swallowed the disappointment and thought, maybe I can still persuade her.

189

In the black night, the deep dark of hours unseen by everyone save the last of the drinkers and the night workers, a flame flickered, then died, then flamed again. The fire was a small thing, but hungry, and the wind fed it as it rose, fanning and flattering, caressing it into greater and greater acts of daring and destruction. Taste it, ash on the breeze, falling like petals like autumn leaves carried on a storm after the longest, hottest summer. Ash carrying burned essence of what was once life, and living, breathing and laughing. Where are those voices now? Do they whisper between the layers of hot air and cold air, the falling rain of all that is left when everything else is taken? Do they cry out in regret, soundless screams that linger, longing, forever?

We came running at the shouts, half-dressed with pyjamas and jackets and shoes unlaced, from upstairs rooms, but the alarm didn't sound, not until were outside on the pavement. In the cold night I pulled my children to me, waited as the sirens howled closer, flashing blue fracturing the night, the wailing siren obliterating the other noises, the sudden rush and roar, the billowing smoke, gold-black and orange, the breaking windows. Fire so fast, life so fleet, men in breathing apparatus, monstrous dark shapes as Terri enfolded me in a blanket, people drawing me away, come away now, come away, and we went, Shahid and Abdullah flanking Aisha, reassuring her as she stumbled, mute and terrified. Pippa standing on the edge of the road. Neighbours coming out to draw us into front rooms and offer tea and coffee and a place to sit, and then Pam, in a nightgown and feet bare, screaming down the street, that her sister was still in there. We ran back out to see Flora being folded into a waiting ambulance, Elonie, smoke-grey and ghost white, stumbling behind her, and the screaming continued. Was it my voice or hers, this mother whose child was missing? The worst news, the worst prospect, it could not be, not really, they would find them, the firefighters with their big machines and their water and the tanks of life-giving oxygen, they would find them and we would all be safe.

But there was no safety, there was no security. Hadn't life taught me that yet? How could I even have dared to taste happiness and freedom, to fly in the face of everything I had known, of every scrap of evidence to the contrary? Was this my punishment now, to live with this forever, because when we came running, my baby, my little one, my Aisha, she wasn't in her room, she came running *up* the stairs to find us, and what if we hadn't found her? Then it would be me in that ambulance, me screaming and raging, tearing at the walls and the paramedics, howling and desperate to throw myself into the flames and save my child.

It should have been me.

They took us to a hotel, in the end, to wait. We had no proper clothes, no money, just my phone that I left in the car, and Shahid's wallet, which was in his coat pocket. We sat close together in a bland room, the six of us, not speaking, not at first. The hours stretched out. Aisha dozed. Yusuf slept with his headphones still on. Terri went outside and smoked, came back in again, went out again, then returned.

At last Shahid said, "I don't understand it. I don't understand what could have happened. Everyone was in bed. We checked the house, me and Penny. There was nothing left on, nothing left out."

"Electrical, probably," Terri in her lofty, knowing tone.

"They'll get them out," I said. "They have to."

"What happened to the fire alarm?" Terri demanded. "They had an alarm system, I saw it."

"I don't know." Shahid again. "Maybe it was faulty or something."

"Where did it start?"

"I don't know."

The next day there is still no news, and we returned to get our cars and weep at the smoking, steaming and charred ruins of the house, the trampled garden, all cordoned off with yellow tape. I wanted to stay, but there was nowhere to go. As Terri said, the children needed me.

At home, Aisha and Yusuf in bed, we all paced, restlessly. I tried to lie down, but the horror and the fear left me rigid and tense, and in the end I got up and started cleaning.

Then my phone rang, unknown number. Samara, ringing from the hospital, informing us that our worst fears are realised. They are gone. Penny and Jenna. The fire reached them before the firefighters could, it reached them and took them and turned them to ash.

I remember the clunk of the phone when it hit the floor. I remember waking up with my face on the tiles, wondering why he was hitting me again. I remember taking myself off to paint, but I don't remember anything more until they took me in for three weeks and assessed me and gave me medication, strong drugs to calm me down and force me back to reality, to make that reality not hurt so much. Terri looked after the kids, visiting me every day with updates, but I couldn't reach her, couldn't feel her and her passion, I felt nothing, not even when she told me about Aisha and school, and how the boys were doing, not when she told me about the fire, and the inquiry, and the inquest, or when she warned me about social services. They were looking at taking them off me, the younger ones, but I was a good girl and did what I was told, and I still do. I still collect my prescription every month though I don't take the tablets because they make everything so flat, they make me flat and I can't paint and without my painting what do I have?

And so I picked myself up and got back to living, but nothing was ever the same again. Penny was dead, and little Jenna, and Flora had to be institutionalised, she was falling apart, and no one knew how the fire started, the questions kept coming, had someone been out smoking in the garden, left a cigarette end maybe in the bin where the fire began? The fire had started in a paper recycling bin, but the cause was undetermined. The fire service could find no evidence of foul play, but no other reason for the fire to have started. No stray cigarette end or discarded match in the vicinity.

Blossom House was gone, the abode of rats and feral cats and junkies, burnt timbers and blackened bricks collapsed into mounds already overgrown with nettle and thorn, the stumps of the charred cherry trees fenced off with yellow tape. It was there, on Google Earth, not hard to find. After the months of my own darkness, I had to see it, because it all seemed so unreal. I could smell the charred earth and the melted plastic and hear the shards of sooty glass cracking under my feet, as if I walked there still, a ghost of lives past, wailing and moaning in my grief.

The insurance company fought the claim, and Pippa and Pam moved together into a little flat, a council flat in an over-50s development. Molly moved into a shared house with friends from her student days. I couldn't even begin to imagine them without Penny, motherly, round and soft Penny, who was unable to leave a child behind and who had perished trying to save a girl with wild curly hair and the sweetest smile. What were her last thoughts as she cowered under the window, desperate to get out? Did she pray for someone to save her? Did she know she was dying?

I remember sitting on my bed, the mattress sinking under the weight of this new burden, horror crushing the fibres together under me and melting my flesh into the plastic and foam, and Aisha running in to me because she had missed me while I was away. I remember holding her too tight, and sobbing, and thinking of Flora and flames and the smell of burning flesh and hearing screams and I remember saying to Aisha, "It was all because of you. That's why I left, because I had to save you. You have to understand that. I had to save you. Is that why you did it?" And she looked at me with horror, thrusting herself away from me, shaking her head, running from the room and taking a lifetime of love and warmth with her.

Things were never quite the same after that.

Purple Lake

Beep, swish, strange noises, dream steps, feet on stone, on sand, on wooden stairs that creak and sway, a swaying house like a thing alive, moving to compensate for the weight of its inhabitants, the feeling of being trapped, suffocated, squeezed and held tight by these moulding walls, the scream dies in my throat as the pressure mounts, fear that I will never be free.

An agony of minutes waiting for the paralysis of sleep to pass, the frozen terror to abate, for my arms and hands to follow their instructions, pick up my phone, for my eyes to open, to focus.

Carl <What happened?>

Jarelle <Hey girl, don't let it get you down>

<Where are you? Why aren't you up yet?> Carl again.

And a string more messages, including Kat.

<I msged that bitch and warned her off, but she won't take it down>

Fumbling, dropping the phone, slick metal and glass and plastic and my fingers numb and alien, nothing seems to work like it should, thick hands like a glove, and then I see it, see the notifications, on Instagram, on FB, on Snapchat.

It's a photo of me, slumped in the chair at the coffee house. Someone has photoshopped a plate of half-eaten cakes in front of me, and added a smudge of chocolate around my mouth. Nice touch.

<Fat pig>

<You think you would stop after one>

<Drunk or just passed out from eating too much?>

Spiralling on, the cruel words, and then messages pouring in from Jarelle and Carl and I don't know what to say, don't know how to answer, just say I'm OK, ignore it, rise above, but it's real, it's there now, and I can't un-see it. Roll onto my back, pull at the hated skin and flesh, then the sickness, suddenly, hurling me across the corridor and into the bathroom, acid retching, bile in my mouth, burning my throat, my gums, my tongue, good, burn out my taste, all of my senses, make me nothing, let nothing touch me or hurt me again, spiralling nausea and violent heaves, let the pain swallow me up from the inside out until I am small enough. Thin enough.

Stand on the scales, yes, three more pounds lost. Three hateful, horrible pounds, but it's not enough, it's never enough, still there is so far to go, so many parts of me to cut away, to scour away the greedy flesh.

Weak, legs wobbling, is this shock, this fear and dread and loathing, still I can shower, and dress, dragging the bodyshaper over my belly, breasts tender in the binder, are they bigger? What am I doing wrong? I have to eat less, have to exercise more.

The flash and beep of a message.

<come for a coffee?> Carl.

<K but meeting Jarelle later>

<K but come for coffee NOW> stern face.

<Can't face it. Too many people.>

<Right, you have new friends now. Nice>

<Not like that, FFS, just trying to get going>

<So meet me in the park then>

<K>

There is a lie they tell you, in school, a lie that anyone can be anything that they want to. Except they mean only the things that you are supposed to be. Good. Quiet, Compliant.

Thin.

They can't stop what I am, what I have been. They can't make my skin not-brown, my features Caucasian. They can't stop me knowing everything I know, after all that reading, the books that used to fill all the cracks in my life, the echoing spaces where other kids had friends and parties and games consoles and Brownies and sleepovers and playdates and all of it. All I had was my brothers, always one step removed, always indulgent, and my mother, and the books in the library; the facts and the stories and the worlds within worlds that changed me, that spoiled everything because how can you go back and pretend you don't know about the things, about history and war and people dying, about the way we use everything up and throw it away, about how they make things, nothing untainted, nothing is clean, and even after turning vegan it still wasn't enough because everything is wrong. Everything is rape in one way or another, what we take, what we use, means we destroy something just by living and none of it matters now because they still hate me and it will never stop, not even when I try to fit in it doesn't stop just this endless agony of wanting and not getting, of just wanting someone to say it's OK, but they never will, because I will never be like them.

Slow steps, messages from Kat and Nina, support and then distraction, yes, but are they laughing at me, secretly? That would make sense, if they're only friends with me so they can laugh at me. Maybe it's all a joke, but what do I do now, I'm too far in, I can't just drop them now, anything could happen, maybe they're all laughing at me and maybe even going to that coffee shop was a total set up but surely they wouldn't be like that, no, Jarelle seems to like me, but then she likes me best when I am over at her house studying, helping her do her coursework, maybe that's it, she's using me, but then we're all using each other. Dusty hedges and drifts of dirt and dead leaves and old bits of rubbish, swollen tarmac and the crumbling concrete pillars that lead to the park. Has it been two weeks, or three, or four, I don't know, there is a time before and a time after but I still can't make sense of it.

Carl, somehow he looks older, different, there is new caution in his eyes, or wisdom, or something, and it's like seeing him for the first time, and wondering, what does he see in me? Am I a pity-party, the duff as they say in American films and tv shows, "designated ugly fat friend?" Is that what I am to Jarelle, to Kat? Have they made me their project?

But no, it's not like that in real life, it's never like that, and that's why I get so angry because I am doing everything right now, not eating, barely eating, and always exercising, and to prove I am right, to prove I am right I ran up and down the stairs five times before leaving the house, and here is Carl, sitting on the swing in the park and squinting suspiciously at the clouds forming above us, occluding the sun and the washed out watery blue and the sense of space, eating up the air and sinking down with the promise of cold rain.

"Well, it lives." He stands. Always, the sarcasm. But he cares about me, I know he does.

"And how are you?"

"Fine, busy as always." The camp shrug, eyes sliding away, avoiding me.

"Busy with men?"

"Beating them off with a stick darling." That bitchy drawl. Yes, that's Carl. But it never seemed so harsh before, his voice so brittle.

"Sorry, you know, not being around as much. I started hanging out with Jarelle and Kat. I didn't think you'd mind."

"I don't mind. But I'm surprised."

We walk, slowly, scuffing the weather-bleached, pitted tarmac.

"Why?"

"I didn't think you would ever want to hang out with that crowd."

"What crowd?"

"The *in* crowd. I thought you were like me, you know, the lone wolf. That's why we had to stick together."

"Had?"

"Well, you don't answer my texts, you suddenly get yourself a new phone and you're all over social media but you don't seem to have time for me."

"I'm sorry, OK, you know I love you, but it's nice to have some other friends. Friends who are girls."

"Right. So now I'm not good enough because I have a dick? Seems you were interested enough in dicks a few weeks ago. What's changed your mind? Going to bat for your mother's team now?"

Stinging tears, hurt, hollowness and a roaring in my ears.

"What the fuck? Carl, what did I do to you?"

"You made yourself a target and you dumped me to join the bitch gang. You know what they're like, Ash, you know how they treat people."

"They were nice to me. They made friends with me. And there's nothing wrong with having lots of friends. And they aren't the really mean ones, they're nice, honestly, Jarelle and I have a lot in common, and it's nice. Doesn't mean I won't hang out with you. Doesn't mean I

199

won't be there for you. You could hang with all of us. Come out today, we're going in to town."

"Oh, yeah, I'd really fit in, with Jarelle and Kat, the veiled sisters. Not my scene darling. You *know* what people like them think of people like me."

He strides ahead, but my legs are almost as long as his and it doesn't take much to catch up. "Carl, stop. Please. Look, I'm sorry if I wasn't around sometime when you might have needed me, or whatever this is about, but I'm here now."

"Well, I'm honoured you could squeeze me in to your busy schedule."

"Please, don't." Tears, yes, burning, and it's just not fair. Why's he doing this?

"It's OK, I know, people grow and change, people move on." He squares his shoulders. "It was fun, but hey, nothing's forever."

I know he is quoting again, and I haven't the heart to match him.

"You're my best friend."

"And everyone can be replaced."

The space where he was is filled with the ghost of our friendship, of late night phone calls and text sessions, of film marathons and confidences, and it feels wrong now, to think of him just not being there. I've hurt him, somehow, but what does he want? For me to abandon my new friends for him? He's a friend but he's not always there, and he can't know what it's like for me, what it is always like, this feeling of never belonging, that there is always something I've missed, something missing.

Prussian Blue

A changeable day, thick grey clouds and clots of rain clearing to patches of blue sky and cotton wool fluff, wind kissing the windows with spatters of leaves, as winter fought with autumn. A brief, violent fight, red leaves bleeding in gutters and along the edges of the roads.

I'd just been out looking for work again, and fruitlessly trying to find something that I could do part time and still paint. Strange feelings, memories chasing me, angry ghosts and wailing women and all the questions, what if, why, maybe, when... The myriad thoughts that chased me then, that still chase me, down all the long corridors of what was and what might have been. Looking for purpose, and finding little. Nothing felt right, then, only the times I spent in my bedroom, painting without thought, accessing that flow state, that place that holds no words. No need for words or for framing thought, just the expression of colour, depth and form. And then, in the evenings, watching Aisha become more surly and withdrawn. Realising that she spent more time in her room than in the family room with me and wondering when that had happened.

This house was the last in a long line of options, weeks of fruitless searching, and disappointing viewings. New builds with no character, ex-local authority homes that reminded me too much of my childhood; nothing within our price range seemed big enough or alive enough to make a home, to build an inheritance. I was working a few hours here and there at the gallery on campus, studying for my degree, home always in the afternoons to make meals that Aisha grunted at and more often than not took to her room. I was trying to adjust to the boys moving out, one by one. Small losses but still, that sense of change. They were closer to me, for a while, in the first years after we left the Kingdom. Well, all of them except Mahmood. And now he never contacts me and only answers my texts after the third or fourth message. He blames me for our situation more than the others.

I thought buying a house would be the answer. We could put down proper roots, rebuild some of what we'd lost to the fire and the endless moving around. It was finally time to stop running.

And then I found it. It was out in one of the villages, semi-rural the estate agent called it, sunk into the curving hollow between two hills, in the liminal space between town and country, the last vestige of a forgotten past. *Four bedroom detached house in need of extensive renovation.* Can a house hold a soul, connect to a human heart? I had never thought so, but crawling out of Terri's two-seater I was confronted with deeply set windows and high gables, wood rotting around cracked panes, climbing vines dug deep into the brickwork. A high, pitched roof, surrounded by huge old trees.

It was a throwback, a ghost, a last remnant of the village that once was, dissolving slowly into the overgrown garden, once glorious, now long past its prime. Brickwork pillars and a sagging gate, a yellow bricked path mossy and uneven, rosebushes grown into fairy-tale briar jungles and great towering holly and bay trees.

There was a space in the brickwork beside the porch, where a stone had once been set.

"The name of the house would have been there," Terri said, assuming the pose of instructor, as usual. I wondered, given that she had no children, whether she was like this with everyone. The windows, high and wide, reflected the sky and the trees. From the road the house was well screened, and yet the windows let in a lot of light.

202

The bloated wooden door yielded eventually to shoving and kicking, and then we were inside, a hallway thick with dust and smelling of mould. But under the carpet were beautiful tiles, and the kitchen was large and long, and the rooms, old, yes, with peeling paper and paintwork, but still, it seemed sound enough.

"...get the windows sorted first, if you can bring the price down." Terri was talking as she picked at doorframes and kicked skirting-boards. I creaked slowly from step to step, drawn upwards, always, and there it was the bright front bedroom, the huge windows, all that light.

We went to a local pub to talk about it.

"I don't know, Terri, it seems a lot of work," I said, nursing a flat pint of cask ale and a packet of salt and vinegar crisps. The sting in my mouth seemed to wake me out of the fug I'd been in since the fire.

"It's not that bad," Terri drank her own pint, lager with a splash of lime, and rolled herself a cigarette. "The structure is sound. It wouldn't take much to make it comfortable."

"I wouldn't have any money for major building work."

"I know people," she shrugged. This is how they get you, I thought suddenly. This is how they make themselves indispensable. Sunlight and shadows, the deep fireplace and the smell of beer, laughter from a group of young men by the fruit machine, a baby crying in the dining room.

"I don't know."

"You like the house?"

"I love the house."

"So what's stopping you?"

"The past. My own doubts. Every choice I make, somehow it seems to be the wrong one. It seems like every choice has a price. And this place... None of my boys are carpenters or anything."

"I told you. I know people. And I can do a lot of the work. I can find you new radiators, cheap paint, bathroom fittings. We could put a downstairs toilet in that understairs space, next to the kitchen."

"What about the garden? I wouldn't even know where to start. It's huge and so overgrown."

"I can do that, and your boys can help. We can clear it enough to make it useable; you don't have to decide everything straight away."

On and on, me worrying, her reassuring, and my heart singing, because I could already see myself there, painting in the morning sunlight, see Aisha sitting in the garden or doing her homework in the kitchen. I imagined a long kitchen table, and all of us sitting around eating big meals, doing family things. Four bedrooms was big enough, one for me, one for Aisha, two for the boys, as it had always been. They could all come to stay, for weekends and holidays, once they had lives of their own. There was a big sitting room, and another room they could have for a games room, smaller but big enough. It could be a home.

"You would really help me?"

Terri almost broke a smile, such a rare occurrence. "You know how I feel about it," she said. "There's money in bricks and mortar."

It was decided, with doodles on the back of a beermat and Terri holding my hand briefly across the table. At last we would have an anchor. Maybe, at last, it was time to stop running, and start living, properly, for a change. Maybe now I could be happy, in what was, instead of always being fearful of what might be.

Deep Rose

Jarelle meets me at the bus stop. "Kat's in town already. We're meeting her at Mango Shot."

Bus smell, diesel and wet dog. I fork out the £3.50 and wonder how much I have left.

"It's a juice bar," Jarelle continues. We sit at the back, the motion and swing of the bus making me feel sick again. Will I ever stop feeling sick?

"Right."

Gossip; Jarelle and her mother and her cousins visiting and her UCAS application and predicted grades, the nauseating bus lurching forward, juddering to a halt, swinging around corners and that drunken sleepy tiredness I always get on buses and I don't know why.

Kat at the juice bar, smell of fruit and coffee, I decline anything but tap water, too much sugar in juice.

"You're not on a fast day again! Not on a Saturday!" Kat laughs. "Wow, you must be really focused, yeah? I mean, I admire you and all, but seriously, I couldn't do a weekend day!"

What to say, have I transgressed some other secret rule of being with these girls, of being a girl?

I wish I could be a boy, be invisible, be accepted, be expected to do something practical with my life, not stand out like this. My brothers never had to worry about what they looked like.

"It's the sugar," Jarelle cuts in. "And you should watch it Kat, it's bad for your skin as well as your belly fat."

I know it's supposed to be fun, shopping like this, but it bores me. Each shop a maelstrom of colour, clothes, shoes, bags, scarves, music, preening teenage girls and slouching boys in doorways and on the street. We march past the bookshop and into a chain coffee house. My feet hurt. Hunger still, inescapable, maybe I should eat something, but the fruit salad is almost five pounds. A plain tea is the cheapest, so I have that, no milk, two sweeteners, and ignore the biting and yawning ache and burn of hunger, but right now, I want to lie down, and sleep, let myself slip away, even my nightmares would be better than this, the acrid thin and bitter tea, chemical sweetness, but I have to stay alert, and listen, and talk, and all the while I can see people looking at me, and I know what they are thinking.

I miss Carl. I could text him, but no, he had no right to say what he said, and if I text him he'll just tell me to fuck off again and I can't face that, not today, not when I feel so weak and hungry, when it's taking everything I have just to stay upright.

No.

Another shop, slender mannequins and colour-coordinated displays; the assistants look askance, and I don't try anything on, not because I can't afford to buy anything, but because I don't want to see myself, naked in those mirrors in the changing rooms, the ones that don't let you miss anything, I don't want to see the bulges and the swollen skin, and I don't want to know what size I am and I don't want Jarelle and Kat to know, when they are picking size sixes from the rack and laughing through the half-doors about the clothes and whether they should get that top in two different colours and whether the jeans are too tight or whether they have a pair of shoes that would go with that skirt.

"Here, Ash, you should try this on," Kat pulls out a pinafore dress, short, denim, something that would look really cute on anyone but me.

"No, I don't wear skirts," I say automatically.

"Yeah, but you can wear it over leggings," she insists, rifling through the rack. "What size are you?"

No way am I telling her I am a size 12. "It's OK, honest, I..."

"Leave it, Kat," Jarelle is at my side, instantly, the heat of her and that scent, flowery and fruity, almost making me dizzy. "I don't think that would suit Ash. She's so tall – I think she'd be better off with something like this shirt," and she pulls a silky sort of thing off another rack. "It's more her style, don't you think?"

I glance at the price tag. "I'm not buying anything today," I mutter. "I... er... I bought some new jeans last week and my Mum had a go at me so... She'd notice if I spent money on clothes again this week."

"Sneak it in and tell her you got it ages ago," Kat says. But Jarelle saves me again. "No, it's OK, though if you want me to get it for you and you pay me back?"

Flush and shame, she knows, but of course she does, everyone knows, that I'm not just gross and fat, I'm poor. "Oh, thanks but I'd better not."

Walk away, pretend to look at a high rail of denim jackets, hide the sudden tears and the drop into that dark pit. There's no way out, even if I get thin, even if I have friends, I can't do anything about my mother, and our house, and never having any money.

"Have you thought about a Saturday job, or something in the evenings?" Jarelle speaks quietly. Kat is two racks over, texting furiously.

"I don't know, to be honest. My mum always stopped me. Now I don't think she'd care. What would I do?"

"Well, anything, really. I mean, I was going to take a job in the salon in town, just cleaning up and making tea and

207

stuff, but my mum wouldn't hear of it. But there's always something."

"Yeah, I suppose."

"Don't work every Saturday though, cos then we couldn't do this." She links her arm in mine. "And smile, Ash, nothing's worth losing your smile over."

Fake a smile, but is it fake? Because it feels good to not be alone, and even though I am so, so hungry, even though I feel monstrous beside her, it's like this is what I have been missing all these years.

After the shopping, coffee again, the usual place, hot smell of coffee and sugar, and the dizzying display of sticky sweet cakes and buns and crisps and so much food, so much food, what happens to it all, if it doesn't get eaten? I almost say it aloud, as Jarelle and Kat buy a banoffee muffin to split between them, and I sit, sipping green tea and hating it, feeling myself crumbling into the aching hunger inside.

Kat and Jarelle talking about some box set on Netflix, laughing and arguing about the characters, about what happens next.

Smile, nod, pretend that it is all familiar, and then a woman walks in, older, a little spotty, and Avad, Kat's cousin's friend.

General hellos. The woman is Avad's friend, but she studies here. She seems to be the reason he comes home so often. He introduces her, Sakinah, and she sits and lets him fetch her a pineapple grapefruit smoothie.

"You're Ash?" A thick voice, liquid honey, heavily accented.

"Yes."

"I am pleased to meet you. Are you feeling better?"

"Sorry?"

"Avad told me you were unwell the other day." Roar of the smoothie machine, voices, music that sounds Indian, or oriental, with plunky strings and nasal female voices.

"Oh, yeah, just felt a bit rough."

"I see. You have beautiful hair."

"Thanks."

"Mine is curly," she smiles. "I always wanted sleek, straight hair like yours. Mine is like sheep's wool."

I smile. "I always wanted curls."

"It's always the way."

We talk, about school and her course in university, and the town and its limitations. Avad brings drinks. Kat and Jarelle alternate between joining in and texting furiously on their phones, that peculiar focused attention as if there's no one else nearby.

"How are you now?" Avad asks me. I feel myself blushing. He is...beautiful is the only word for it.

"I'm OK, thanks. Thank you for taking me home the other night."

"It was no bother." His voice is accented, soft.

"Avad is a good friend," Sakinah smiles into her drink. "And he only did what was right."

Is this a Muslim thing? They talk a lot about what's right, what's moral. This is nothing like I thought it was, hanging out with these people. Mum won't even talk about religion, and Mahmood does nothing but tell me I'm going to hell. Words fly away, no sense, something I want to say, to ask, slipping through the oil-slick layers of my consciousness.

Jarelle and Kat draw Avad into their conversation about the show, something to do with zombies, and they're flirting slightly, I can see it, touching their hair and laughing a little too loudly.

"Ash, can I ask you something?" Sakinah is watching me, smiling slightly.

"Go ahead." Almost relaxed, this almost seems normal.

"What is Ash short for? Do you have another name?"

"Aisha."

"Ah, a beautiful name. It is the name of one of the Prophet's wives, peace be upon him."

"I had heard that, yes. But everyone calls me Ash."

"May I also ask...why don't you wear *hijab*?"

"I'm sorry?" I stare at her, at the beautiful cream silk scarf she wears with its pattern of pale blue flowers.

"The veil. You are Muslim? I thought Kat said..."

"Oh! No, I mean, I was born Muslim, but we left when I was two so, no, I don't see myself that way."

"Ah, my mistake. I apologise."

"No need to apologise, I have nothing against it."

Her smile deepens, and as the light hits her skin, I am momentarily fascinated, fixated on its soft surface, and the craters and pits of acne, not repulsed, but fascinated. What must it feel like? Yusuf had spots, lots of them, but I never did, and I never needed braces like him.

"I wonder," she says, softly so I have to lean closer to hear her. "Have you ever wondered about it? About your faith?"

"I don't know. Sometimes. But not really. It's like, well, Mum doesn't talk much about it, but my brothers talked to me sometimes of what life was like when we lived in Saudi Arabia." Her eyes widen.

"Ah, the Kingdom. Such a holy place. Tell me, did they ever visit the Kaaba, in Mecca?"

"I don't know. But I think my mother did, once. "

"I am visiting there after I finish my degree. We are going to make a pilgrimage. I am from Pakistan, but I have some cousins who live in the holy city."

210

"I can't remember anything about it.

She finishes her smoothie, her perfect lips pursed around the straw.

"Do you think about it at all? Islam?"

"No. It doesn't seem to be a positive thing for women."

"Ah, but that's the thing. Most people think that. But tell me, do I look like someone who is oppressed? Do I seem unhappy, or abused?"

"No."

"Does Jarelle? Or Kat?"

"Not really."

"Women are held in high honour in Islam, Ash. High honour. It is a simple faith, clear rules to follow. Life is much easier this way, instead of always wondering what is wrong and what is right. But it's OK, it's not right for everyone. But I would think, perhaps, you might like to come along to my women's group sometime? We hold it on campus, not far from here. We meet once a week, to discuss things that women need to discuss, to give each other support, and solidarity. You are the only daughter in a house full of brothers, I can imagine you would welcome some female company."

"Oh." My stomach turns over, not hunger this time, excitement. Is she really asking me to go to a women's group? To be part of something? Perhaps, in a group of older women, university students, I wouldn't have to worry so much about what I say, about how much I've read. Perhaps they might have some answers.

"Well, here," and she hands me a card, with a phone number and an address. "We meet here, every Monday night. We women, we have to make our own way in the world, and it can be lonely. People often don't understand us, yes? But perhaps you will find friends here, as I have."

"I'm not sure."

She reaches out, tucks my hair behind my ear. "Jarelle tells me you are a great reader, that you have a passion for knowledge. So do we. That's what we are, just a group of women sharing what we know and learning from each other. We share books too, reading and discussing them. And we talk about everything that's wrong with the world, and what we can do to make it right."

Does she actually get it? Does she feel like I do, about this shitty world that everyone has fucked up for us?

"I..."

"That strikes a chord?"

"Yes. Yes, it does. I just..."

"You feel powerless."

I nod. "It just doesn't seem fair. You know, you grow up getting told the world is black and white, and it's not. And the more I learn, the more I know, the worse I feel." No, stop there, don't tell her what it's like watching the world of celebrities, seeing through it all, nothing but fake. Fake people, fake bodies, fake images.

"You don't feel like you fit in."

Another nod. "I don't. I mean, Jarelle, Kat, they're good friends... But..."

Sakinah leans a little closer. She smells of perfume, light, floral, sweet. "But they don't talk about all the thoughts and feelings crowding into you head, do they? How hard it is when nothing seems to make sense. When you just wish someone would come along and put everything in order?"

"I suppose so, yeah."

"Well, that's what our women's group is for. We're just a bunch of feminists trying to find a way to fix things. We just use the logic and the gift of science, of knowledge, and the holy words that Allah has given us, to forge a path. Please, Ash, say you'll at least give it a go."

"OK."

She sits back, satisfied. "Good. That's my phone number. Call me any time."

Avad is standing up, eager to leave, and Sakinah immediately rises, picking up her bag. She steps in close, speaks softly into my ear. "Come, Monday night. If you cannot get to town, call me, and I will drive out to fetch you."

"Thank you."

"Don't mention it. But don't be alone, Ash. There is no need to be alone."

In Jarelle's airy room, Kat picks over the shopping bags as I open the physics homework and work through it, and Jarelle flits between us, copying my answers and trying on clothes. We drink coffee and there is a tray of little cakes. Hunger a beast swallowing me whole, there is nothing else in the world for a moment other than the smell of them, heady lemon and vanilla and sticky sugar, I can taste them through my eyes, through just looking at them, can feel the sticky thick sponge on my tongue, the slight resistance between my teeth... Oh, who knew that food could be so fucking tantalising, and I can't eat anything, I daren't, because once I start I won't want to stop, I won't be able to stop, I'll just eat and eat until I swell up like a sweaty, greasy slug and somewhere inside I'll be lost, suffocated in all that fat.

"You should eat something," Jarelle insists, sitting next to me with a cake in her hand. Almost faint with wanting, I shake my head. "No, really Ash, you haven't eaten all day, and it's getting late. We're going to call out for pizza, if you want in."

213

"Oh, no, no, honestly, I couldn't. I should get home, anyway..."

"You don't have to."

I scramble to my feet. The physics homework is finished, and I can't do it, I just can't, sit here and watch them eat pizza, I won't be able to hold on, I just won't.

"I should get back. See you Monday?"

Jarelle behind me on the stairs, am I ruining it? There's a black shape in the corner of my vision, a nightmare shape, and I need to get home, need to find something to eat that won't make me feel weak and cowardly and fat and out of control.

"Look, I've got a family thing tomorrow," she says as I find my shoes. "But why don't I come round to yours after? That book you mentioned the other day, you could show me that..."

"Oh. Um. Uh, yeah. I'll see what I am doing. Message you later, yeah?"

"OK." A swift hug, too quick to notice, press of her elfin body against mine, oh, can she feel my sweaty skin, my horrible bulges, I hope not, but it feels good to get out, into the evening drizzle, to be away from scrutiny. I almost run all the way home, I just want to be shut away, no one looking at me, no one noticing, and I race up the stairs at home before Mum can catch me, slamming my door to sink onto the floor, great retching sobs and icy tears and the emptiness, dark empty hollow inside me, nothing can fill this, nothing can make this better, I can't I just can't I need to eat something but if I do I've failed again and I just can't do this anymore. I just want someone to take it all away, take it away and hold me and rock me until I stop crying but it's not fair, it's not fair, why does everyone hate me I just want it to stop it's not

214

fair why won't it stop? If I am so fat why am I so hungry why why do I want to eat when it will just make it worse why do I have to eat when will it stop when will I be thin enough, why can't I be thinner, she's thin, it's not fair why....just why...please make it stop I can't do it any more, everything hurts just make it stop...

Late night horror-dream, demons crawling from the cracks in the ceiling to drop onto my bed and suck at my flesh, and I let them. Shouting, screaming, but waking; the sound is a whimper. Sweat soaked, reach for my phone, no one online. I wait, frozen and terrified, until the sun rises. I find the number, text Sakinah, and she miraculously she is awake and texts back, and asks me if I am OK, and I tell her about the dream. Her answers, the long messages, they make sense of it, she talks about the dreams bringing messages, and after a long time and a lot of texts I drift away and sleep through the morning thinking of some God in the sky sending texts that turn into dreams and become shape and colour and movement as they enter my brain.

Chrome Green Deep Hue

"You can't blame me." Terri's voice, a slightly nasal, Hertfordshire accent, with a hint of Bristol.

Terri and her bulk, half-comforting, half-threatening, but I loved her body and the way she held me like I was precious – not fragile, but valuable. Something to be savoured. At least, sometimes. But there were days when she looked at me as if she didn't know me, as if she was waiting for something to happen.

She stood in the kitchen trying to repair one of the broken cupboard doors, which hung half off its hinges, the softened, damp chip board refusing to bear its weight.

"Blame you for what?"

"For getting fed up of this."

I followed her wide hand gestures. Terri was volatile, loud, expressive. Everything she felt or thought was written on her body, on her face, and she was always thinking things, feeling things, and the pressure to keep up, the pressure to respond appropriately, was immense.

Yes, the place was a mess. Aisha was always so messy, too clever for her own good, always needing to be stimulated. Shahid and Abdullah had moved out, into a shared house, using their earnings from their work to gain their first real independence, and Aisha was now in their room. Although negotiations for buying the old house were ongoing, I couldn't wait to give her the room she wanted. So I painted the walls pink and got her a princess bed with the pink, heart-shaped headboard and her pink plastic drawer sets and the pink wardrobe, a pink rug in the middle of the room, pink fairy-lights around the windows.

I hated pink. I hated it but I wanted her to be happy. Still she brought destruction in her wake, a tide of uncapped felt pens bleeding onto fabrics and surfaces, crayons left to melt on radiators, half-eaten chocolate eggs and jaffa cakes ground into carpets. If I turned my back she made a mess, and even when I was watching she made more mess as fast as I could clean it up. Terri had been badgering me for days about the kids' rooms – Mahmood and Yusuf's stank the way only boys' rooms can stink, and she complained loudly every time she walked past on the way to the bathroom.

"I thought you were watching her."

"Christ, Mand, she's eleven years old, she shouldn't need to be watched every minute of the day. Besides, don't you think that's shirking your responsibilities, expecting me to watch her while you do other things?"

"I told you I was going to clean her room."

"And she should have been cleaning her own room, or at the very least, helping you to clean it."

"And you know that as fast as I cleaned it she would have been making a mess."

That shake of the head, the superiority, the judgment. How had this happened, that she felt she could stand in judgement on me, on my parenting? But there was always something. Yusuf leaving the toilet seat up, Mahmood not cleaning the bathroom after showering and trimming his beard, Yusuf leaving crumbs in the kitchen after late-night toast, Shahid speaking too loudly on the phone to his girlfriend late into the night. I spent more time responding to her constant criticism than anything else.

"Well, you got that right. I don't know why you've let her get away with this for so long."

"She's always been like it. It's a sign of high intelligence and creativity."

"It's the sign of a pampered princess who expects to be waited on hand and foot."

"All you had to do was tell her no."

"She's not my kid."

"So you watched her make all this mess?"

"No. I was working on the bike in the porch. I left her to it."

I suppressed the anger, the frustration, the feelings of being let down.

Then I walked into the living room and surveyed the chaos, a multi-coloured cacophony of mess. The dolls she used to love a few years ago had been painted with nail varnish, and there were blobs of it on the carpet and the coffee table, and books strewn haphazardly on the floor, the sofa, the table in the corner, the TV stand – where the TV was tuned to the Discovery Channel, and penguins made death-dives from cliffs into blue-black water – and half eaten yoghurts with spoons stuck to cushions. Pens and pencils and bits of paper littered the floor, and I could see where she has been reading books and marking them up with yellow pencil and green crayon, and where she had been copying out quotes.

Aisha was asleep in the corner, face pillowed on an open book about the Brontes, and she was covered in glitter. A line of glitter snaked like a slug trail across the room. She was wearing a pink tulle skirt and a denim waistcoat over a pink t-shirt, and her beautiful long hair was in an untidy plait. She had shadows under her eyes, and I wondered if she was sleeping badly, that she could fall asleep like this in the middle of the afternoon.

I picked up the papers she had been scribbling on. It looked like she has been trying to write a story of some kind, about a princess in a cave, with pictures of strangely bulbous people and odd, animalistic trees, but there are a mix of quotes from different books and something strange about chaos theory and that was when I started to worry. Not because she was

218

writing, but because the kind of things she is writing were far too advanced for an eleven-year-old.

Terri was standing over me.

"This is what happens when you spoil a kid," she said again, and looking into the anger, the disdain, I thought, without warning, how did I ever really think I loved you? How did I ever really think that you loved me? Is this how it always has to be? Too tired to process these thoughts, I tried to let it go.

"That's not helping, Terri. Do me a favour? Make me a cup of tea. I'm knackered but I daren't stop before I get this cleared up."

"I'm busy with the bike." Of course. How stupid was I to think that she would do something for me. She hadn't made me tea in years. Every day I got up first and made tea and coffee, because coffee is her drink, and then I got the kids up and made their breakfasts, and Terri's breakfast. All the time I'd been doing my foundation degree I packed myself a lunch along with theirs, little pots of rice salad or pasta salad made from leftovers because there was never enough money. Terri refused to contribute anything more than our agreed ten percent of her income to the household budget. She also refused to be a parent to the children. "They've got one mother. That's enough," she said, several times. I managed the mornings, and sent my children off, Yusuf taking Aisha to school on his way to the high school, Mahmood heading off to his job at Tesco where he was spending his gap year. And I managed tea time, with Terri only condescending to cook from time to time. And I managed as much housework as I could, avoiding her acerbic tongue by pre-empting her complaints where I could.

And while I sat on the floor picking up the various bits of rubbish, I thought of how it was a lot like the art projects some of the younger students did, the art I could never

219

understand because it just looked like mess to me. Like kids' paintings, not conceptual at all, just chaotic. And I thought, art is supposed to make you feel something, and looking at Aisha sleeping in the corner I felt a powerful sense of love, but also of something else, something that wondered and worried at the vast world inside of her that I had no understanding of. I knew from the stuff I used to read about psychology and symbolism that we all created the world according to our own reality, our own perception filters, but it was the first time I realised just how alien she was to me. This child, flesh of my flesh, my last child, my daughter, the one I left everything to save, the child I thought I would know best because she was female, like me, and because I took her away from that other world that my boys inhabited where men and women lived separate lives.

Yes, I knew she was different; she never slept well. She needed constant attention, constant supervision, was not easily entertained. She was the most demanding of all of them, never leaving me alone. The only time she seemed happy was when I picked her up after school and took her back to campus with me, and sat her in the library while I studied. She picked up books and read them, and brought her scribbles to me, mimicking me writing my essays. She did her homework, and then we caught the bus home together and sometimes got chips on the way home, and I laughed at her strange, unfunny jokes.

"Why did the koala fall out of the tree?"

"I don't know."

"Because it was dead."

"What's black and white and red all over and can't turn round in a phonebox?"

"Uh, I don't know?"

"A nun with a javelin through her."

"Why was green?"

"I don't know."

"Because black told him to."

At school they complained that she was disruptive, that she wouldn't settle. They tried to put her in the special needs class, refused to give her more books to read once she had finished the set books on the curriculum. All this against the backdrop of Terri's constant scrutiny, her accusations of 'pandering' to her, that she was just a naughty child and needing punishing, not listening to.

I looked at her, my baby, face relaxed but still, somehow, concentrated, as if she even slept intensely. Aisha felt everything, did everything more intensely, with an all-encompassing determination, than anyone I had ever known.

"You should wake her up and make her clean up this mess."

"That's not helpful. I'm knackered. You know if I wake her up now she'll be in a foul mood and I won't get anything done, and I'll just end up doing it myself anyway."

"She's like that because you let her get away with it. She should be taking responsibility for herself by now. At her age I kept my own room spotless and helped around the house every day. If you keep making excuses for her she'll end up dependent on you her whole life."

Anger rising again, after yet another insult about my parenting. Nothing was ever good enough for Terri, not my cleaning activities, "You leave the floors far too wet, you need to wring the mop out properly," not my cooking, "This rice is too greasy," not my discipline of my children, "If you don't put proper sanctions in place they're going to walk all over you."

Anger and frustration and suddenly, completely, resignation. Defeat. There were just weeks before I started my BA Fine Art, the degree I'd wanted to do for so long, and the thought of it, of coming home to this persistent drip, drip, drip of negativity made me want to scream and leap out of the window and run, run, run until there was no breath in my body, no skin on the soles of my feet. No barrier between myself and the land, I could melt into the earth, into the stones and the bones of it and never have to feel like this again.

All through the two-year foundation degree she had treated it like an indulgence, and I did all my work at the library and in the studio before coming home to cook and clean and sit with Terri while she watched her programmes. Even though I ignored the waves of disapproval coming from her when I read textbooks while she watched soap operas, and didn't complain when she insisted on turning off the lights to watch TV so I couldn't read. Even then, it felt that I was always trying, every day, to please her. How had it come to that, anyway, that someone else wass calling the shots again? How had I let it come to that?

When you have kids, when you feel that unconditional love, you can't run away. There are no escape routes. A mother doesn't run unless she takes her children with her. And I have been running for so long, it seems I will never stop. I thought, when Terri moved in, when life became almost normal, two parents, I thought, two sources of love and comfort. Someone to come home to, someone to love me and keep me in one place long enough to set down roots. But there was no security with Terri, only the incessant insecurity of her scrutiny and her commentary on everything that was wrong with our life. And then, the secret thought, the relief that I would have my own house soon, and that meant I would be in charge. I would call the shots. I would never have to run again. And if Terri didn't like it... but no, I wouldn't think like that.

I had most of the books back on the shelves and the papers stacked together and neatly put into the box in the cupboard under the TV. The dolls were piled together in the toybox, and the pens and pencils and crayons back in their cases. I fetched the cleaning bucket from the kitchen – Terri liked things done a certain way, and there were special buckets and bowls and cloths for each task – and chipped and scrubbed at the wax from the crayons, and the yoghurt, and washed every surface down carefully with the appropriate cleaning product, rubbing the carpets and fabrics dry with a towel. All the while I was too aware of the looming energy of the woman who filled the spaces and corners of my world with her disapproval.

An hour, that's all. One hour. But there are hours that feel like days, or years, cardinal times that mark the beginning and ending of things. There are moments that seem fixed, that will always exist, as if time had rooms, side-abutting alcoves into which we can step for a moment, revisiting that one point, that one place or experience, as if it had never changed. I knew, even as I felt her slip into the room with her cigarette in one hand, that this was one of those moments. Heart pounding, breath coming short, the mingled scents of bleach and fruity cleaning spray and carpet cleaner. Fixed moments, mutable time, some things don't change and some things are always changing or being changed. I thought it would be different this time, that having gone into things with my eyes open, with a toolbox full of experience and lessons learned, it would be better. It would work.

"I thought you were going to make coffee."

"I will. I'm about done." Straightening up, slowly, old aches and new, waiting. I kept my voice low, as did Terri. We both knew what would happen if we woke Aisha before she was ready. "But you could make it, you know, given that I've been busy."

"And reward you for being a fool, for letting your kids walk all over you?"

"I don't. I just don't punish them all the time for being themselves. They're people in their own right, Terri, not slaves or indentured servants."

"Oh, listen to you with the big words! Been reading more of those books on feminism? I know all I need to about your kind of feminism. Call yourself a feminist? When was the last time your sons lifted a finger in this house without being nagged?" She shakes with the effort of keeping her voice quiet.

"And when was the last time they did anything, breathed even, without you finding some fault with them? They're good boys, and Ash is a child. If you're so annoyed by their behaviour, feel free to confront them about it."

"I told you in the beginning I won't parent them. That's your job."

"Which you won't let me do, not the way I believe to be right."

"That's because your way of parenting is setting them up to be spoiled and entitled."

"I disagree."

And there it was. The raising of the hand. Pause. Freeze-frame, as in the movies. Her hand raised, and I knew that turn of the arm and wrist, just so. I knew what she was threatening.

"You should have woken her up, made her clean this herself."

"Why? So she can feel upset and beaten down and so I can squash her creativity, her individuality? Is that how you think I should parent?"

"I can't stand this, the way you give way to them no matter what."

Step away. Pick up the bucket. She occupied the doorway, her favourite attitude, penning me in one place. I shouldn't have been wondering at an alternative escape route right then.

224

"Well, if you can't stand it, I suggest you leave." I growl the words.

"Watch what you're saying!"

"Or what?" The anger seized me and drove me to face her. "Or you'll hit me?"

The hand dropped.

"I..."

"I know what you think I should do. You think I should hit my children, and punish them with emotional distance, just like you do with me."

"I don't do that."

"What about the five weeks you didn't talk to me because I accepted the place on the foundation degree? We'd discussed it, you knew I'd be taking it up, but I dared to say yes without asking your approval first. Five weeks, Terri, five weeks of agony and fear and hurt, when you wouldn't even acknowledge my existence, and then one day you just acted like nothing had happened. Do you think I should do that, leave my kids in an emotional wasteland until they feel the keen edge of fear that misbehaviour will threaten my love for them?"

"You think that just because you are going to Uni to be an *artist* you are superior to me? Don't use that language with me. You're no cleverer than I am."

Time stopped, still, that moment, and fear in my mouth because I knew how dangerous it was to say no. It was always worse when you tried to get away.

Then the anger was back, and it blazed through the fear. No. Not again. Never again. I walked right up to her, nose to nose. I hissed the words out, keeping my voice low so as not to be heard by Yusuf upstairs, and to avoid waking Aisha.

"Terri, just go, will you? Just leave. There's nothing here for you. Nothing about my life and this house makes you happy. I can see that now. You don't like my kids, you don't like my

225

habits, and you don't even like me. I can't understand any more why you stay."

She backed off, into the hallway, allowing me to follow her and shut the door. Her voice, raised at last, fury and cruelty.

"Well that's nice, isn't it? I waste four years of my life looking after your house, your kids, cleaning up your mess, and what, you think you can kick me out? Yeah, right, as if. Too fucking late love, I am going, and you'll be sorry, believe me. You think I want to be here with *you*?" The venom in that last word. Of course. "You and your dirty, spoiled kids, you're just as bad as them, lazy and dirty, you don't even shower every day, and believe me, you need to!"

"I'm not engaging with this Terri."

She turned towards the stairs and I slipped past with the bucket and cloths, my arms full of bottles. Shaking, putting the things away, emptying the bucket, then tea, I made tea at last, and I didn't make her coffee. I wondered how long it would be before I stopped automatically taking out two mugs and taking the lid off the coffee jar. And then I thought of her touch, and it made me weak, my legs almost giving way to think of never being kissed like that again, of never being touched like that again, and I wanted to run to her and say no, stay, we can work it out, but this was just one in a long line of arguments and we'd crossed the line.

I took my tea into the sitting room, watching Aisha sleep, a puddle of girl in a corner, listening to Terri packing, her feet heavy, doors and drawers slamming, creaking floorboards and words I sensed rather than heard, words of hate, of disdain.

Machine-gun fire of feet on the stairs.

A gap. She was watching, of course, that silent threat.

I stared at the wall.

"I'm going." Loud, mean. Did I ever like that voice with its shrill, eldritch edge? "Good luck with paying your own bills."

The front door slammed. Out of the window I watched her slinging a case onto the back of her motorbike and strapping it in place with bungee cords. Rucksack on her back, bulging. I looked around the room. She made it like this. All this furniture, bright and light, the pale cushions that stain so easily, the pale cream curtains, the blonde wood and the pristine white voile. And the fairies. The bloody fairies everywhere. I used to like them, but they came to annoy me with their sugar-sweet smiles and perfect bodies. The grumble rumble of the bike, the look of pure evil she cast back at the window.

The engine revved. I knew, as well as I knew the rising threat and the menace and the fact that sooner rather than later she would have done more than simply raise her hand to me, that she was waiting for me, baiting me, willing me to come out and beg her to stay, only to give her the chance to roar away in rejection.

Slowly, deliberately, I closed the curtains. I double-locked the front door and shot the deadbolt.

Then I looked at my daughter, and gently covered her with the blanket from the back of the sofa, and lifted her head to put a pillow under it.

I was still watching, my tea long cold beside me, her when she woke.

"Mum?"

"Yes, sweetheart?"

"Where's Terri?"

Always, always she cut straight to the quick. Always wild, a natural child, always making me feel that she saw and knew in ways I can never understand.

"She's gone, lovely."

"You had another argument."

"Yes."

227

She stretched, long legs, and that bit of puppy fat that softened her sharp edges.

"Why do you always have to argue with people?" She stretched again then jumped up, not noticing that I'd cleaned up the mess she made. "Is she coming back?"

"No, honey. I'm sorry." I reached to hug her, to comfort her, regretting most having let someone else into her life, someone who was fated to leave. She pulled away, shrugging out of my arms and storming out of the room. Alone, I looked at the now-tidy room, the neatly aligned throws, inhaling the scent of furniture polish and bleach. Too late. Too many questions. So tired, bone-achingly tired of the constant pressure, cleaning, cooking, cleaning again, balancing their demands. For what?

Long, stiff-legged steps into the kitchen, table laid for a meal no one wanted, cottage pie in the oven, pans on the stove, all ready to go. Pointless, all that work, that effort. They never thank you for it. They just leave.

My fault. Everything my fault. Everything I've done since coming back, every choice I've made, has been the wrong one.

Of course. That was the answer, all along.

Orange Mist

I wake screaming, the burning hunger a brightness. Another day of fighting and failing, of wrapping myself tight and holding myself in as if there's a tight band around me, tighter than the binding, stilling my words and suffocating my thoughts. Messages from Jarelle, walking to school, I can't find my voice. Something off, something not right, a dancer out of step with the chorus, a strange day that still tastes of ash and burning.

The streetlights' flaming glow fills the misty, drizzly air, like the sky itself is smouldering. Skipping school was easy this afternoon, and then there was the interview with the woman at the café on the corner, opposite the gate to the park, where I saw the "help wanted" sign, and now I have a job, washing dishes and waiting on tables and clearing tables and cleaning the kitchen after closing, and whatever else needs doing, every day after school for three hours and a half day on Saturday.

Smells of hot bacon and coffee and toasting paninis but I'm strong, I can do this, I had a handful of oats this morning with boiling water, enough to keep my stomach from hurting so much, and I had an apple on the bus into town, 90 calories, it's OK because that's it for today, only 90 calories. I should be fine and it makes me feel really full, a whole apple. The bus made me nauseous but that's OK too because I'm here now, my phone finding the right way to the Woolf building after work. Big old wooden doors, carved panels, set into deep stone walls, worn stone steps with a hollow where hundreds of feet have passed, students pushing past me. This is real life, it smells of dust and something else, something that takes me right back, back to when I was little and mum and I used to do things together. But this is a different uni, a different world, and I'm not 10-years-old any more, and I can do this, following the signs for room A21, as Sakinah directed me, telling me to come, telling me I'd be welcome, this adult woman treating me like I'm just like her.

I see a woman ahead, in a veil, and follow her, but daren't approach. Outside the door I have to stop, catch my breath. Don't be breathless, fat people are so unfit, don't let anyone see me panting, am I sweating? Blot my forehead, my neck, no, maybe I should go, this isn't right.

"Ash!"

Sakinah, reaching out, taking my hand. The room is tired-looking, with old bits of blue tac on the walls where posters have been and some worn chairs and tables, and several women milling about. To one side someone has set a kettle and an array of mugs and drinks, and there are plates of biscuits and fruit, and boxes of dates like sticky, bloated, dead insects.

"I am so glad you could come. Let's get a drink, and we can sit down."

Two women are setting the chairs out in a semi-circle, and another is unpacking a box of leaflets. An older woman, wearing a long black coat, something like the things I have seen my mother wearing in old pictures, is leafing through a pile of papers. Suddenly I have a cup of black coffee and Sakinah is ushering me to sit down.

"How have you been?" she asks.

"Oh, fine, thanks, um, you?"

"Oh, the usual. Life is too full, too many things to do all the time, I sometimes wonder if I will ever have a day when I don't feel like I am running to catch up!"

"I never asked, do you work?"

"Yes, I work here, in the library, part time, and I am doing my degree, obviously, but it's all the other things..."

I want to ask more but a shorter woman interrupts, "Sakinah, it's Aidah, she can't work the projector."

"Excuse me," Sakinah presses my hand gentle. Sudden touch, startling. "That's our speaker for tonight. But this is Su," I look into Asian features, and a wide smile, as Sakinah slips away.

"You're Aisha, right?"

"Yes, but everyone calls me Ash."

"Sakinah said you'd be coming. You'll like it – there are some great women here, really amazing women." She is bright, bubbly, earnest, her voice is high, like a child's, and her eyes are everywhere. "Tonight's speaker, she's so famous, maybe you've heard of her? Aidah Sabin? Her books... She was on Woman's Hour last month. I can't believe we actually have her here."

"I never..."

"Well, you'll see. Oh, I'd better go and shut the door."

She disappears into the growing crowd. The room has filled with women, there must be around 20 or 30, and they set out more chairs and collect drinks and talk, English, Arabic, my stomach clenches as someone passes me with hot chocolate, veils moving with them, some without veils, then Su shuts the door, and a few women take off the coverings on their faces and the sound of conversation rises, a wave, a tide, warmth, and another woman sits beside me, smiling gently.

It reminds me of when I was younger, before the world turned and seemed to turn on me, when I sat in a new classroom and another girl would sit next to me and smile, and both of us would be wondering if we might be friends, before the name-calling started, before they all started to run away from me, or taunt me, or push me over in the hidden parts of the yard, or wait for me in the toilets and drop my pencil case down into the loo, and throw my homework on the floor. That moment of possibility. And still I want it to mean something. I could run, I could go before they get the chance to lure me in and then cast me down as unwanted, unworthy. But maybe now, maybe this one time it'll be different. Maybe just once I'll find people who want me for me, not just out of pity or because I can do their homework for them. And then Sakinah comes back and sits down, and leans towards me.

"It is good to see you. You are going to enjoy this. I am sure we are going to be great friends."

And I believe her.

Can you taste it, or smell it, that state of knowing and of being fed, not physically, but mentally, of having your mind teased with tasters and then filled, again and again, with new understanding? Breaking dawn insights, rupturing a lifetime of night-dark ignorance. Oh these things, if I'd known these things, known about how and why and what they have been doing to me all my life, all of them, it hurts to know, it hurts to think like this, to see how I have been punished and taunted and teased for no reason.

"This is such an important topic," Sakinah says. "When we talk about knowledge, we understand that everything that is there to be known, to be understood, has been put there by Allah. It is our duty to know ourselves, and the world around us. Don't you feel that?"

How can she know the struggle inside me? "I guess so. I..."

The sympathetic smile, a pouring forth of compassion. "It's harder when you're on the cusp of everything. I know that it is easy to feel lost, to feel rudderless."

Yes, I think. Yes.

"I think we will have a lot to talk about."

She touches my hand again. A strong feeling, like happiness, like affection floods me.

Aidah's book is about the beauty industry; she talks about the rise of Western ideologies in Muslim life, the pressure for women to be thin. I don't understand some of it, some of the words and phrases, so alien. The commodification of the body and Cartesian Dualism, gender theory and Islam and ethics. But I can understand what she means when she poses the question, "Is it better to wear the burqa, or to lie awake at night calculating what weight you need to lose to be considered attractive, acceptable?"

Images of women, the shame as I look at the rolls of flesh, the wide hips, she talks about diets, their inevitable failure, I wonder, is she talking to me? About me? Is she looking at me now? Questions, hands raised, earnest voices, one woman's thick accent as she frames the words, "But in Islam, you must not indulge or deny the body. It is a sin to abuse what Allah has given to you."

A sin to abuse it. Is she saying that diets are abuse?

No, this isn't right, everyone knows being fat is the worst thing, the ugliest thing, all those news items with fat people eating huge burgers and piles of chips, that's what I look like.

"Dieting, and the control of the female body, are uniquely Western problems," the speaker continues. "Fighting wars, being bombed by insurgents or terrorists, women are fighting terrible crises, struggling to survive, to find food. And yet here, in this very country, women are being harassed on the street, accused of inciting rape because their clothing is too revealing, or denied medical treatment because they are considered too fat."

Spiral arguments, a medical student speaks up.

"But being obese is unhealthy, it causes cancer and heart disease and arthritis."

Someone shouts her down. "That's a falsehood. Lifestyle causes ill health, not just body size. You're just parroting what the system tells you."

It excites me. Sakinah is speaking, saying that we should be valued for our work, the mental work and the emotional work we do to carry our families, I don't understand it, but I want to. There's a whole world of something here I don't understand, so hungry still, always hungry. When will it stop, this feeling? It has to stop soon; I'm strong, yes, they use those words here, strong, and powerful. Look how strong I am, I want to say it, but I can't. Look how strong I am, I haven't eaten in days, that apple was my only weakness, even in the café I didn't eat, I am better than anyone, even these clever, glamorous women turning back to the tea table and the cakes again, but not me, never me, I can rise above this.

As I stand to one side, Sakinah sighs. Has she been watching me.

"Just think," she says, "if you turned all that willpower towards something worthwhile!"

After the talk, Aidah is surrounded by admiring women. I stand awkwardly, drinking black tea.

"This is Aisha," Sakinah introduces me. "She's new to the group."

"Good to meet you," Aidah pulls me to her. I feel the softness of her clothes, the soft caress of her headscarf against my face. "Did you enjoy the talk?"

"Very much." She moves so easily. I want to look like

234

that, to move like that, liquid smoke, wafting across the room. I follow her, heavy and clumsy, but trying to mimic that slow sway of her hips and the set of her head. She wears her veil like a crown, a headdress of power of some secret cult. Would I look like that, veiled? Would I seem so unassailable?

"You haven't tried the cake," she says as we sit at the edge of a group of women.

"Oh, no, thanks."

"Aisha, it's OK to have some cake."

I shake my head, "No, thanks."

That smile. "Aisha, can I ask you another question?"

"Sure." Bitter, dark tea, acid in my gut. Ask me anything. No one has ever really listened to me. No one. Not even Carl. He threw me away when I wasn't what he wanted any more.

"How long have you been starving yourself?"

Such a low voice, slightly rough. Eyes, like mine, brown and deep and knowing.

"I..."

She lays a hand on mine. "I know that look. I've worked with women like you, so many women, punishing themselves, hurting themselves."

No. You don't know me. You don't know anything about me. No one does. This is my secret, my superpower. I can make myself into something different, I can make myself not me, nothing like me, if I try hard enough.

Aidah sighs. "Do you have anyone to talk to at home?"

"I have four brothers. They've all left home now. There's just me and my mum."

"And you don't talk to her?"

"No. She's crazy, she's just wrapped up in herself. None of this would have happened... I mean..."

235

"I understand. Sometimes we can't talk to the ones closest to us."

The rising tide of conversation, different voices, different accents, then Sakinah, emerging from the throng, lifting her headscarf to tuck away an errant curl, smiling. She plants herself beside me, that scent of hers, flowers and spice. I want to close my eyes and lose myself in it.

"Here, just taste this," Aidah has a piece of cake in her fingers, and the sweetness burns my nostrils as she coaxes. "Just try it, Aisha, just one bite. It's my own recipe, courgette and lemon cake."

Soft fingers, warm moist cake, warm fingertips brushing my lips momentarily, and then the bursting thick sweetness and the stickiness and my head spins, the world righting itself again. No, a part of me shouts. No. Pleasure, deep and hot, rushing through my veins like lightning, burning and heady and so, so dangerous.

Pull away, turn my face away, why did she make me do it? Now it's done and the barrier is down and there is nothing I can do to stop what will come next.

"It's so good," Sakinah is eating the cake with enthusiasm. "You must give me the recipe. I love baking. Don't you, Aisha?"

"No, I don't bake. I cook sometimes, but nothing much, just stir fry and pasta and stuff." My head is reeling from the rush of sugar. "My mum, she doesn't cook much anymore, not since my brothers all moved out. She's so wrapped up in her work. So I cook. She... paints. She spends a lot of time painting, or at shows. I cook, because she forgets to. But..."

Sakinah is nodding, but it's Aidah who holds me with her gentle smile. Encouraging. Waiting. As if what I have

236

to say might matter. "But she went vegan a few years ago, she doesn't eat anything normal, for fuck's sake...oh, Sorry."

"It's OK."

Sakinah finishes her cake. "Another slice anyone?"

"Yes, please." Aidah nods. "Aisha?"

"Ash. My name is Ash. No one calls me Aisha."

"But it's your name, isn't it? And so musical, so lovely. Get her some cake, she needs it."

No, I don't need it but somehow I can't resist Aidah's insistence.

"Tell me more, about your mother, about your family," Aidah urges.

"Nothing to tell."

"You said you had four brothers?"

"Yes, the twins, they're the oldest. Mechanics, both of them. They live in their own house. They visit, sometimes, but Shahid has a girlfriend, so he doesn't come home so much. And Mahmood, he's still at university, studying theology. He...doesn't get on with Mum, or with me, really. So he's not home much either. When he does, he and Mum argue. He doesn't approve, he said that to me, of her lifestyle. I mean, he messages me, sometimes, but it's like a stranger. He's obsessed with God and always trying to get me to go to church. Which isn't my bag. Shahid, Abdullah, they message and stuff but they have their own lives."

"I would have liked a brother," Aidah nods. "Yes. I have three sisters, and they're all older than me. I've watched them grow up and marry and move out, but I never felt particularly close to them. Now they belong to someone else, someone else is the centre of their lives. Husbands and children."

"Are you married?" I straighten up. I want food. Now. More cake. As much as I can eat. When Sakinah brings back more cake, and some dates, I eat, not too fast, but steadily, crushing the sticky sweet flesh, caramel thick, between my teeth, devouring the crumbs of the cake.

"No, I'm not married," Aidah laughs. "I have scandalised my family by refusing to marry. But I'm happy, doing the work that I do, working with women to find their confidence. And I would still do this if I was married. I'm sure I will marry someday, just not yet. I feel that Allah has some other purpose for me."

Thick heavy weight, the warmth, like embers, a radiating glow, slowly melting the hard iron inside me, treacle-slow progress of the sugar through my veins.

"Let's get you home," Sakinah says. Her voice seems distant. I slump, so tired, leaning into the chair, my head spinning with the sudden rush of sugar and the inevitable nausea. Voices speaking over me.

"Come, Aisha, let's get you home. I can see you are exhausted."

I let her lead me out, put me in her car, and drive me home. The streetlights pass over me, wave after wave of amber washing over my face and arms, turning my skin livid. I imagine that it's burning away everything that I don't like, about myself and my life.

She walks up the driveway with me, in through the battered front door, taking in the bare bulb in the hallway, the lack of carpet, and my room with its floorboards and rag rugs and the rickety clothes rail and stacks of books.

Is mum home? I panic and cross my fingers. She won't appear if she's painting.

It's the first time I have brought anyone other than Carl here.

238

"You said your brothers are working, right?"

"Yeah, most of them."

Sakinah sits beside me on the bed. "Can't they help out with some of this? I mean, you've made it nice in here but you could use some more furniture. Maybe some paint? Why does your mother let you live like this?"

"She doesn't come in here."

I look around, panicking suddenly, but there's nothing to give me away; no empty wrappers, the bottle of laxatives hidden in the bedside drawer.

"Is she home?"

I listen. Faint strains of Fleetwood Mac. "Yes, she's in her studio. Music means she's painting."

"This is neglect, Aisha." She shakes her head. "I know it's hard for you to hear, but it's true."

"I'm 17, nearly 18, I'm not a child anymore." I want her to leave, suddenly. Seeing her, sitting on my bed, it's not right, it makes me feel uncomfortable. Does she want something from me, something I haven't thought of until now? What is she doing here? "Umm, thanks for the lift, I'm going to...umm, have a bath and go to bed."

"You're welcome. I'll see myself out. See you next week?"

"Yes, I think so."

"Good. It's OK to have friends, Ash. You don't have to be alone. I'll pick you up next Monday."

"I'll be at work. Can you pick me up from there?"

"Of course. Message me the address."

When she's gone, the room feels empty and cold, as if she has taken all the life and warmth with her. I feel sick, so much sugar, but it's too late now to bring it all back up, it won't come. It will hurt more, the acid will burn and numb my tongue and roughen my teeth and make my

239

throat sore, and I just can't face trying. Water, stale and dusty, and six of the laxatives, and my bed, my sweet bed. My phone buzzes. Messages from Jarelle, from Kat, from Abdullah, checking in on his baby sister. But I'm not his baby sister, I don't know what I am but not that, not a baby, not a child, not since... since she drove away everyone who ever seemed to like me, to care about me.

Mahmood said once that our father tried to see us, that she went to court to stop him. He says we would have been better off living with him, or our uncles, that we would have had a proper home, and a big family, and we wouldn't have been teased in school and we could have stayed in one place.

I can't imagine what that's like. I always thought, with my brothers there, that I would never be alone, that no matter where we lived they'd look out for me. But they're gone, all of them, they left me too, just like everyone does, and somehow I'm supposed to build a life for myself over and over again from the ashes of her last fucking mistake, and I don't want to do it anymore.

Sugar-fuelled dreams of flight and fight and being followed by a huge black shape that blocks out the light, that brings cold darkness. I flee through an empty landscape, searching for something I cannot name, only knowing that I'm lost without it. I wake too early, to sickness and self-loathing, and the cycle starts again.

Terra Rosa

The sweet-sickly smell of linseed and oil paint, the sun rising to find me dishevelled and aching, empty. How many days since I'd eaten properly? But the paintings, oh, the work that I had done, like waking from a long, hazy dream. And there they were, glorious and glistening and yes, there was time to wonder that I could do this, me, now, Amanda. Oh, if I'd only known then what I'm capable of. If only I'd known that there is, there always was, this great well of power inside me, these images and ideas, this imagined world and the ability to make it manifest on canvas, on wood, on paper. If only I had been able to see this future and this beauty. But even when I didn't know, it seems that this was always what I believed in, this is hope, *this* is the freedom I had been moving towards, all these years.

My life, the story I have been telling myself, the way to make sense of it all, first this happened and then this, and that's why I was there, in my house with its holes in the roof and its half-finished renovations and its echoing rooms that smelled of damp; my children mostly gone from me, and all the time at last, all the time in the world that I always wanted to just not think about anyone else, not serve or service anyone. Episodes, swimming to the bloated surface of the sea of my thoughts, time crushed into gobbets of memory: Aisha leaving for school, her first day in uniform; Shahid, his face shining, his wide grin, passing his driving test; Abdullah bringing home a girlfriend who giggled as they sat in the corner of the sofa together; Mahmood announcing he was becoming a Christian and denouncing me for drinking, hinting at my immorality for having a female lover. Terri making me breakfast on my birthday, Dee stroking my face in the middle of the night and whispering that she couldn't

241

believe I was real, couldn't believe that I could love her, could want her. Yusuf with his gangly limbs and too-large teenage teeth, trying desperately to learn the violin and being so, so bad at it that even his brothers turned on him and threatened to throw it in the canal if he carried on, and then he switched to piano and it was as if everything suddenly made sense to him. And then he grew up and started travelling and making a living from his music.

Real life. Real lives. My boys, men at last, men who forgot to call their mother and didn't answer my texts, fading away into that huge wide world, and the only thing that kept me from panicking every day was knowing that *he* couldn't hurt them.

I didn't know how much they saw, or understood, when they were little, but it amazed me that they all turned out so well. I'd read the books, I knew the statistics, but there they were, my boys, each of them working and earning and surviving, thriving even, and when I did see them, together or individually, when I spoke to them, when they remembered to send their mother a quick message, it always ends with, "Love you, Mum." And that's enough.

I thought I was winning, I thought success was simple survival, I thought the measure of my strength was my ability to endure. But I was wrong, because there was also the beauty of the desert and my life before that, the green of the Welsh hills and the dark brownish grey stone of the primary school where I ran and played and never thought of anything other than all the possibilities of a distant future. Flowers in my garden the precise colour of the school uniform I wore for seven years, turning up the skirt at the waist to make it shorter, hiding behind the science block to smoke. There is the pink of my mother's favourite cardigan, the same colour as the flowers on her grave, and there is the green-grey of Jan's eyes – my only regret was that I never saw them again, her or my father, because after Blossom House I knew they weren't safe, and in that stroke of the brush, that curving vine, the exact shape of my belly when I caught my reflection in the smoky glass, the very last time I was pregnant, when I was so full of despair and hope was a star-speck glimmer in a whole world of darkness.

I took Terri back, of course I did. She came back with her tail between her legs, two weeks before the house move, full of apologies.

"You can't just say you're sorry," I was abrupt with her, busy with packing and cleaning. The house had taken all of my money bar the cost of hiring a van and a few thousand left to start renovations.

Her bulk seemed diminished as she hovered in the hallway. "I *am* sorry Mand. Really. I just... It's a lot to live with, all of you. I love you, and I love the kids. I just get a bit..."

"You knew we came as a package."

"I know. And I know I was wrong. I miss you."

"I miss you too."

Defeat, shoulders dropping, I knew the fight was over, that from that moment I would be unable to resist. I did miss her, the company, the closeness of another body in bed, of having someone to talk to.

"It can't be like it was before."

"It can't," she agreed. "But it would help if you didn't shut me out when I talk about the kids."

"And it would help me if you didn't criticise my parenting."

"I was trying to help, not criticising."

"Didn't come across that way."

She moved closer, that hopeful smile, her eyes bright. "I guess I can learn to be a bit more careful how I put things."

I looked at her for the longest time, that familiar, long face, the creased and crinkled edges around her eyes, her mouth. I had forgotten why I was so angry at her.

"Fine. You're just in time to help with the move."

"What do you want me to do," she said, heaving her cases inside and closing the door.

"Just hold me for a moment," I replied, and moved into her warmth and felt her solidity and let it be enough, just for that moment.

I stand and I paint, and I catch sight of the dusty frame which holds my degree certificate, such a flimsy symbol of freedom. Gone now, empty house, Ash, my little one, womanly and still as wild as she always was, so angry now as if I have let her down somehow, as if growing up is a foreign country and I should have provided her with some kind of guidebook, taught her the language, warned her about the vagaries of native customs. Anticipated all those questions.

As if I ever had the answers.

Iridescent White

The dreams stop when I eat, but each day is a nightmare when I do. Waking is remembering, realising that I ate the cakes and the sweet stuff again last night, my third night at the Muslim Women's group, while I listened to Su talk about her cousins in Syria and Sakinah introduced me to Helen, a Muslim convert, and we studied the Koran, and talked about the oppression of women and suddenly it makes sense, all of it. What do I do with this anger now? And then I forgot to take the laxatives, forgot all of it.

Doomed to be fat.

Helen's house. I smell of the café, of burning cheese and bread and bleach, everything aches after running to clear up and wash dishes, and the scrubbing and cleaning, my hands raw, my nails broken. Mrs Green, the owner, checking everything I do, tutting and pointing, but now I'm free again, with £20 in my pocket and a return bus ticket and here I am, at this house, all the curtains closed, otherwise it looks like all its neighbours, pale brick and bland façade, holding its secrets.

"Aisha!"

"Helen."

She has her headscarf on, but her face is uncovered. Narrow corridor, small rooms, white walls with no pictures, blonde wood floors and pale sofas in shades of cream. A TV on the wall, a laptop on the floor, a corner lamp. Three other women there, I forget the names as soon as I'm told them, but Helen says that I am another "seeker" and then the conversation swells and pulls me in, someone is asking my opinion, words hanging in the air.

"What? No, I'm not Muslim, I mean, I was born Muslim, but not now."

"What's stopping you?"

"Have you internalised all that Islamophobic bullshit as well?"

"Don't you know that the mass media's using Islam as an excuse for imperialism?"

"Or is it that you still think Islam oppresses women?"

Books come out, they show me passages, read me words, and suddenly this makes sense. I seize the books, pick up one that has caught my eye, start reading.

"Don't you have a sense of purpose, Ash?" asks Helen. "Can you not see something greater in your life than simply existing?"

"I honestly don't know."

"What is it that haunts you?"

She holds my chin in her hand, green eyes locked on mine. "Whatever it is that you're carrying, this burden, whatever it is that you've done in the past, none of it matters if you believe in something greater. The past can be healed, Aisha."

I shake my head, wanting to pull away or bury myself in her arms, burrow into her flesh as if diving into this pure certainty she embodies. As she drops her hand I feel a chill.

"It can all be healed," she repeats.

They keep talking, more to each other than to me, but these books, thick and heavy or light and well worn, stories and ideas and then one book, *Women and Islam*, I can't stop reading.

"You can borrow them, if you like."

Helen. Her headscarf has slipped, showing pale hair, reddish gold. How old is she?

"My husband will be home soon," she says, and everyone gathers their things. "Aisha, I mean it, borrow those books. I can see they've caught your imagination. And here is my number. Message me and I'll add you to our group chat."

"I..."

"Where's the harm? We're just women asserting ourselves, asserting our right to know and to understand. I can see your confusion, I see how alone you are, how hurt and how rejected the world makes you feel. But you're not. We just have to hold together, find strength in each other. This is a good place to start. We're all your friends, Aisha, all of us. We just want you to be happy."

"I... well, thanks."

"Good. Now, we'll see you soon. I'll let you know when we get together again."

Suddenly I have so many friends and I don't know what to do with all of this, but I take the books with me, and read on the bus. At home I can hear Mum in her studio so I take them upstairs and read and read until tears come, and then I go downstairs and make toasted bagels with coconut oil and lots of jam and go back to bed, crying with the sweet, sweet pleasure of the sticky, doughy bagels and their crunchy edges and the jam making the saliva run, eyes burning as I read more and everything falls away; the lies and the half lies and the way I've been made to feel, because it was never about me, it was about them, all of them, always wanting to control me. And then I go to the bathroom and throw up for what seems like hours and end up sobbing again on the floor, aching and empty and so very tired.

I've been hating myself for so long, how do I stop it?

"You look different."

Jarelle catches up with me at the bottom of the steps

into the main building. What does she see? It hurts now, to eat, and I feel sick all the time, every day, and some days I want to throw up as soon as I've eaten, but I try not to. I try to let the anger flame instead, flash fires of feeling and the resentment of realisation. My body aches, breasts sore in the binder, and then Jarelle is off on her usual rant, and mentions Auntie Flo visiting, and I realise it has been a while.

Two months and nothing.

Or is it longer? Three, maybe four months?

Fear tastes like acid, like the way my mouth feels when I throw up. I have been feeling so sick, I thought it was from not eating, then letting myself eat again, and maybe it is, maybe this is just a reaction, my body in shock still after starving for so long. I can't talk to Jarelle, no, who can I trust? There must be someone, there must be something I can do, someone to tell me what to do, not Mum, fire and flame and shame of it, she'd love it, tell me "I told you so". This isn't happening, I'm like all of them, no different, no.

"Hey, Jarelle..."

"So what's up with you?" She falls into step beside me. "I thought we were going to town on Saturday?"

"I know, just wasn't feeling up to it."

"Avad said he saw you with Sakinah Monday night."

"Yeah, I go to this women's group, at the uni."

An arch look, one perfectly curved eyebrow. Fear again, who can I talk to about this? Not her, no, not her. I can't talk to her and not Mum and not my brothers, Jesus no, never my brothers, not about this..."

Small talk, keep smiling, joking, go to class, make notes, meticulous notes in neat handwriting, the pen boring into the paper, Jarelle on her laptop typing swiftly. Kat walking with us to PE, I run to change in the toilet cubicle as always.

"Hey, that diet's working," Jarelle bumps me with her hip as we walk into the hall. We do PE as part of the Advanced Baccalaureate, all of us in our regulation sweatpants and polo shirts, boys as well as girls. Jarelle wears a long-sleeved tee under hers. I wish I could too. Today is kickboxing, We pair up, on the crash mats, and practice kicks and punches and blocks. Everything aches, and I feel heavy and weak. My superpower has left me. Every Monday night I lose control. I remember that Dee taught us this stuff, ten years ago maybe, or more, or less, how we used to go into the big room in Blossom House, which always smelled of rice cooking, and curry, and laundry, and I remember copying my brothers and wishing I was as big as them, that I was a boy like them and would never have to sit down and be quiet and be a good girl.

Perhaps if I exercise hard enough, perhaps I can make whatever's happening stop. I throw myself at Jarelle, and she fights back, her kicks and punches harder, and I let her land a good kick in my gut, knocking the wind out of me, and I laugh as she pulls me to my feet.

"You kick like a girl," I tease her, and she rewards me with a roundhouse that I don't even bother to block. The pain, the blow to the gut and then the rough graze of the mat on my palms. I want it to hurt. This is what makes it real. Like when I purge, and the pain rips me from the inside, and I love it, that feeling of emptiness. As if the hollowness at the centre will swallow me and shrink me until I fit into this world. Maybe the bruises will soften my flesh, make it easier for my body to scour away all this hated fat.

"So, you hang out with Sakinah now?" Jarelle pants as we pause for a minute. "That's new!"

"Oh, I just like those talks on a Monday. Plus, she picks me up from work and then brings me home. So I don't have to get the bus. It keeps me out of the house."

"Still bad then?"

I shrug, lifting my hands ready to spar again, feeling the moves coming easily to me. I used to be good at this sort of thing once, before I realised how much ammunition it gave them to bully me; call me a fat dyke, bull dyke, butch. "Nothing changes."

"How's the job?"

"It's a job." I grunt as I dance away from her next kick. "It's OK. She wants me to do Saturday afternoons too, so I'm thinking I might."

"But we don't see you so much as it is!"

I stop, panting, after a combination of kicks and punches that has driven her almost to the wall. "I know. But, you know. I like having some spare cash."

And I do. I like the money, the fact that I can buy clothes now, and books, and pay for music on my phone, and plenty of data. And I can buy my own food. Not that I need to, not so much since I took Aidah's advice, and had a long chat with Abdullah and Shahid about Mum. Now they get food delivered each week, and when I get home there's a freezer full of stuff and loads of stuff in the fridge – real cheese, and milk, and all her vegan stuff, and decent bread, and baked beans in the cupboard again. And now I'm working most evenings she has to cook for herself, and Abdullah checks in on the phone every day now, making sure she eats and takes care of herself. I don't tell her that half the time she thinks I'm working I'm with Helen, or Sakinah, or Aidah. The group chat is always active, every day, and we meet at odd times, in different houses, always talking about the same topics. Hardly an hour goes by where I don't get a message from one of them.

"How did you get on with the chemistry test?"

"Oh, OK," I shrug. I'd almost forgotten about it. There's all the pressure now about UCAS forms and uni interviews. I thought I wanted to go to uni, to get away, but now I don't know. Having friends, for the first time in so long, I'm not sure I want to give this up. The Monday night group... They act like they really like me, like I matter, like what I say is important. Warm, like being wrapped in a thick blanket, the feeling of belonging.

"I only got a B," Jarelle confesses, standing with her hands on her hips and breathing heavily. "And I worked really hard for it too. I can't have Bs. I have to get an A*."

"You will. It's only one little test. I'll go over it with you if you like."

"Oh, yeah, great. After school?"

"After work." I pick up the pads, mirroring the actions of the teacher, and hold my hands up for Jarelle to punch the thick, plastic covered padding. The thud and thunk of each blow is strangely satisfying. "Meet me after?"

"Yeah, OK."

In the café, I glory in my power, renewed now, the ability to ignore the food, the hunger, the deafening roar of desire. Black coffee and water, that's all, while I scrub and clean and serve others, clear tables, wash dishes, sweep floors. All through the bus ride to Jarelle's I triumph in it, my control, my power. We work through the chemistry, watch a film, and I walk home, fast and swift with my earbuds in, loud, fast music, back to my room to exercise again, a cup of some vile herbal tea with fennel in it, to kill the hunger pangs that won't stop. Lifting a bag of books, star-jumps, squat thrusts, sit ups, press ups, arm raises. Yoga pose after yoga pose, then the kicks, the blocks and punches, until there is no breath, until my head spins and my vision darkens and I have to collapse at last, fighting to breathe, pain in my chest, my belly, pain everywhere but this is good, visualising my body devouring this hated fat a hundred thousand cells at a time.

Late night, the phone buzzes over and over, messages in the group. We call ourselves the recipe club, but we don't talk about recipes. I flip the phone over, key in my code, scroll down. Aidah's final message hangs in the air like spirit writing. "Remember, only through the true knowledge, given by Allah, can we find the keys to unlock the understanding of our past, our present and the means to access our future."

The pain of something unfolding, birth pangs of potential being and becoming.

In the liminal space between waking and sleeping, when the monsters of childhood and the demons that live inside me flame into remembered life, I see it, almost, a land just beyond reach, a newborn world just flexing its muscles and learning its own shape, form and boundaries.

The future.

Perhaps.

Mars Black

Deep night, no sign of Ash. Maybe she was with Carl. I thought he was gay but you can't always tell. The younger ones, they don't seem to come out or make a big deal about it, they don't need labels, they just do what they want, girls wearing androgynous clothes and boys wearing heels, like the waiter at the art show two weeks ago with his black stilettoes, like something I used to wear in my teens. The house was different without her, emptier, less disturbed. But usually she was home by 10.30. She was never one to break the rules, not like the boys, especially Shahid who never could follow a rule if it was laid out in front of him. Gone eleven and no sign of her. What should I do?

Her phone was switched off. Did she have other friends, except Carl? I had his number, didn't I? Didn't she text me from his phone sometime? Yes, there it was. Text or call. Call. Then it's easier to tell if someone is lying.

"Hello?"

"Carl, it's Ash's mum. She hasn't come home yet, is she with you?"

"No, sorry, she's not. She and I haven't been hanging out much lately."

"Oh? I didn't realise. Sorry to disturb you, but you haven't got any idea where she might be, have you?"

"No. I haven't spoken to her for a few days."

"No? But hasn't she been at school?"

"I haven't seen her there, to be honest."

"Right. Well, thank you anyway."

"Wait, Mrs Said, just...look...she's been hanging out with some girls in school, Jarelle and some others. Maybe she's with them."

"OK."

"Just so you know."

"Thanks."

I went into her room, had a quick look around, barely registering the usual teenage mess. Her old phone was there, and its charger. I took it with me and plugged it in. Yes, texts from someone called Jarelle.

I rang Jarelle's number. No answer.

I checked the contacts: a mobile and a home phone. I wrote both of them down, tried the home phone. Still no answer.

Silence a muffling fog seeping through the house; a rising mist that grows colder as it creeps up from the skirting-boards and along the surfaces, filling the air thickly, stopping my breath. Where was she? I should be rational, she's a teenager, they come home late. But something was wrong. It wasn't just that hadn't come home yet. She felt...gone. I tried to remember when I last saw her. She was gone before I got up this morning, but she was here last night, wasn't she? I was painting until late, but she came in, didn't she? Didn't I hear her?

I texted the twins, to ask if they've heard from her today. Messages winging into the ether. No point texting Mahmood, she didn't talk to him. Yusuf was away, I didn't want to worry him. Surely she would be home soon?

Shahid's answer was brief. Not in the last couple of days.

Restless, pacing, up to the studio, some empty plates on the table, a couple of mugs. A wineglass with a dead fly floating in the dregs of Malbec. When did she bring me that toasted sandwich and the mug of soup? It must have been yesterday, surely? I remembered her coming in, and how thin she looked. I should have known better than to say anything. She'd been so moody lately, and that look, witheringly adolescent, because what could I possibly know about

254

anything? What was it she said? "Don't start noticing things now, when it's too late." But that was just teenager stuff, wasn't it?

Was that yesterday? Was that today? Where was she? Why hadn't she come home?

Images and fears and feelings and that underlying terror, the waiting demon-ghost of the past which was always there, always present, the fear that one day, one of them, him or one of the family, would come for her. Almost 18 but she wasn't like the boys, nothing like them. They were independent long before this. She was less confident, less self-assured. As much as I had cultivated an air of nonchalance towards her and tried to just accept her for who she is, I worried then, my mind scuttling from one thought to another, that I'd gone too far the other way and she might not feel connected, or loved, or *something*. I thought I was doing the right thing, letting them all be themselves, not placing any expectations on them. Maybe I should have put more boundaries in place, but she was always difficult, always different, always resistant to everything that I did, everything that others did. And I knew that if I'd said anything about her being out so much lately she would have turned on me, "There's no pleasing you, first you complain I spend too much time alone reading, next you complain I'm out too much. You'll never be happy."

And maybe she was right. Maybe I had no right, because I had left her to her own devices, but then I didn't want my mother riding me when I was a teenager and I really didn't want to drive her away. But there I was, wondering if I'd done just that.

I had dreamed of her the previous night. I went into her room and she found me there, digging amongst her things, and the anger and betrayal on her face was palpable. But I hadn't done that. I never went into her room. I was supposed to trust her. That's why I never asked to see her laptop or phone or to know her passwords for all those apps, because I wanted her to feel like I respected her.

Outside: inky blackness in the garden and the faint twinkling of the solar fairy-lights under the old oak with the gaping gash like the woman-parts of an ancient hag, brooding over the rambling camellias and the bay tree and the mossy lawns and their clots of primroses and dandelions. Where was she?

Time, too slow and too late, and the only thing to do was wait. I couldn't sit and do nothing, I hadn't been able to since Blossom House. Too much time and too much silence and I start to see things, so it was better to just paint and keep on painting. In the studio I chose a new canvas, and although I was thinking of autumn and though it was spring outside and though the night was deep and drawn with shadows, grey on inky-black, this landscape was white, bright white and grey-white and silver, trees and boughs, and frozen grass and flowers, all crystalline with frost and snow, all beautifully dead. And when I emerged from that place I went to when I painted, where time and sensation did not exist, there she was, the woman in her black shroud, not in miniature or in shadow, not half-hidden behind the bole of a tree or ghosting between clouds, but full front and centre, the delicate silk ribbon edging the headscarf reflecting the icy landscape. The eyes in the slit between the sooty black edges of the *niquab* and veil were brown. And I realised that I'd been painting her all along. I thought it was me, my ghost, the woman I should have been, still haunting the edges and the liminal spaces of every painting I had produced from past until present, but it wasn't.

It was her, always her.

Cadmium Yellow

"I need to talk to you."

Sakinah floats up to me, serious, taking my arm as she does. She always touches me, and I wonder at it, because no one else touches me these days, no one bridges that gap between me and the rest of the world, except in the dreams I keep having; wild, volcanic dreams, land splitting apart. But I'm the land and it's my blood pouring out as molten lava and the fear that I will burn up, burn away and blow away as ash on the wind seems to drag at my heels all the time.

In all the weeks I've been coming here, making the journey to the Uni, weaving through crowds of students, envying the girls in their short-shorts as the summer heat casts a haze over the college buildings, Sakinah has always made a point of chatting with me. We have had talks about the Koran, talks about morality, about politics, and last week a woman novelist read from her book and reminded us that we lose nothing by embracing womanhood, by being mothers or wives. If we're respected for that, our work is as valued as that done in laboratories and offices and hospitals and schools. I can't get it out of my head, that everything women do is work; mostly work that no one pays them for.

"I don't have to rush off."

Sakinah smiles. "My friend, let's wait until the others are gone."

I help to put the chairs away, wash the mugs and tidy up. They drift away, one after another. A weight, suddenly, the knowledge that something is about to happen.

"I've been watching you, Aisha," Sakinah says, sitting down and patting the seat beside her. "I wanted to talk to you, as a friend. I think, well, I know you have been visiting Helen, yes, and her friends?"

"Yes. I go after work, a couple of times a week."

"I see. I just... Well, that was the first thing. I wanted to say, please, be careful. Helen is a good woman, but she is very... devout. As is the way with some converts, and some of her views, well, let's just say we don't all share them. Please, I don't wish to interfere. But please be careful."

"OK."

"You know what people think of us. You know what kind of world we live in. I am not sure how much you identify with Islam, but you must see that it is not just a religion, it's a way of living, of seeing the world, a way of knowing and understanding how the world works."

"I do see that. I think, sometimes, that it's what has been missing. Nothing makes sense to me, but I come here, and it starts to."

"Good."

The pause fills with something, there is something more she wants to say.

"I hope, well, please, I hope you will forgive me, but there is another thing. You see, I come from a large family. My mother had thirteen children, several of my sisters have had children, and I have been around pregnant women all my life. I don't know, it seems you don't talk to your own mother much, but I wonder, is there something you need to talk about? You can confide in me. I only want to help you."

Hollow, make me hollow and let me fold in on myself. I know what she's asking. It makes sense that she should ask it, she caught me vomiting last week and I made the mistake of telling her I feel sick all the time.

Her breath is loud as she draws it in. "At first, well, I

258

wanted to talk to you about the fact that you seem to eat so little, that you usually refuse food, but you seem so pale and tired. And then... I don't know."

"I...what?"

"Aisha, do you have a boyfriend?"

"No! No, I don't."

"I speak as a friend."

"I don't." Stand up, move towards the door. "It's OK, everything is fine, I don't... I mean, I haven't..."

"I'm sorry! I didn't mean to upset you, to assume..."

"It's OK, it's OK, but no, there's nothing... I'm not..."

Run now, run fast, feet slamming into paving stones, ankles hurting from the shock of it, run until I can't breathe, chest hurting, heaving, fighting the bindings, belly aching, run and run and never stop, run far, run fast, don't look back, but the only place to go is home and at home I cannot hide or pretend and suddenly I know, I know. This body, this hateful monstrous body, I can see everything now like a film playing out as I hobble and try to jog through the park, as I stumble onto the bus, the life that will come, the way she will be with me, no, it cannot be and it won't be and I won't have it and that's the end of it because it's not real it's not true it was just one time, just once, just one time and it's not fair how can it be like this, no I don't believe it, it can't be, it isn't, but it's been more than three months now and nothing and I know what that means I'm not stupid

If I.

Could only just.

Breathe.

I find myself at Helen's house, no memory of how I got here. The door opens and Helen smiles. "Aisha. My dear, what has happened?"

Inside, jumble of voices and noises. "I..."

"Don't worry, I can see you're upset. I'm glad you came to me. Some of our sisters are here, but let's go into the front room and we can talk." She looks beautiful, her kind eyes and the silky texture of the scarf framing her face.

"I don't know what to do." The deep sofa is comfortable, but I perch on the edge. Everything is numb. "I don't know what to do."

"Wait here, and I will make some tea and we can talk about it."

As she leaves, she pauses. "Here. Something to read, while you wait."

I take the book and hold it, barely taking in the words. It is another of her books about Islam."

"Aisha?"

"Sorry?"

A stranger, a small woman in black, her *hijab* plain, with bare feet as brown as mine.

"Helen has been called away for a few minutes. My name is Zara. I joined her discussion group a few months ago, but I don't think we have met before."

"I... hello."

She sits next to me. A sweet smell, like cake. Awkward, my lumpy body seems so out of place in this place where women drape themselves so elegantly in black. "I understand you are upset. Would you like to talk?"

"No offence, but I don't really know you. I mean, you're a friend of Helen's, but we've never met."

"I understand. Helen tells me you are perhaps considering what to do next with your life?"

Great, Helen talks about me? Maybe I should go. I start to rise.

"Please, sit, it's OK, I won't ask any more questions."

260

She puts a hand on my arm. Warmth. I miss it, I want to be touched, I want to be held, this churning, these thoughts, the fear like clouds, like fog, I can't see beyond it, what happens next? Where do I go now?

"Would it be okay for me to just sit with you a while?" Zara asks. "I don't think you should be alone."

I nod. She sits there, so calm, just staring ahead. She doesn't look sad, or angry, or even happy, she looks peaceful, it's like peace and quiet and calm are just flowing out of her and I want to feel like that, I want to stop these feelings I have, the thoughts, I am so sick of it, of hating myself like this, of everything feeling wrong, but I don't know how. I will never be like them, I will never be able to be like them now.

"You know, sometimes, it is good to pray," Zara says after a while. "Would you mind if I prayed with you?"

"I don't pray. I'm not religious." Small voice, hoarse, hard to force out against closed throat and dry mouth. Nausea too, spinning and unsteady.

"That's okay. I will pray for both of us."

For a moment I think of Mahmood and his bloody prayers and his criticisms and his absolute bloody belief that he is right, he is always going to be right because God told him so, and I want to pull away again, but my legs won't move, my body too weak, there is nowhere else to go carrying what I know.

She chants quietly, words that I almost feel I should know. The room still, just her moving a little, and the musical flow of syllables blending one into the other, rising, falling, like waves, like breath, like sleep, and I breathe out with her, and it all rushes back, the pain and the hurt is there, the numbness goes, I'm crying, no, don't let me cry, don't let them see how weak I am, but I can't

261

stop. Burning, rasping sobs, hot, searing tears, and then Zara's arms around me, strong, capable, and she pulls me to her, and there is nothing left to do but to sink into this warmth. Her hand strokes my head as I sob against the black fabric of her headscarf, tears soaking in, crying like a baby, that's what they say, wordless noises, drawn from the deepest well of all I have been keeping inside. A release; I become boneless and heavy, and she holds me, strong and gentle, against her, holds me up, cradles me, and let her take my weight, take my tears, and at last, at last, I can let go.

Silver

The hours from sunrise to 9 o'clock dragged, and then I rang Terri at work. Yes, it had been years and she was still angry at me, but I was still angry at her too and I could get over it. I needed her. I needed someone who knew us, someone I wouldn't need to explain everything to. And not my boys, not yet, because then I would have had to worry about them too.

"Terri Corescine."

That voice, deep and gravelly, with its broad West Country tones, the flat intonation on the drawn-out vowels.

"Terri, it's Amanda. Please don't hang up."

"What do you want?"

"Look, I know you hate me, but I need your help. Ash didn't come home last night, and I can't reach her and I don't know where she is."

A pause. Office sounds in the background.

"What is she, seventeen, eighteen?"

"Seventeen. Nearly eighteen."

"So she's probably out partying and doesn't want to come home yet because she knows she's in trouble."

"But she doesn't do this! She never has! She spends all her time in her room or hanging out with her friend Carl, and he says he hasn't seen her."

"New friends, maybe?"

"Yeah, Carl said—"

"So follow it up. I can't help you. You made that perfectly clear when we were together, and after the way you behaved, I can't believe you would honestly think I would come running."

"I never meant to hurt you."

"And yet you did. You got me to open up to you, you let me waste years of my life loving you, and then you dumped me like toxic waste."

Breathe. Don't argue with her, not now.

"I'm sorry Terri, I didn't know who else to call. And as I recall, it was you who walked out. Not me."

"And I came back. I came back and I spent two years supporting you while you moved into the house, and helping you do it up."

"I know."

"Call those crazy friends of yours, the ones who had so much to say on the subject of our relationship."

When she rang off I felt a kind of chill, but I tried Jarelle's number again. No answer. I tried the home number and asked for Jarelle.

"She's not here," a woman answered.

"This is the mother of her friend Ash."

"Who?"

"Aisha."

"Oh, Aisha! Such a good girl. How can I help you?"

"Has Aisha been there? I'm looking for her."

"No, Jarelle went to school this morning and Aisha didn't come to call for her."

"Has she been there recently?"

"Yes, she was here three nights ago, doing homework with my daughter, like usual."

I could tell from the tone of her voice she was wondering why I didn't know that my daughter had been at her house.

"And you haven't seen her since...Monday?"

"No. Sorry I can't be more helpful."

"Could...could you give me your daughter's number, please? Ash didn't come home last night, and she might know where she is."

"No, that wouldn't be acceptable."

I gave her my number instead.

"Please ask Jarelle to call me. I just need to find my daughter."

Pacing the kitchen, chewing my lip and then I thought perhaps I should go and look in her room, properly this time. But I was scared to break the barrier I'd built between us, and even more scared of the answers I might find in there.

Instead I cleaned up a bit in the kitchen, telling myself it was probably nothing. She would appear at any moment, hung over, no doubt, and sheepish, and I would hide my relief and give her a proper telling off for staying out all night. Chipping away at the months-old grease and stains, wondering when I last did this, and when I heard the front door go, I ran to the hall, because had to be Ash.

"Terri."

"I still have my key." She held it up sheepishly. Terri with her throwback 80s mullet and her too long-spiked hair, and the beetle-like dark eyes and that mouth so set around with lines and scars that it seemed she would never be able to smile. Terri, tall and broad and her skin tanned brown, weather-worn, her hands in the pockets of her creased Levis.

"I thought you were at work."

"I was. Joanie, you remember Joanie? She's running the bike shop with me now."

"Oh."

"I can go if you don't want me here."

"I do, I do, please, come in."

"So, any word?"

"No." I put the kettle on, fished out two clean mugs, found the real coffee, the kind Terri liked, and the sugar pot, which still had some white sugar, in a semi-solid lump, clinging to the bottom corners.

"Nothing? What about school?"

I shook my head. "I rang Reception, they said she hasn't been in since Monday."

"And they didn't notify you?"

265

"They did. I had a text. And another one yesterday. I didn't notice until today. I was painting."

"Well you know what I think of the school system."

"I do." Memories, bittersweet and laced with whisky and wine.

"What about the boys?"

"I didn't want to worry them. I asked if they'd heard from her recently, but I didn't say she was missing."

She took my hand where it rested on the table I had attempted to scrub clean, the stained pine still sticky with cleaning spray, smelling of lemon.

"Amanda, she might be with them. If she wanted to run, it's the most logical place she would go."

I knew that, didn't I? I knew she'd go to them.

"They would have told me, wouldn't they?"

"You haven't contacted them because you're afraid that's where she is, aren't you?"

Fuck you, I wanted to say, fuck you for knowing me better than I know myself. But I didn't, because she was there, at the very least solid and practical and of all the people in my life right then she was the one most likely to be able to do something about this.

"Yeah."

"Let me call them, yeah?"

I drank my tea, which tasted stale, and listened as she called Shahid, then Abdullah, then Mahmood, and finally left a message for Yusuf.

"Yusuf's somewhere in the middle of the Caribbean," I said absently. "She can't be with him."

"But she may have contacted him."

None of the boys had seen her. All three of them asked to speak to me. I tried to reassure them; yes, I'm fine, no, there's no need to come home, not yet, yes I'll let them know when she shows up. Concerned reactions, except for Mahmood. I ignored his insinuations about my parenting. We all show stress in different ways.

"You're still trying to take care of them, aren't you?" Terri shook her head and finished her coffee, and my hackles rose.

I always hated the way Terri made me question myself, doubt myself, tried to rewrite my past to make me the villain, not the victim. How she would listen to my stories and say, *I don't think that was how it was at all, Amanda, I think you did this,* or *I think you did that*, and how everything was always my fault, every story an opportunity for criticism.

"I always will."

"So what next?"

"I don't know. The police?"

"They won't be interested yet, you know that. Do you want to take a drive around, see if we can find her?"

"Yeah, but first... I want to check her room, properly."

How could I have forgotten how annoying it was when she tutted at me, like I was the child and she the parent?

"You mean you haven't done that yet? For fuck's sake, Manda," and she was out of her seat and up the stairs and as I followed her I thought, yes, I'm a coward and I obviously didn't know my own daughter, because in her room were stashes of carrier bags full of food wrappers, chocolate wrappers, mouldering remains of chips, half packets of stale, soft crisps, and a smell of mould and staleness. It was clear she hadn't been in this room for days, not to sleep, not to do anything. The wardrobe door hung open.

"Are her clothes gone?" Terri asked. How should I know? I hardly knew what she wore any more, it all looked the same. But yes, there were only a few things hanging in there, school uniforms, and some old bras on the floor, and an old coat and some other bits. Nothing I'd seen her wearing lately.

"Looks like."

"Right. What about her rucksack?"

"Her what?"

"The big rucksack I gave her when she had to go on the year 9 bonding trip? Did she still have it?"

"I think so."

Terri moved through the room, picking up rubbish and piling it outside the door, remaking the bed, looking under and in and around and behind everything. "It's not here. And there's no phone charger."

This room, the rag rug, the curling posters on the walls, and the long mirror Terri got from a skip, a weighing scales in the corner, and in the drawer, jumble of bits of rubbish, including several packets that once held laxatives, old tampon boxes, paracetamol boxes, and bits of paper.

"Her schoolwork's all here," Terri said. Files and books were stacked on the table under the window. "Look, the last date on this notebook is two weeks ago."

"Shit. How didn't I know she was skipping school? She was so motivated, I thought she liked school."

"Yeah?" I tried not to hear the judgement, the criticism in her tone. "So what the fuck has happened?"

There were no clues, no real indicators of where she might be.

"Try her phone again," Terri said as she fished around under the bed. More rubbish

"Just leave it," I said, trying Ash's number once more. "Nothing."

"Then go check the bathroom. See what she's taken."

Her toothbrush was gone, and the little bag of makeup and her face cream.

"She can't have gone far," I said to Terri, the stairs creaking under us, down, down back into the lemon-scented kitchen.

Terri lit up a rollie and I automatically opened the back door. It was as if the years apart never happened.

"What makes you say that?"

"There would be something. Some trace."

"Everything's done online nowadays, Mand. All she needs is a bank card."

"But she doesn't have any money."

"Are you sure about that?"

"No."

"Right. So you don't know anything about your 17-year-old daughter who has now gone missing."

"Terri, this isn't helping."

"Sorry."

"I guess we should call the police."

"I told you, it's too early. They won't do anything."

"I don't know what else to do, Terri. I can't just sit around."

"Have you slept?" That strange shift to solicitousness, to caring. "You haven't, have you? Come on, let's go and have a lie down. I can see how tired you are."

My bedroom, with its old velvet curtains pocked with tiny moth-holes, and the bow-backed bed with the Ganesha hanging above it, rag rugs on the floorboards, the clothes rail and the stack of trunks and boxes against one wall. The familiar feel of her body wrapped around mine, pulling me in against her, stroking my hair off my face, tracing the outline of my earlobe with one finger as she told me to rest, to sleep, that she was there and she'd keep me safe.

Sleep came faster and more easily than it had done in all the months since she was living here with me, sleep like peace, dreamless and deep and seductive, the great pretender, persuading me that everything's OK, for a while. But she could always do this, Terri, could always soothe me and make me feel that she would make everything OK. Somehow, though, she never followed through on those promises.

Raw Umber

Strip off the clothes, strip off the binding, stare at my breasts, my curving, stubborn belly, are my nipples darker? Is my belly sticking out more? Is this it, is this why I haven't been getting thinner, is this why I feel like shit all the time? I hate this room, I hate these clothes, why am I even here? I should have gone somewhere else, I don't know where. Maybe I should call Carl, but no, he wouldn't help, he hates me now, maybe...

Maybe.

The leaflet on the floor where I dropped it, Misconceptions About Islam: What do you Really Know?

Helen gave it to me.

Helen, she said she'd help me. She's a convert, she knows, she understands what it's like to grow up in this pig-fuck awful world where nothing matters except what you look like and boys just look at you as another hole to be filled, a whore to be fucked. I never wanted this, never wanted any of it. There must be a way out, there must be a way but I can't, I can't tell anyone. No, it's not real it can't be real I would rather die, burn it out of me, burn out my flesh, make me sexless like one of those awful dolls, make me plastic and hard and let there be nothing inside me but air.

I can do something about it, I know. I can go to the GP or contact a clinic. I can get rid of this thing inside me.

But it's alive. It's a bundle of cells, but it's alive. How can I do that? And then they will all find out, someone will find out, someone will know that Ash is one of those girls, the ones who can't even keep her legs closed. Stupid, so stupid, I could have stopped this before it started. But it was one time, just one time, it's not fair, I can't do this, I shouldn't have to, and there will be no way to stop myself getting fat now, fuck, fuck, this is not fair!

Purple and lilac, dark print and light, telling me that Islam honours women, telling me that *hijab* empowers a woman, emphasising her inner spiritual beauty, that's what Helen said, that what matters is the intellect, not superficial appearance... Tears, sobs now, aching and crying because I just can't, I can't do it any more, can't fight any more against this, I am so hungry, and so tired, everything aches, everything is so hard now, my arms and legs always so heavy, so much effort to do anything, I can't live like this forever, I just can't...

The phone, strange in my hand, fingers failing to grip it, nerveless. There was a book I read once, a science fiction book, a girl with progressive paralysis. Is that what's happening to me now? My mind skitters down path after path, throwing up information from all the books I ever read, and images of bodies and internal organs and no, God, no! Not that anything but that but I do a search anyway and there is a clinic, but I don't know, I don't want to do that, it's a baby, I don't want to do that, swipe it away, tap the screen, Helen's number. There have to be words, there has to be something, a way out, something to be done now, vomiting bile and acid and that burning on the back of my tongue on my teeth and my lips, give me some way out, something other than this, something that means something, wrap me in black and hide me away from the world so I never have to see myself like this, crawling on the floor in pools of my own vomit, sobbing, silent convulsions, smell of it and the vile smell from the rubbish under the dresser and it's been so long since I ate properly or felt anything other than this disgust and

271

I.
Just.
Want.
It.
To.
End.

Numb, a fake version of myself, pulling together light and shadow to project something that is made of Ash but isn't me, not now, waiting until I can run, until I can flee, somewhere, but the messages and the posts haunt me now. Nina commenting I look rosy, positively blooming, and Jarelle saying she's never seen me look so well, and as soon as lunch is over I duck out, slip through the gap in the back fence, catch the bus and keep moving, keep moving, running. I have friends, other friends, I can go to them, but where will this leave me? Will they want me now? Such lofty ideals, these women who are so driven, Helen with her fervent faith, will she turn me away? Oh, I wish I had it too, that faith, that feeling that someone, somewhere is watching over me, that there's something bigger than me that can make this better, I would give anything now for someone to come along and just make this go away.

Just make it stop.

Rush of traffic, the bus, familiar streets now, just make myself move, walk, make myself take one step and then another, keep walking, point myself towards where I need to be.

Helen's house, curtains always drawn. She opens the door, looks into my eyes, notes the fear and the tear track stains and her eyes look deeper and it's as if she sees something else, something no one else sees. She nods.

"Ash. Please, come on in. We've been waiting for you."

The soft, scented blush shadows swallow me, and I disappear.

So many nights like this. I pretend I am going to work, it's easier, though I've given up the job now, but Mum doesn't know that, so I come here instead. The familiar, pale walls, the comfortable furniture, and the women, soft voices and gentle words and smiles, that welcome, listening to me, no one has ever listened to me but they don't judge me, they just talk to me and let me talk and it feels so good to say these things.

"You shouldn't hate yourself so," says Zara when I first turn down the dates and sweet cakes offered around. "You have every right to feed your body, and to enjoy doing so."

Eating as a ritual, a rite of self-celebration. I can only nibble bits, at first, but they coax me to eat. Zara, Jane, Helen, Mariam, the women who meet three or four times a week to pray and to talk, they bring small portions to me, talk about the recipes, about their families and who likes to eat what food. Each evening there is a topic to discuss. Food, often. Clothes and appearance. They debate the wearing of the veil, the headscarf, the long loose coverings that hide their bodies. They talk about the freedom of it. Of choosing.

"We all choose, one way or another," Helen says, offering around tea. "But is it really choice if you are told, always, that only this way, or that way, will be acceptable? If you are not really shown that there are other ways to be? None of us is forced to wear a veil, but we do so because it frees us from that scrutiny. It liberates us."

"I never knew that," I say.

"You struggle with how you look," Zara adds. I nod. I can

talk to these women. Nothing seems to bother them. "I did too, for years. I was like you, always denying myself food, always punishing myself for not being thin enough, attractive enough. My mother was a Muslim convert and told me it was up to me if I wore *hijab* or not. And it wasn't until I examined my faith, and found peace with myself through wearing *hijab*, that I actually lost weight and focused on being healthy. I found my purpose, do you see?"

"No one talks like that," I argue. "None of my friends or my family talk about having a purpose. It's just about survival. And popularity."

"And that is one purpose," Helen concedes. "Survival is the very basic purpose, but life is about more than that, surely?"

"Maybe our purpose is to do what is shown to us to do," Mariam suggests. She is older, with a wrinkled face. Her children are all grown, and two of her sons have gone back to be with family in Syria.

As the sweet sugar floods my brain, and the soft scented women sit around me, listening to me, considering my opinions, I wonder, at last, is this my purpose? What could my life be if I no longer felt like this? What am I being shown to do?

Alizarin Crimson

Waking like finding myself at the high point on a swing, swooping down and landing in my body with a thud, the pillow hot beneath my cheek, Terri still wrapped around my back, snoring none-too-gently into my ear. The light was fading. How long did we sleep? Long, lost hours when I could have been looking for Aisha, my little Ash, but I was somewhere else, and I didn't feel better. If anything, I felt more tired, my whole body weighed down as if gravity had increased while we slept.

"Hun?" I pulled away and she rolls over, rubs her eyes, looks at me. Accusation. "I slept."

"Yes, we both did."

"Time?"

I fished out my phone. "Nearly four."

"Shit. I'm supposed to be helping Joanie. I should have phoned her. Bollocks."

"Call her now. I'll make a cuppa."

Always the cups of coffee regular as clockwork, sometimes more regular, coffee and fags every half an hour or so.

She was smoking as she came into the kitchen, talking on her phone. "No Joanie, I didn't. But if you look in the van, under the seat, the invoice book is there."

I put the mug in front of her, her favourite mug, thin porcelain with a picture of a horse.

"No. I can't. Something's come up. Yes, it's Amanda. No. No, I'm not. Don't start. Aisha's missing, and yeah, I have to be here. I'm not the kind of person who abandons somebody even if... Yeah... OK... Let me know when you get back."

I watched her, noting the familiar expression of fatigued patience. "Are you and Joanie an item?"

"What?" Her colour darkened. "No, not really, no."

"Ah. But you're dating again."

"Well, yeah, yeah I am. What, did you expect me to sit around like a fucking nun?"

"No, not at all. I'm just surprised. You said you wouldn't be bothering again."

Shrug. A flash of something in her eyes. "Yeah, well things change. And it's been, what, four years since the last time you threw me out? I wasn't going to keep on coming back you know."

"It's OK, none of my business anyway. I just thought that we were going to be friends."

"Yeah, it's not that simple is it?"

"Let's not argue. Can you take me to the police station?"

"Still not learned to drive?"

I let it pass.

"Please, Terri? Do this and then you can go home. I'll be fine."

"Come on then."

She took me to the station in her car, a two-seater so low I had to crawl in and out on my knees, its seat and footwell crusted with dirt and oil and cigarette ends and ash and empty cola bottles. I used the journey to answer the frantic texts from the boys.

Terri waited while I sat for hours on a horrible plastic chair, while I completed a report, got told nothing would be done until the following day, and eventually got sent away. Then she drove me home via the kebab shop, and dumped a bag with a felafel wrap and garlic bread into my lap. "Go home," she said at my gate. "Eat. Try to sleep. Keep trying her phone. Sooner or later there'll be news. There's nothing more you can do right now."

"Thank you."

"Yeah, whatever."

It was like coming home to a stranger's house. I struggled with the latch on the gate, tripped on paving stones on the dark path, and somehow couldn't seem to get my key into the lock on the first or second attempts. The rumble-roar of Terri's car pulling away left a gap, an ache. Something was missing. I rang Marcus and Fliss, but they were away at a festival. Just voicemail, no comfort. I felt the urge to talk to Pippa, or to Pam, but we hadn't spoken since the fire. They wouldn't even let us come to Penny's funeral.

The space stretched around me.

No messages on the landline. The studio was brighter than the rest of the house. The sodden paper around the wrap was difficult to remove and the smell turned my stomach, a heaving, wrenching feeling, like the sickness that came when I was pregnant with her. It had been different, that pregnancy, different from all of the others. That was how I knew that she was a girl. I'd been sick with every one of them, violent sickness with the twins, early morning sickness with Mahmood and Yusuf, but with Aisha I had a constant sense of nausea, all day, and rarely wanted to vomit. I ate more with her than any of the others, because food was the only thing that stopped the persistent nausea.

The falafels were dense and dry, the salad limp, the garlic bread greasy, but I ate it all, every bite. I slept a little on the futon in the studio, curled up against the thin mattress like a baby monkey clinging to its mother, anchoring myself to something solid, while in the centre of the room she stared at me, the black-cloaked figure of my dreams and nightmares, and I knew that it meant something. But what?

Rain weeping down windows, pooling in the corners of the old wooden frames, tap-tap-tap on the blown stone in its age-drawn wrinkles and layers. In a dream she came to me, not a woman, but a child, running across the desert to me, and I called out, because her bare feet were on the stones and the shale and the hot sand. She was wearing the veil and the *abaya*, but her face was free and she was laughing, running to me without a care in the world, 8 or 9 maybe, before everything changed and she became like a stranger. Dusty, hot sand smell and that hot, dry air, how could I have forgotten how it was? But she never knew this life. Why was I dreaming of her there?

The tinkling sound of the phone. The police. They would be coming to interview me, with the family liaison officer, and they wanted to take a look in Aisha's room. Morning with a foul mouth and a heavy head, thick with sleep and worry and that dream of the desert and the thirst it brought. I drank a glass of flat lemonade, days old probably. The world receded to simple sensations, standing, peeing, cold air on my ankles in the bathroom, dancing tap, tap of the rain on the window halfway up the stairs, the hard unyielding tiles in the hallway, smell of lemon and old food in the kitchen. What should I do, what should I do?

And then Terri was there. She took me upstairs, put me in the shower, brought me clean clothes and even brushed my hair, styling it in that efficient, no-nonsense way of hers. We sat at the table with the police officers, looming and huge in their uniforms hung with all their accessories, wider and larger than life. I held a cup of tea between numb fingers, but forgot to drink it, as they asked question after question, as they wrote things down and said things into their radios. Terri showed them Ash's room and they asked permission to search the house, and I said yes, yes, but don't touch the painting on the easel, it's still wet. When the taller man came back he looked at me oddly, and I knew there was something wrong.

When did you last see your ex-husband?

When did you last have contact with him or any of his family?

Does Aisha have any contact with him, or members of his family?

And then there were more looks, and conversations between police officers, and the family liaison officer sat with me while Terri alternated between sitting opposite and going out to smoke and use the phone. And then it came, the rage and the fear, as I realised that it never stopped, it never really does stop, the horror, not even when I tried to make it stop, because even then, fifteen years later, fifteen years of leaving and fleeing, of running and hiding, of recovery and of fighting back, even then he could still hurt me.

I wanted a life for the twins and then their siblings, I explained to whoever was listening, I wanted them to be safe and to have a family, I thought I was doing the right thing, but it was wrong, so wrong, every choice I have ever made has been wrong because he got to her, in the end, didn't he?

"No," said the FLO, blonde, female, small and compact. "Not necessarily. We don't know where your daughter is, but, given the history, we have to follow this up."

The tall one came back. "They're running passport checks now," he said. "We have all their details on file from the previous investigation."

"What about her friend, Jarelle? And Carl?"

"We have officers at their houses right now." Ann, the family liaison officer, grim and final.

Taste the atmosphere, slick and thick and slow like time itself had decelerated, the world had stopped turning, nothing more could happen, not when that this, this almost-worst thing had happened, and the fear, like ashes and dirt in my mouth.

Terri made cup after cup of tea and coffee. I wanted to run away, wanted to paint, as they asked again about my past and I had to dig over that old ground again and again, each question like a fork through years of earth and soil, a decade and a half of defences and determination. If I could paint this, it would be dark red and black and that white mist of fear and not knowing.

My baby girl. My little Aisha. Turn back the clock, make her six or seven again, playing on the swings and running between the different parts of the playpark on her long legs, not caring. Make her ten or eleven, when she still wanted to curl up against me on the sofa and watch Disney films over and over. Make her my little girl again. Take these images away, the horrors I was imagining.

"Mum."

Abdullah and Shahid, looming huge in my kitchen, these young men, these boys of mine. Shahid smelled of cigarette smoke, Abdullah of sweat. They were so handsome, with their chocolate eyes and coffee skin and dark, dark hair and their smiles like winter sunrise, unexpected in their simple beauty.

"Did Mahmood come?"

"No, he's working. He said there wasn't much he could do but we should be sure to tell him if there is any news." Abdullah's bleak look told me his feelings about his younger brother.

"What happened? What's happening?" Shahid demanded.

Terri took them aside, explanations, questions, always more questions. Police people in and out, then a call from the one who had been searching Ash's room.

"We found this."

"What is it?"

A piece of crumpled paper, cheap, flimsy, coloured on one side.

"Mrs ..."

"Amanda. Please."

"Amanda. I need to ask you," Ann, looking up at the boys then back to me. "Are your children Muslim?"

"No."

We said it together as if this was some awful play that we had been practising for.

"We're not religious," Abdullah said.

"Mahmood is, he's going to be a vicar," Shahid added, looking at me in a kind of half-guilty way.

"And you?"

"Not for fifteen years," I replied.

"Please explain."

I look at the paper. A Muslim women's group, and she had scribbled on it, in her cramped handwriting, a name and a phone number.

"Amanda, please, we need to know. Is your daughter a Muslim?"

And it started again. "I got pregnant, and Muhammed was a Muslim, and he said we should get married, so I converted. But I haven't followed any faith since I left the Kingdom fifteen years ago with the children. Aisha was brought up with no religion."

Then the boys went into the sitting room, one at a time, to answer questions.

Then we waited.

Terri rustled up some pasta and garlic bread after sending Abdullah down to the shop. The day waned.

"So close," I murmured to Terri as she cleared the plates. "So close. She's almost eighteen. I nearly kept her safe."

"You did a good job of keeping us all safe, Mum," Shahid reached across the table. I watched his brown hand closing over my pale one, and I remembered how I envied the children the beauty of their skin colour which always seemed so much lovelier than my pasty magnolia skin. "We remember, me and Abdullah, and Mahmood, though he'd never admit it. We remember what it was like."

"Do you?"

281

"We couldn't play loudly, couldn't laugh, couldn't speak English when he was around. Couldn't defend you, either. I mean, we were happy, I remember lots of happy times, but I remember him hitting you, too, knocking you to the floor. I remember his gun, and I remember his rages, and when we left, I remember how it felt to be free of him. I missed school, my friends, I missed the family, but it felt good not to be worried about what he might do."

"Oh, Shahid," I squeezed his hands. There's engine oil under his nails and around the nail beds. "I'm so sorry."

"I'm glad Aisha never knew him," Abdullah piped in. "Things were hard enough without that."

"I just don't understand it," I laid my head on my son's shoulder briefly. How strange, that he should be the strong one, that I should lean on him then.

"She was always strange, though," Shahid said, making yet more tea. "You know that, Mum... Always off in her own world. Don't you remember the problems in school, when she was what, six, seven?"

"After we left Blossom House."

"It went on for so long. And remember the fire..." The urgent look in Abdullah's eyes, trying to shut his brother up.

"What?"

"Nothing."

"Don't nothing me, Shahid. What are you not telling me?"

Hot tea, dark and stewed. He splashed in too much soya milk, then added sugar. "Nothing, Mum."

"Shahid!"

The twins held one of those silent exchanges I always resented, excluded from their private world. "Fine," Abdullah picked up his own mug. "After the fire, she kept having those dreams, saying she saw a man in the garden."

"I remember."

"There was no man, Mum. I was awake that night."
Abdullah looked sick. What had they been keeping from me?

"I saw Aisha, late that night, after we had all gone to bed.
She was at the bottom of the garden, playing in the fire pit."

I remembered how she loved to make fires with Dee in the
little brick-lined fire pit. How she always said she was cold,
the house was cold, and she liked how the flames danced.

"I told her off, sent her back to bed. She was, what, 8, 9?"
"Nine."

"And she did that thing she does, turning her head and
lifting her chin, not listening to me, flouncing off to bed as if
it was her idea in the first place."

"Yes." I recalled it clearly, how she used to resist us all so
successfully.

"I was awake, looking out of my window. No one came into
the garden. The house was silent. And then I saw the light go
on in the utility room, and it was her, Mum. Aisha. The last
person up and about that night, when the fire started, as far
as any of us can remember, was Ash."

I shook my head. "No, it couldn't have been her." I couldn't
have them believe this.

He shrugged. Shahid sat closer to me. "Mum, think about
it. Who did Terri come down hardest on? She was strict with
all of us, but it was worst with Ash. It was like she'd never
leave her alone, never stop watching her. Like she was just
looking for something to criticise."

Yes, that's how it was.

"But she wouldn't burn the house down."

"I don't know. But I think she made up the man in the
garden so we wouldn't know it was her."

"None of this matters, now," I insisted. "None of it.
Someone has to do something."

"We'll find her, Mum. Someone has to know where she is."

Ivory Black

The last night I will spend here, and she doesn't even know. Sweet heavy smell of turpentine and frying onions. I am cooking her favourite, a dahl fry that she learned to make when we lived in Blossom House. Farewell cooked into every stage of the recipe. Will she taste it in the bittersweet garlic, the slow burn of the green chillies? Will it taint the thick earthy caress of the creamed coconut? Will she know that this is the last time?

It was always leading to this, I think, the inevitable slide into self-awareness. But now I have the answers, the ones you refused to share with me, Mother, Mum, Umma. I have them from women like the ones I should have grown up with. The knowledge you had all along but held away from me, like a bully holding aloft a favourite toy. If only I'd known what you knew, perhaps none of this would have happened. But maybe this was meant to be, anyway, this path, maybe this had to happen to send me out into the world and to finally understand what it's all about. And now, at the moment when it ends, I ache for you, for the loss of you, for what you'll feel when I am gone.

Fight the tears, this is a familiar pain, it's not as if she knows me now, or cares, really, or she would have noticed, like Sakinah, and Helen, and Zara. She would have realised before I did, and she would have done what they did and taken me into a long, laden hug and told me that everything would be all right. At the last, I can only look at her sadly, the air heavy with everything unsaid between us, all the questions and recriminations that will never be breathed into life, not now. I know what I am going to, what my path is. I only wish she hadn't kept me from it for so long.

Although I am eating more, now, I still struggle with it, and today nothing, though I should, Zara will text and ask if I have eaten, she never misses a day. All of them, texting me, supporting me, reminding me I have the strength for this, that I am strong, and worthy, and there is a place for me in this world, but my hands shake and my legs feel weak, and I throw the last of my remaining energy at this final moment.

"Thank you, love," she says, taking the bowl, the toasted flatbreads. The scent makes me dizzy. "Will you be eating with me?"

I sit opposite her, with a smaller bowl, and pretend to eat, and listen to her talking. Despite everything, I know I'll miss her.

Pewter

Day and night and day again, time-loops, Abdullah and Shahid leaving to go back to work, Terri curling up with me in bed while I tried to sleep and tried to wake from feverish drowsy half-dreams of terror. She whispered to me that she was sorry, sorry for all the times she resented my kids and resented Aisha's teenage tantrums.

"I guess I wasn't ready for it," she sighed into my hair.

I shook my head. It wasn't the time for it, but there was no time, just this nightmare landscape. Phone calls from the police. I cleaned the house with Terri, one room at a time, something to do. She worked in the garden while I sat in the study, staring at the last painting, wondering.

Terri. Looking at her through the window, her familiar broad shape, the strange way that she moved, it seemed as if she never left. I didn't think she'd finally end things, didn't think she would take her anger and pack it up into a ball and throw it at me as she marched out of the door. She came back the first time, and the second. She never stayed away longer than three or four weeks. And then that one time, that last time, when Ash was about 13, yes, that last time, she just didn't. Oh, we tried to stay in touch, we even slept together a few times, but it was just out of habit. The arguments always followed, and I retreated.

Everything ends. Everybody leaves, and everybody lies, and when her shadow passed the window as I sat, numb, I hated its familiarity, hated her coming back to remind me of the all the good parts of what we shared. I hated that I missed her closeness. I hated that just having her here made me want her.

There was a strangeness in becoming accustomed to being alone. Not that I was ever alone with the kids, but then, the empty house, ringing with absence, the rooms and walls that spoke of what could have been, the high ceilings and wide windows begging to be filled with noise and laugher, with the dreams of many. And all that was left was me; watching the grey clouds from my window, staring at the distant ridgeway in silhouette, thinking about my life and my children and knowing that she was gone, somewhere terrible, somewhere unthinkable, far beyond my reach, and not knowing if I could bear it.

In all the years I had been a mother to these children, I had borne it, the pain and the sorrow and the anger. The frustration and the unending boredom of the same routines and the same arguments and the same repeated words, "do the dishes", "clean your room", "pick up your laundry", "take the bins out", "who left that mess in the bathroom", and underneath it all was the love for them all, and mostly, for her, because I could love her for myself alone. She never belonged to *him*, to that place, she was always mine. I should have known I would struggle to let her go, unlike her brothers.

I hadn't felt lonely, not until that moment. I know Terri was there to help, but what happened when she left and I had nothing but these empty arms and what if... What if something's happened to Aisha? No, those thoughts sent the world spinning down into a jumble of colour and impossible thought. Don't go there. Hold on to this, to the moment as I dragged my limbs up the stairs to my bedroom, and found that Terri had changed the sheets, made the bed, and cleaned and tidied the room. She'd even put a hot water bottle in the bed for me.

"Can I have a shower?"

She was there, solid, smelling of outside, of rain and cut grass and dirt. Terri.

"Yes. Of course. Thank you for this."

The usual shrug. "You should try to sleep. You're exhausted."

"Will you sleep with me?"

"If you want."

"I do. If I can't sleep, can you at least hold me?"

She held me as I ached for my missing daughter.

It never stops, not once they start to grow inside you, not even when they're grown up and living their own lives. Still, they're always a part of you, these pieces of your flesh made from dreams and hopes and inevitability, seeds planted by life itself and its drive to continue. If I could paint that feeling, I would paint this as grey and green, green for life and its drive, grey for the things never said, the warnings never given, the best kept secret of life, the best kept secret held by all the women who have held on to this knowledge forever. None of us would submit, perhaps, to that kind of future, if we knew that we were trapped for life, enslaved to this other flesh which must always be alien, and yet is always a part of us. I wished I could let go, I wished I could not care. But if I hadn't cared I would have stayed in the Kingdom, breathing dusty air and drinking in the winds from the desert, and submitting, always submitting, to something else that claims to be greater and more powerful than me. And I was good at it, the submission, the acceptance, good at shaping myself to fit. Until he threatened my children.

The past is written into us, invisible tattoos of what was and what we wished for. Hidden in the shadows are the ghosts of my mother, my father, my sisters; Jan, open and hopeful, Karen, bitter and hateful. And there, beyond them, my children's father and his brothers and their wives and children, and his parents, the only family they really knew. And they are cut off from all of them, adrift in the world with no anchor but myself and each other. A line from an old activist song they used to sing at Blossom house comes back to me, from the poem by Khalil Gibran.

Your children are not your children. They are the sons and the daughters of life's longing for itself.

I always thought it was true, that I was bringing them up and teaching them love only to be ready to let them go.

Permanent Magenta

Waking is worse than sleeping, the dreams are better than this consciousness, this inner knowledge and despair, but they say I must not despair, that there is a way out, there is a way to make this better, to move up and beyond and through and to become more than I have ever thought of becoming, more than I have dreamed of. They say there's a purpose and the voices that surround me whisper of something bigger, something so much more than this pathetic body, this flesh, I never wanted it, not really, I didn't ask to be born into this world, to be doomed by my own biology, to face a life with no choices, doomed, yes, fated from the moment of conception to repeat the same patterns, the same horrors, life after life after life of it. I swore I'd never be her, never be like her, but I wonder now because the face I see in the mirror seems naked and the bones are more prominent, more like her than ever as I awkwardly fashion the veil.

Helen pins it for me, a last service before she sends me off, Frankenstein's bride or some such nonsense, the vampire's victim perhaps. This is my chance for eternity and to escape this body that binds and fetters me, that traps me and ties me to a future I never wanted. This is the way out.

It happened so fast I can hardly believe it, just a few weeks, the time it took for my passport to come through, that's all. Time enough to try to eat more and to learn a few Arabic words and to rehearse the stages of my journey into my new life.

The final checks. Passport. Rucksack. Coat. Helen murmurs the plan to me again. I have a photograph, and a letter.

"You will join the Sukhtis in London," she reminds me. "They'll be waiting at Euston." I nod. The soft lamplight blurs her features. Or is it the sickness I feel? In the days I've been here I've only eaten a little. "Umm Musab will take you home, and then on to the airport. She will travel with you. Remember, you are going to visit your cousins."

I nod. I have rehearsed the story again and again. She settles the long coat over me, and then the face covering, and at last I'm anonymous.

Does everyone long for this, to start again, to begin life anew, a clean page with no mistakes in it?

There's a man waiting for me in Syria. He will marry me, and then I will be free. Helen says it doesn't matter about the baby, that it will all be sorted out. All these years and I never knew it could be like this, seeing the world as something other than this, this life as a fleeting moment, the space between one breath and the next. I don't know what I believe but I know there's nothing else to be done, nothing for me here and I don't want to live anymore, so this is the way to do it; to do it properly and to do it right. I will die in fire as I have lived. The dreams, always waiting for me, always there, on the other side of night, more real than this is now. There will be fire and heat and I will be cast upwards into the sun to join something bigger and more wondrous than this earthly mind can imagine.

All the days and weeks and months I wouldn't eat, and then there was Helen. Helen nursing me, spooning soup into my mouth, trying to get me to eat so I can do what I was meant to do, what the dreams were always telling me to, if only I had been able to understand them. She wants to make me strong again. It was never about being thin, it was about being something other, not this ugly fat girl but the embodiment of something greater, something

291

pure and good, not landlocked by skin and bones and pulsing vessels and earthly desires.

I was built for higher things, that's what they say to me. And it makes sense, because they have haunted me, these shapes, these draped women and their accented voices and the words that echo from the time before, before I knew language and speech, before I understood girl and woman and before I found myself on that path and fell into the lie of believing that it was what must be.

No more painful binding. I'm wrapped in soft clothes, comfortable, loose fabrics and the veil covers all, even my face. No one can see my eyes, the world a haze of shadows and distant noises and nothing can reach me now, here, and she will never find me now because I can fly away and finally, this time, I can disappear.

Indigo

Banging on the door made us both jump, Terri swearing and then feeling for her cigarettes as usual. In the dusty lounge, midday sun-shafts and the shabby, pocked walls and the broken-backed sofa swallowing me.

"Answer it, then."

"I can't." Every hour, every day of my life passing through me, ghosts, memories and dreams and all the reasons I gave for everything I'd done.

"Fuck's sake," Terri was up and moving, but I felt as if I would never move again.

Policeman and woman, both tall, looming, and then the FLO, Ann, and I knew that something terrible had happened. I knew it because they all looked at me like they were about to end everything that made sense in my life.

That feeling, the hard wooden chairs and that moment, framed in time, nothing could change it as the words coalesced, taking form, as if I was seeing them not hearing, tasting them in the air I tried to suck into my lungs, and Terri was bundling me up, finding shoes and coat, taking me to the police car. Talking, questions and explanations hanging still in the crystalline air, bullets waiting to meet their target in my flesh, the self that had betrayed me one final time.

A police station, a room, cheap, nasty tea, lukewarm. Then the boys came, Abdullah and Shahid and Mahmood too, and we waited, and they talked, but I thought only of Aisha, my baby girl, shaking my head, this cannot be, it must be a dream because this was never meant to happen, no news, soft biscuits and plastic-smelling sandwiches but everything was ash in my mouth and we just waited, and waited, boys in and out for phone calls and cigarettes and then she came again,

Ann, and I held my breath for it, that final shot, and it almost felt like a relief, because it would all be over soon.

"We've found her, Amanda. We know where she is. She's safe, for the time being."

Timeslip. My baby girl, her first day of high school, my heart in my throat, realising that it would never happen again, that everything I was doing with her was for the last time. Last first day of school, last 11th birthday, last 12th, last Christmas with toys, last trip to see Santa. So many last times, but the last time I saw her, I didn't know it was the last time, when did it stop signifying, when did I lose track of it all?

"I should prepare you." Ann settled opposite me, glanced at the boys. Not boys, men. "I'm not sure, do you want–"

"They can hear whatever you need to say, it's OK." Was that my voice, cracked and unsure?

"Well, we finally got hold of this friend, Sakinah. She runs a Muslim feminist society at the university. A sensible woman, she told us everything she knew, and that put us on to another friend, a woman called Helen. I'm sorry to say that Helen has links to extremists in Syria."

Clearing her throat.

"It seems that Aisha believed herself to be pregnant."

"Oh."

"Yes. Sakinah thought she was, and tried to broach it with her, but Aisha ran away, it seems, and went to Helen, who has, umm, convinced her to run away to Turkey and marry, with the aim, I think, of crossing into Syria."

"Oh my god."

I let the boys ask the questions, roaring, buzzing, hornets of questions and denials and rebuttals, and the answer, finally.

"We don't know if she was pregnant. This woman, Helen, told her that she had done a test, but she hadn't. As far as I can tell, your daughter was in a bad way, psychologically, and

Helen used that to turn her mind. We have arrested Helen Dunworth and several of her associates. She has links to an ongoing investigation."

"But Aisha was never a Muslim."

"I don't know what to say. This is how it happens, they pick on the weak, the vulnerable, they sell them a story of purpose, of greater things, I don't know what it is that finally works for them, what tips these young people over the edge. But anyway, she was secreted away four days ago to a location in London, and there she got on a plane for Turkey. She's living in a women's hostel, she's not yet married."

"Not yet? After four days?"

"That was the plan, that she would marry. You must understand, Amanda, these women have everything paid for by extremists. She will have been told she will get a house, appliances, food. She won't have been told about the unreliable electricity, often poor sanitation, and that she will have to live under strict Shariah law."

"No." This was everything I didn't want for her. How did I get it so wrong? Was this path laid out for her, a long time ago? Why did I put us through everything I did, if this was going to happen anyway?

"The Turkish authorities are helping with the investigation, and there is a link to a mobile phone, but it's not always switched on. We can't bring her home. You are going to have to try to do that. And I suggest you do it soon."

"How? When?"

Hand on my arm. "Calm yourself, Amanda, there will be questions, she will need to be debriefed…"

"Please, just let me see her. I need to see her, need to know she's all right. I have to go!"

Significant looks. "Someone from the Home Office will be coming to see you. Counter-terrorism unit."

None of it registered, the ringing in my ears blotted out the sounds so that they came piecemeal. Words floated, meaningless. "Will they arrest her? Do we need a solicitor?"

"Not at this point, although you are at liberty to have one."

"What will happen to her?"

"If you bring her home, we'll question her, obviously, to find out how this happened. But as far as we can see she has been simply dragged into something she doesn't fully understand. We're currently accessing her mobile phone records and social media accounts."

"How can this happen?"

She shook her head, patting my arm and letting me sink into a huddle with my sons.

They came later, the counter-terrorist investigators. We were questioned, separately, for hours. Our phones were taken, and I could hear the white-hot fury in Shahid's voice as he demanded answers. It flowed over my head, all of it, the hours spinning out. Guilt.

All my fault.

"You need a solicitor." Terri and I in the waiting room, her anger thick and dark and palpable.

"We all do."

Terri, in the background, on the phone, making arrangements.

When they came again, more questions, I put my hands flat on the table. "Bring my boys in. I am not answering anything until you bring my boys in."

There they were, the children of my body: the twins, greyish and tired, and Mahmood, looking thunderous. They had contacted Yusuf. His texts were frantic. He would fly home as soon as he could.

"I want to go and get my daughter." I said clearly. "Whatever she has done, whatever happens to her when she comes home, I want to go and get her."

The boys argued. "We can do it Mum. We can go and get her."

"What if she won't come?"

"We'll find her and make her come." Abdullah, uncharacteristically angry.

"No," I heard my voice from far away. "No. It has to be me."

Gold

Pinkish gold and amber, peach and mango light, clouds like snowfields touched with dawn, this is what it's like to fly, then. This is how it feels to be so high you can almost touch Heaven. If there is a Heaven, though Helen says there is, and a world beyond this one which makes so much more sense, so much beyond us, beyond knowing. I thought if I read the books, if I learned how to be like them, like the others I could fit in. That being thin, that ability to shape myself, would make me feel right, at last, would let me belong. But it's not about that, is it, not about my body, this body, which doesn't matter in the end, because there's something so much greater than this, something more powerful and more terrible. Something pure and clean and simple for me to reach for now, just one goal, just one path into the future. If I take this final step, then the pain and the fear will stop and I won't have to think and I won't have to try. If there's a purpose to all this, if I've been put here for a purpose, then please, God, Allah, somebody, show me. Let this be the end of it.

I'm so tired, so very tired, aching arms and legs and body. Let this be the end of it, of waking every morning hating myself, of lying down at night in pain and always wanting. Let this be the end of it. Finally, somewhere to run to, somewhere to be other than this, somewhere no one knows me or her or what has happened, the things I've done, where the dreams can stop at last, where the ash can fall away and I can see myself, and the world, made new.

Please.

Slate Grey

The arrangements took very little time. The solicitor cautioned me. "But it's just a holiday to Turkey," I argued, "we are just a family on holiday."

"They will watch everything you do," she warned me. "Everything. They'll be watching you all the time. When you come back, Aisha will be arrested, and questioned. And you might be too. Is that what you want for her?"

"She doesn't know what she's doing," I insisted. "She's not herself. Her friends, they think she's been... She hasn't been eating, she's..."

"The police know this. They've seen her engagement with the online anorexia community. If we can get her back, and seen by a doctor, then a diagnosis like that could save her from a prison sentence. We can argue that the balance of her mind was disturbed."

It had been days. My baby, my precious girl, I thought she was safe. I thought I'd saved her.

Dusty White

Dear Sakinah

Thank you for the email, this is the first time I have been able to answer. I got an international 4G phone in Turkey, as Helen suggested, and although the electricity is intermittent here, I have managed to charge it at last. All is well here. I am very busy, much absorbed in my studies of Arabic and the Koran. This is the second *makkar* I've been in since I arrived last week. We don't go out, though. If we want anything from the shop, we ask the house owner, and she arranges for it to be brought.

In answer to your question, no, I am not yet married. The brother who was due to marry me has been sent elsewhere. It means I cannot go anywhere without a *Mahram* but there is no one to ask. I don't mind. I am so happy, with so many sisters around me, sharing their stories and their faith. We spend all our time together. I am learning so much, my sister.

Helen was right, the past can be healed. Since coming here, I have been cooking and sharing food with my sisters, who make sure that I am eating well so that I can be healthy and strong for the tasks set before me, and everything is back to normal. I am happy to be surrounded by so much love and support.

Please send my very best wishes to the sisters there, I miss them all,

May Allah guide us all.

Ash.

Dearest Ash,

I cannot tell you how happy I am to hear from you. We have all been so worried. People have been asking after you. Please know that we only wish you the very best. And that you can always come home, if you wish. If you feel that your place is here, rather than there, then we are waiting to welcome you.

Your sister in faith

Sakinah

What else could I write? I only read my messages and reply when there's no one else around, sneaking furtive glances, hiding this phone in a hole in the wall underneath my bed. Still I can't say anything more than that. I can't go on my social media, or message Jarelle. No one can know where I am.

I am so rarely left alone. I keep waiting for it to feel like it felt when I sat with the women in Helen's house, that joy and certainty, that sense of strength. I keep waiting for something to change. I wash my clothes, I cook with the other women, strange foods often, but some of it is familiar. I still feel sick after meals, and they all say I don't eat enough. I tell them it's the heat. I can't help it. I try to keep the food down, but more often than not it comes back up. Helen warned me it would take time for my body to get back to normal. I hope she's right.

A small room, stuffy, hot, I sweat constantly. The only place I can feel alone, though the others follow me here if I am gone for too long.

Outside, there are noises and voices and vehicles, there is the sun and the velvet night, but my life is these walls, copying the others as they pray. Every day the same, and finally, the heat that I have always dreamed of, the air hot and dry like bonfire sparks in my throat, laid like flames on my skin, as I am consumed by everyday tasks. I thought I would be learning, I thought I would be fighting, doing something. I thought I would be shown the way forward.

I feel that I will fly apart if something doesn't change.

Jet Black

I swore I would never do this again, but here I am, older, pale and puffy from the flight, picking up the black fabric, fastening on the *abaya* which closes in the memories and the scars, covers the woman and leaves just my head free. And then the veil, slow wrapping and fixing, tucking the cloth in at the side of my cheek. Hands moving without volition, muscle memory burned into me by day and night and day again in the desert and the dust and the heat. The same kind of heat here, not as bad but still that dusty, toasted earth smell and the weight of fabric on my hair, the tightness around my face, the brushing fabric affecting hearing. Cover my face, hot breath, how I always hated this, but she mustn't know, no one must know, so I will go cloaked and veiled and I will bring her home.

After the long journey, the train, the flight, the waiting, so much waiting and remembering, it feels strange to stand on solid ground. To move from past to present. I have to put aside the guilt and the torment, cast off the regrets, the questions. I have to get ready. To be ready to act, at last.

Huge mirror in the bathroom at the airport. Older, perhaps, but I am little changed. The policewoman said she was here still, in the city, in Istanbul. There was nothing they could do, only I could claim her, she's still 17, still my child, only I could try to bring her home. Sweet Goddess I hope she hasn't married already, please not that.

Shahid's face as he sees me, my precious son, and Abdullah turns, and they are boys again, little boys crying for their mother. So long since they have seen me in *hijab*. This is the worst thing, shrouding my face like this, but she might run if she sees me coming, she might run and hide and now I need to find her, that's all, I need to find her. Then I'll know what to do.

It was me, all the time, it was me, in every canvas, that black shape. I was painting myself, my future, the woman I always was and always will be, the shadow in the background. But I am no ghost. I am flesh and blood and fire and heat and I am strong, stronger now than ever. That's my daughter they have taken, my child, and I will find her. I will find her and claim her and bring her home with her brothers to be safe. This quest, this fight, it never ends. I have worked and striven to make a life for her and I will not allow this to happen, not now, not ever.

She is my daughter. And I love her. And she will know that, in the end, and that is what will save us both.

Hot plastic taxi, hot air, the chaos of streets and the noise of it, a nameless cheap hotel, sweat on my face, pooling in the small of my back, soaking the jeans and t-shirt underneath the all-encompassing shroud I must wear, disguising everything but my eyes, twin coals of anger and determination. I *will* find her. We have the address, another taxi, Shahid dredging up his long-unused Arabic and Abdullah clenching his fists, but it is I who will achieve this final goal, I know it.

Dark Brown

I dream of the rumbling volcano, hot ash breath from the cracks that open up beneath me. I wake to the sweat and stickiness, the stench of my own body, which bleeds sweat like an eternal wound, iron tang and the longing to wash. Across the room, a *sukhti* called Umm Haritha stirs as well. In the bathroom I wash in tepid water, put on the clothes I've been given, loose trousers and a tunic, the long abaya. No more binding, trying to shrink to fit. It is too hot to wear so much. Even after washing I can smell myself.

There is a commotion outside, the sisters huddle in the kitchen, the house owner, Umm Esa, goes to the window to look, gesturing for us all to be silent. I feel it then, a pressure, a desire to burst through the door and run away. I have been confined for weeks without change, stifled by inertia, and the thought of running, wild and unrestrained, is intoxicating.

"The brothers have sent word," Umm Esa says, returning to the kitchen where we are frying chicken. "Aisha, your husband is waiting for you in Syria. Pack your things and prepare yourself. They are coming for you. It is time for you to go." She hands me my passport and some papers written in Arabic, tells me to hurry. I know this always happens last minute; three other girls have left like this, given only minutes' warning.

Race upstairs, hot air in my chest, life is turning, the change will happen now, this is when I will feel the shift in every part of me, when I will no longer dream of fire, and ash, this is the moment when I will become all that I could have been. When the past will be healed and the future mine at last. I put on the face veil, pack up my few things: the clothes I brought with me, the headscarves

305

and the other long robe I was given. I leave the phone in its hidey-hole under the bed. I will not need it now.

The moment of panic, uncertainty, comes out of nowhere. Is this really what I want? My legs are shaking, I can hardly breathe. Really, is this what I want? Once I take this step, there is no going back.

The knock at the door. I straighten my veil, shoulder my bag.

It is time.

Lemon Yellow Hue

She is not at the first address, closed doors, suspicious faces, but we knew this might happen. The police gave us other addresses. Where is she? Where is my daughter? Doors and walls, more streets, the press of people,

We find our way to another house, a few streets away, through hot dry air, Abdullah using his Arabic to speak to people, one after the other. A different place, but somehow familiar to me, spinning me back in time. We have some names, we have money to use. We hurry, the boys flanking me, *Souk* smells, a market place with spices, old memories, no time for this, no indulgence, find the street, the building, through an iron gate and up stone steps, dark shadows and the darker avenging angel sweeping upwards to wrench open the door.

A shadowed room. Three people. A man and a woman. And closest to me, a third, a figure, in black, tall and slender, the veil tucked neatly, the *niquab* fitted tightly, she turns to me, my mirror-twin, and I see myself, I see the slow grace as she moves her hands, the huge eyes, the recognition, hands up now, in rejection or supplication.

Step forward, I take a breath, reach out my own hands towards her.

"Ash?"

More from Honno

Great writing, great stories, great women
Founded in 1986 to publish the best of women's writing from Wales

The Seasoning *Manon Steffan Ros*

On my eightieth birthday, Jonathan gave me a notebook: 'I want you to write your story, Mam.' Peggy's story is the story of her Snowdonia village but not until everyone's story is told does Peggy's story unfold...as thick, dark and sticky as treacle.

"...a charming, heartbreaking and captivating novel"
Liz Robinson, Lovereading

ISBN: 978909983250   £8.99

Albi *Hilary Shepherd*

A poignant, compassionate glimpse into the life of a child caught up in the Spanish Civil War, in a country at war with itself.

"A wonderfully drawn portrait...utterly convincing"
Chris Stewart, author of *Driving Over Lemons*

ISBN: 9781909983748   £8.99

A Different River *Jo Verity*

Miriam had been freewheeling into a comfortable future, but after a bitter betrayal she's stuck between the dual spectres of maternal servitude and obligation to her octogenarian parents. She is given an unconventional route out of her comfort zone – is she brave enough to take it?

"This book is yet another winner for Jo Verity... Jo's characters leap off the page and make the reader empathise with their situations." Amazon reader

ISBN: 978190998376   £8.99

Short stories; Classics; Autobiography; Fiction
All Honno titles can be ordered online at
www.honno.co.uk
twitter.com/honno
facebook.com/honnopress

ABOUT HONNO

Honno Welsh Women's Press was set up in 1986 by a group of women who felt strongly that women in Wales needed wider opportunities to see their writing in print and to become involved in the publishing process. Our aim is to develop the writing talents of women in Wales, give them new and exciting opportunities to see their work published and often to give them their first 'break' as a writer. Honno is registered as a community co-operative. Any profit that Honno makes is invested in the publishing programme. Women from Wales and around the world have expressed their support for Honno. Each supporter has a vote at the Annual General Meeting. For more information and to buy our publications, please write to Honno at the address below, or visit our website: www.honno.co.uk

Honno, 14 Creative Units, Aberystwyth Arts Centre
Aberystwyth, Ceredigion SY23 3GL

Honno Friends

We are very grateful for the support of the Honno Friends: Jane Aaron, Annette Ecuyere, Audrey Jones, Gwyneth Tyson Roberts, Beryl Roberts, Jenny Sabine.

For more information on how you can become a Honno Friend, see: http://www.honno.co.uk/friends.php